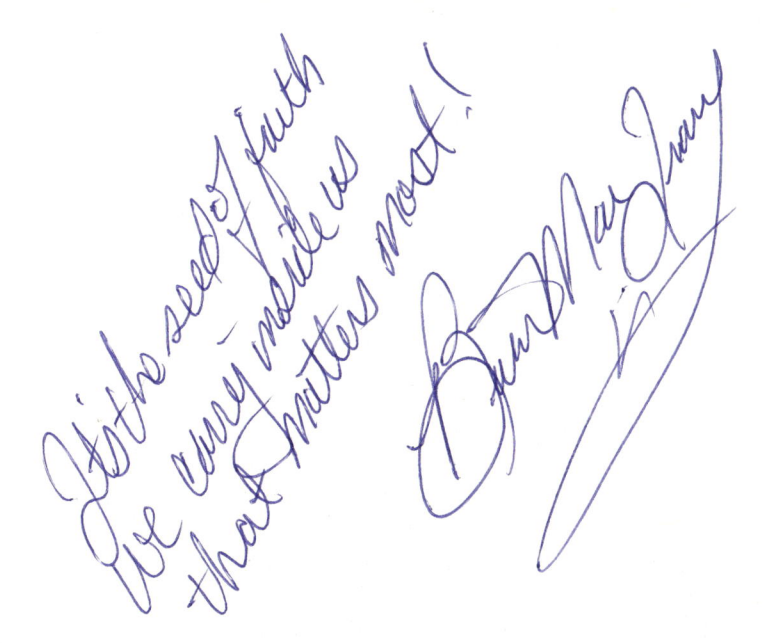

ISOLATION

Brian MacLearn

It is the seed of faith we carry inside us that matters most!

Brian MacLearn

Isolation

Copyright ©2018 Brian L. MacLearn

ISBN: 978-1-54393-846-3 Soft Cover PRINT
ISBN: 978-1-54393-847-0 EBOOK

Published and Distributed by BMac Enterprises
In association with BookBaby
P.O. Box 299, Waverly, IA 50677

ALL RIGHTS RESERVED. No part of this book publication may be reproduced, stored in a retrieval system, or transmitted in any form or by any means—electronic, mechanical, photo-copy, recording, or any other—except brief quotation in reviews, without the prior permission of the author or publisher.

I would like to acknowledge the support of my parents, Charles and Betty MacLearn and my daughters, Katie and Heather. Without it, I'm just throwing words at the wall. Their insights and contributions are vital in breathing life into my stories. Thank you also to Deborah Harmes, Ph.D. for editing and guidance. She made the words dance.

ISOLATION

CHAPTER 1:
Anniversary

Twenty-nine years of marriage and she still got to me. In truth, it is more like thirty-five years when you go back a bit and consider the first time I saw her. Say what you want, I may have been incredibly young, but I knew back then that she was the one for me.

Vicky walked back and forth from the vanity to her closet, trying to choose the best outfit for our anniversary date tonight. As for me, I'd been dressed in a lightweight, brown-tweed suit coat, complete with elbow patches, coordinated pants, and nicely buffed shoes for the past hour. I made myself comfortable while settling in for the wait. Most women would be agitated with their husbands if they sat on the end of the bed, watching them, ogling them — but not my Vicky. Tonight is all about the perfect love we share and in her playfulness, she teases me—*just because she can.*

Our anniversary fell shy of my birthday by just one day. Tomorrow I would be turning fifty and we just missed having both milestones occur in the same year -- my fiftieth birthday and our thirtieth anniversary. I'd been planning for tonight for quite some time. Vicky doesn't have a clue about the extent that I've worked on this to make it a night for her to remember, but then again, she probably does in some hidden corner of her heart. It's the reason she took her time and kept giving me those little sideways glances, the ones that made my heart pound with desire. Andy Griffith had it right when he acted in Brad Paisley's music video, *Waiting on a Woman*. Most men never find that special woman with the uncanny ability to make them feel contented, even when *they're waiting on a woman*. I would wait forever for her -- it's as real as that.

Vicky effortlessly moved from the closet to her soft chair in front of the vanity. My eyes caught every graceful step as she slipped by, her satin-lace slip swishing against her nylons, pulling my gaze to her shapely legs—*my blood pressure edges into high-risk levels*.

Her long and sleek wrist was slightly bent, fingers stretched out in the manner of a ballerina when she used her hands to draw attention to a dramatic pose. The diamond and ruby bracelet that I gave her for our twenty-fifth anniversary dangled daintily against her skin, glistening on her wrist in the soft light. The fingernail polish on her recently manicured nails matched the deep red color of the bracelet's rubies.

Vicky leaned forward to look in the mirror, granting me the opportunity to admire her backside. It was all I could do to sit still, not jump up from the bed and pounce on her. She knew that too and her reflection was grinning at me. I loved her – but more than that, I loved the total package of us -- together. Bounding off the bed to race across the distance between us, I no longer cared what the plans for tonight were -- they could wait.

She giggled like a schoolgirl at the effect she had on me, expertly avoiding my grasp by ducking into the bathroom, closing the door behind her and on the wolf chasing her. She laughed from her position behind the safety of the door as I paced back and forth between the closet and the bed waiting for her to exit from the bathroom, too keyed-up to sit still any longer.

In most relationships, the woman was the one who attached emotional importance to special dates. But in our relationship, I was the softy. I was the one who remembered the significant and important moments of our lives and I was always the one who placed more emphasis on them. That wasn't a criticism of Vicky – it was simply a fact of life. Emotionally, we stood together as equals. I had to admit though, I took every opportunity to dote on her and spoil her.

I had felt like the luckiest man in the world from the very beginning and that feeling was reinforced by my own father on our wedding day. As we stood in the receiving line next to each other, he said, "Son, you are one lucky man. Never, under any circumstances, take that for granted."

I reached down to my wrist and slid my shirt and suit coat away from my watch. The time was six-fifteen and our dinner reservations were for seven. We had a thirty-minute drive to Decorah from Tremont for our dinner reservation at the Water Street Grille.

Vicky believed we were dining by candlelight at Marelli's Italian restaurant and she hadn't guessed the magnitude of the surprises that were in store for the evening. Our two children and their spouses would be present, along with special friends and relatives. The days spent searching for the perfect, updated wedding ring simply added to the specialness of the evening ahead.

I knew Vicky, and she would never have traded in the ring that a big-hearted but poor teacher bought her thirty years ago. But the new ring, the unseen ring, would tell her, "I'm glad you're mine and I'm going to love you even more for the next thirty years." She might have expected something like that on our thirtieth anniversary, but not tonight.

I had enlisted the help of our youngest child, Abby, to help me pick out the *right* ring. Between the two of us we must have searched every jewelry store in Iowa, some in Minnesota and even a couple in Illinois over a three-month period. Steve Drexler, the owner of Wingate Jeweler's in Decorah, called me three weeks previously and mentioned a certain ring he'd seen advertised for inventory clearance at a jewelry store in New Hampshire. Steve called them and they agreed to hold the ring until I had a chance to look at the pictures on Friday afternoon.

I was standing in Wingate's, waiting for Steve to finish with a customer by four o'clock sharp and extremely lucky not to have been pulled over for speeding along the way. All day long and especially on the drive to the shop, I'd repeatedly had 'one of those feelings' -- those instinctive vibrations that poke at your insides and tickle your mind, suggesting that something is up and you'd better pay attention. I was convinced that the ring was going to be just 'the right one' -- yet something else was pushing a long, thin knife into my subconscious and urging me to "Beware!"

Abby couldn't make it up from Cedar Rapids to see the ring so I was all on my own. But it only took seeing the first two pictures in the slideshow before I told Steve to order it. It was the *right* ring and I had it in my possession within a week. The second that I opened the ring box, I knew it was better than perfect.

The hardest part was finding a place to stash it where Vicky wouldn't discover it. First I hid it in the sock drawer, then I moved it to the cupboard in the garage. That hiding place lasted less than four hours after Vicky asked if we still had the stain for the old dresser in the garage cupboard. I jumped off the couch and beat her to the garage door, mumbling nervously, "I know exactly where it is -- I'll get it for you." Vicky is intuitive -- and I probably gave her an unintentional clue that something was up.

I called Abigail once I brought the ring back into the house and had it snuggled safely inside the pocket of an old suit coat hanging in the closet. I told her she needed to come soon and take care of the ring before my worries got the best of me, but took her nearly a week before she found the right excuse to stop by the house to see us. The moment Abby opened the case and looked at the ring was the moment I knew I'd chosen wisely. Then, on the day of the special evening, I called Abigail three times to remind her to bring the ring with her. "I have it Dad, don't worry."

Even though she is the child who is most like me, I'm not sure that Abby completely understands my intense love for her mother. At age twenty-four, she is still in the 'honeymoon' phase of her own marriage. Someday, if she's lucky, she might begin to know what I feel so deeply inside of me.

As I remember the saga of finding the right ring and keeping it safely hidden, I stopped pacing and smiled when I heard the sound of Vicky singing in the bathroom. Like a cat that purrs when it's content, she hums and sometimes sings when she is the happiest. She occasionally sings when she is troubled or worried, but this time it was a happy tune.

On the drive to the restaurant, I reached over to hold one of Vicky's hands. Her thumb moved tenderly across my thumb, tracing its outline. Her touch was magical. Feeling like a lovesick teenager again, I was transported to another time and place where I was the knight and she the fair maiden. The old highway between Tremont and Decorah winds through the hills and forests and our car became her chariot. I was escorting her to her castle after having declared my love to her, offering my life in service to her protection should any dragons or ogres try to impede our progress.

All of those thoughts were unspoken and they vanished as Vicky flipped the radio to a classic rock station, and Journey serenaded us with a powerful love ballad. If there was more meaning to a life than that, I was at a loss to know what it might be.

My fantasy was completely shattered when Vicky shouted out a warning. A large buck leaped out from the ditch ahead of our car, bolting across the highway and into the trees on the other side. I tapped my brakes since the deer was now far enough ahead for it to be a real danger. I slowed down and kept my eyes focused on the ditches on both sides of the highway. In Iowa, where there is one deer, there are likely to be more of them lurking around nearby. Our joined hands tightened their grip, the romantic mood replaced by the necessity to keep a diligent watch out for deer.

I hit the cruise button again and the Camry picked up speed. After two more miles, the car climbed out of the valley and into wide-open farmland stretching as far as you could see. Vicky reached over, her right hand across her body, and gently squeezed my upper arm. The world was right once more. Journey was replaced by REO Speedwagon, singing we "Can't Fight This Feeling" anymore – *perfect – simply perfect.*

Where the old highway met at the intersection of Water Street in Decorah, I turned right instead of left. Through the corner of my eye, I noticed the slightest cock of Vicky's head to one side. Clever woman. She was too coy to say anything and too smart to show any indication that I could have possibly surprised her. All the years of being married to a romantic had taught her to be ready for anything. I smiled -- and I knew she saw that smile. Even though she remained silent, I also believed she had guessed our destination.

There are two restaurants in the direction we were headed, the "Water Street Grille" and "Luther's Pizzeria." The name of "Luther's" had nothing to do with Luther College at home in Decorah -- it happened to be the current owner's real name. It certainly hadn't hurt his business when he chose to display memorabilia from the town's private university inside his eatery and it quickly became a popular hangout for college kids and alumni alike.

I drove past Luther's and signaled for a left-turn into the parking lot of the Water Street Grille. There were times when silence speaks louder than words ever could and this was one of those special moments. The Water Street Grille had been a fixture in Decorah for over fifty years. It was also the place where Vicky and I shared our first date, where I asked her to be my wife, and where Vicky told me she was expecting our first child, Trent. Going there meant that it was more than a simple and romantic celebration of our anniversary.

How I wished I wasn't driving at that moment since I wanted to enjoy her every little reaction. But the need to keep my eyes on the road and concentrate on the traffic didn't allow me to see the expression in her eyes or the smile playing at the corner of her mouth.

Our hands were still pressed together, our palms clammy as each of us had different reasons for being anxious. Easing into the lot, I parked the Camry in the first open spot I could find. Justin and Abby's blue Chevrolet Cobalt was parked a few cars down and I knew that if I had noticed it, so had Vicky.

I turned to look at the woman who not only loved me with all my faults but who had made the world a better place for everyone who knew her. Vicky, never Victoria Ann Rustad, looked back at me with love reflected in her eyes. Her right hand gently caressed the side of my face as I leaned into her and she moved towards me. So much could be said with the eyes -- and even more in a kiss. I tasted her lips, inhaled the fragrance of her perfume, and closed my eyes. No other perfume worn by any other woman had ever affected me the same way as the one Vicky always wore.

Vicky's fingers slowly slid from my face to cup the back of my neck. When we finally managed to pull back from the tenderness of the moment, I looked into those eyes and whispered, "I love you."

"I love you, too, Simple. I always will," she gently answered.

I'm Simpson Gregory Jennings to the rest of the world, but only a handful of people could get away with calling me Simple. Vicky was the only one who ever made me feel proud of the cruel nickname that other children used to belittle me as a kid. She once told me that it fit and I should be proud of the intended meaning of my name. Simple had nothing to do with a lack of intelligence or capabilities but everything to do with heart and soul. Vicky said others might use my name in mockery. But those who understood me, as she did, and who loved me, as she did, knew that my name was a capsule summary of the way I helped others separate clutter into order.

She told me on one particular night when I was less than happy with myself, "Simple is who you are, and it is also part of what I love about you." I had done poorly grade-wise on a paper that I had written and it was a shock since I had put in what I thought was an exceptional effort. Vicky playfully used the

Isolation

nickname just then and I let it get the better of me, nearly ruining our relationship.

That particular night had been during our courtship. I was a junior at Luther College, working toward my secondary teaching degree in history and Vicky was in her sophomore year, working on her elementary teaching degree.

It had been an unlikely dream coming true when we ran into each other at Luther. Vicky had decided to join the prestigious Nordic Choir and I was already a member. This was the same girl who had left an indelible impression on me in high school.

During my senior year at Tremont High School, while participating in the state music contests, a lovely young girl initially caught my attention and later caught my heart. Entering one of the judging rooms to support two fellow classmates as they sang their solos, Vicky Ann Rustad from Waukon happened to be wedged in-between Carla and Pam from my school.

Vicky's name was posted on the door outside the room. At the time, it hadn't meant anything to me since she was just a participant from another school. Later though, that name would be committed to memory and daydreamed about. Sitting next to Rick Parson when Vicky entered the room, I noticed the long brown hair and the way it gently swirled around her shoulders. I was in a teenage trance as I watched her walk to her position at the front of the room. Her full, pink-glossed lips and stunning brown eyes created a shock throughout my body, causing my heart to beat faster and taking away my ability to speak. As Vicky began to sing, I was immediately drawn to her. The girl with the beautiful alto voice, whose name I hadn't yet learned, locked eyes with me halfway through her solo. It was one of those unforgettable moments -- the beginning of a deep connection between us that has grown stronger throughout our lives.

I wasn't the only one who was attracted to Vicky though. My classmate Rick was equally enthralled with her, but for more lustful reasons. Vicky was even more beautiful than she was talented. Her singing touched me and her eyes stole my heart. After our classmate Pam finished singing, Rick and I did a sweep of the entire school trying to locate Vicky -- her name now tattooed in our memories after reading it on the door.

We never did find her that day, but I was unable to forget her either. She was the only one in my dreams for over a year—the mysterious girl who used an invisible hammer to nail a magical first impression into my heart.

Years later at Luther College, I recognized her the second she entered the room and sat down with the other altos. But she didn't see me. That made the rest of rehearsal time painful and awkward since all I could think about was whether or not she had a boyfriend and did I have a chance with her. Would she even remember me? Had she felt the same connection that I did the last time we met?

As soon as the rehearsal for the Nordic Choir was over, I made a beeline towards her. She was tentatively walking my way and she stopped when I approached her. Those brown eyes were sparkling up at me and I knew that smile was meant for me alone. What I wasn't prepared for was hearing her say, "Hello Simpson. I've been waiting to say that for a long time."

"Hello Vicky," I said back without even flinching, keeping my eyes locked on hers.

That had been our first spoken encounter, but neither of us had ever gotten over that original moment together back in the high school contest room. Vicky had been equally affected by our previous meeting, so she had asked around and learned my name.

Geographical distance had managed to keep us apart back then, but no longer.

During my junior year at Luther, I proposed to her at the Water Street Grille. I'll never forget the look on her face when I pulled out the ring—*she glowed*. That look, that glorious look, was all the motivation I needed to commit myself to spending the rest of my life showing her how much I loved her.

We got married the next summer and lived for the next two years in married housing at the college until Vicky had graduated. I began my own career by commuting to Tremont high school each day. I was returning to the school that I had graduated from and taking over the history classes from a newly retired Jack Medfield -- the mentor who'd inspired me to become a teacher in the first place.

We ran into Rick Parson at the Nordic Fest the end of July. Rick yelled out, "Hey Simple!" It was the first time Vicky had ever heard me called by the dreaded name. The three of us spent most of the day together and Rick continually used Simple when talking to Vicky. "Simple was the best pitcher we had at Tremont. Simple once took a dare to jump off the cliff at the quarry. Simple had always been the best friend he ever had."

Over the next few months, Vicky started calling me Simple. It stung, but I loved her enough to let it go without discussing it. Simpson was a mouthful to say, so it was tolerable when she called me Simple. I'd even started thinking about using my middle name once I graduated. Gregory, or even Greg Jennings, sounded much better than Simpson did, and definitely better than *Simple*.

The professor who had given my paper a C- hadn't really intended to mock me. But it was the anger I felt at not meeting both his standards and my own standards on that paper that caused me to overreact to his comment. He had written in red ink, "The progression of your theory is too Simple." That was it, but the fact that he capitalized the word simple made it feel conspiratorial to me.

I couldn't shake the notion he had done it on purpose, so when Vicky tried lightening my dark mood, she called me Simple. I let her have it, loudly and verbally taking all of my frustrations out on her. My anger chased her from the room in tears and it took me hearing the closing of the front door to realize what I might lose because of something so stupid.

As I ran after her and grabbed her arm, she pulled away from me, fear clearly visible on her face. If there was a lower feeling, I didn't know what it might be -- verbally hurting someone to the point that they become afraid of you. I hated myself and I came unraveled -- spilling out my regrets, my pain, and pleading for her forgiveness.

She should have walked away from the crazy man crying at her feet, but Instead, she forgave me. I silently promised to never be that man again. I had tried to explain to Vicky why I wanted to begin using the name Gregory -- but just at that moment, she took both of my hands in hers and stated firmly that my nickname was a sign of my courage and compassion for others, not a put-down about my abilities. "It's a perfect nickname for a man who is straightforward, uncomplicated, and true to his beliefs. So what could be wrong with that?" Then she leaned in and kissed me, closing the door on that argument.

Now, thirty years later I sat in the parking lot of the Water Street Grille with Vicky, touched by the manner in which she endearingly used my nickname. Ever since that night long ago, I had done everything possible to be worthy of her love and to bring value to the name Vicky lovingly used -- Simple. She had been right all along and because of her, I happily wore that nickname with honor.

CHAPTER 2:
The Surprise

THE NIGHT COULDN'T HAVE STARTED ANY BETTER. Everything was going just the way I had imagined that it would. Vicky held my hand as we entered the restaurant to the resounding cheers of family and friends. She was all smiles and when I felt an extra squeeze, I knew I'd succeeded in surprising her. My grin couldn't have been any bigger as I hugged Abigail and whispered into her ear, "She didn't know."

Vicky's maid of honor from twenty-nine years ago wheeled herself forward from behind the group of well-wishers. Melissa Scharnhorst had suffered spinal damage in a skiing accident, leaving her paralyzed from the waist down. Her injury, rather than slowing her down, had pushed her to achieve more than most people could manage in three lifetimes. Melissa held three doctorates and taught Advanced English Composition at the University of Michigan. Watching those two long-time friends, excited to see each other and sharing squeals of joy as they hugged one another tightly, brought tears to my eyes.

As soon as Vicky and Melissa separated long enough to give me a chance to act, I stepped in front of Vicky and reached for her hand. She turned to face me. In her face, I saw all the emotions she could no longer contain—happiness, excitement, and *expectation*. In front of our children, our family, and our friends, I got down on one knee. Vicky's hand had a slight tremble to it, so I gently kissed the top of that trembling hand. Then, looking deeply into her eyes, I proposed, "Will you, Victoria Ann Rustad Jennings, do me the greatest of all honors and marry me again tonight?"

Vicky could have been silly and made light of my proposal, but instead, she replied with all her heart, "The honor has been all mine and always will be. I'd love nothing more than to marry you again."

Rick Parson and his wife Tammy handed each of us a glass of champagne. "Here's to the Bride and Groom! Turning to face the crowd, Rick shouted out across the room, "These are two of the most remarkable people I've ever known -- and together they're perfect."

The group erupted in applause and "Here, here!" Everyone raised their glasses and drank a toast to us. I was all smiles as Vicky's father, Harold Rustad, dressed in his best suit, took those raised glasses as his cue to make his way through the crowd and stand by his daughter. Vicky couldn't seem to help herself as she looked over at me with a devious smile and asked, "What if I had said no?"

Good spirited laughter and clapping continued as Harold first hugged his daughter and then kissed her on the cheek. The moment had arrived when I knew I had surpassed Vicky's ideas of what she thought I was capable of. I took a deep breath and opened the double doors into the party room of the Water Street Grille.

Abigail and Trent had spent many hours during the previous two days decorating that room for the wedding. Our oldest child Trent and his wife Cyndi had flown in from Ohio on the morning before. Vicky smacked me on the shoulder as she ran past me to embrace Trent. He had been waiting, quietly and patiently, on the other side of the door. In a beautiful, slow-motion, movie-like scene, Vicky stopped hugging Trent and stood silently, taking in the surroundings. The party room had been thoroughly transformed into a beautiful wedding chapel, an equal to anything Las Vegas could have done. Chairs lined either side of a red velvet runner which extended from the entrance door to the altar at the back of the room. Standing behind the altar was Pastor Samuel Hennessey. He looked great for an eighty-six years old man. He had been Vicky's confirmation pastor and the one who performed our previous wedding ceremony.

Vicky slowly turned to face me with both surprise and adoration shining from her eyes. I was choked up by her expression and I knew that I would never get tired of looking at her beautiful face. She was more stunning than ever and the delicate lines at the corners of her eyes added a serene look of compassion and wisdom to her face. Clearly touched by what I had done, her lower lip began to tremble when she smiled at me. She planted a tender kiss on my cheek, whispering so that only I could hear what she said, "I love you Simple. You win. I didn't have a clue." I said nothing back to her, hugging her tighter, the love in my hug the only response necessary.

"Let's get this show on the road before "Happy Hour" is over," called out Pastor Hennessey. He was a true Irishman and a self-proclaimed comedian. There wasn't a parishioner around who didn't love the Pastor's sense of humor. It's probably what kept him so young and full of energy.

After the chuckles died away, Rick and Tammy began ushering guests into the *chapel*. Trent and Abigail made their way to the back of the room and stood at the altar. Vicky and her father waited by the door for everyone to enter, and I took my place at the end of the runway to meet my bride.

As soon as everyone was seated, Elizabeth Hennessey, Pastor Samuels's equally spry wife played the "Wedding March" on her portable keyboard. Melissa wheeled down the aisle with Rick by her side. She pivoted her wheelchair in next to Abigail and Rick stood next to Trent.

The hardest part for me was not having my own parents there with us on that special day. My father and mother, Carl and Patricia Jennings, had died six months apart from each other two years earlier. My dad was seventy-eight when he died of a heart attack. Mom, who'd been in poor health for over ten years, simply seemed to give up after dad passed. People had always compared me to my father since the one thing that we shared was the importance of expressing our love and gratitude for our wives.

Some men just know the score, my dad was one of those, and he was an inspiration to me in many ways. He would have loved the idea of the second ceremony, especially the planning of it. It wasn't a shock when my mother passed because the whole family knew that she'd been hanging on for her husband's sake. But it was never easy to lose both of your parents in the same year. However, it was also a trigger-point in my life and I reset my personal goals towards being in the best shape that I could be – both mentally and physically. Life now held an expanded meaning -- a promise to enjoy life and be there for Vicky -- *for a very long time.*

Standing at the altar, I didn't know why, but I felt more nervous that time around. Perhaps it was silly, but I was so young and naïve the first time that I noticed the difference in my feelings immediately. This time around I understood how important Vicky was to me. Luck hadn't been kind to either of our parents. Vicky's father, Harold, was seventy-four and fighting diabetes, while her mother, Amelia, was in the Decorah Nursing home in the advanced stages of dementia. All of the hardships that life threw at our parents only made the connection between us stronger and made my need to dote on my queen and picture myself as the knight-protector even stronger. Neither of us would ever take one single day for granted.

Shifting from one foot to the other, I nervously waited for Harold to escort my beautiful bride-to-be down the aisle. Elizabeth played the lead-in to the chorus extra-loudly and everyone stood up. All eyes turned to the back of the room as Vicky began her walk down the red velvet runner, her face aglow and her brown eyes sparkling, dancing in the flickering lights of Abigail's perfectly arranged candles throughout the chapel. Twenty-nine years ago, Rick had placed a similar hand on my shoulder. I knew what the gesture meant then and what it meant this second time. It was Rick's silent way of saying – 'I'm in total agreement -- *you're a lucky guy because she's a special lady.*'

Stepping out to meet Harold, I took Vicky's hand in mine, ready to lead her the final few feet down the aisle. Harold couldn't hide his emotions, his smile was larger than life, and rather than turning away to take his seat, he bolted forward to hug both of us.

Right in the middle of giving us his bear hug, he said loudly enough for those closest to hear, "I love you, Vicky -- and I couldn't have asked for a better son-in-law, Simpson." He kissed Vicky on the cheek and before breaking his grasp he added, "Sweetheart, you look so much like your mother. I know she's proud of the two of you and she loves you both!"

Isolation

Turning to Vicky, we made our way together to the altar, me with a face covered in smiles and Vicky wiping a tear from her eye – the combined emotions of sadness and happiness giving that moment extra meaning for her. Pastor Hennessey raised his hands in prayer and began the service. Then, right at the point where we were about to share the vows, Pastor Hennessey looked at me, as if he was seeking permission to stop or continue. I nodded and smiled, slightly more mischievously than intended, and gave Vicky's hand a squeeze before looking over at Abigail.

Letting Vicky's hand slip from mine, Abigail and I made our way to the keyboard, now vacated by Elizabeth Hennessey. Abby sat down and adjusted a few of the controls and I noticed again how much Abigail looked like her mother, but with my eyes and chin. When she looked up at me for the cue, I had to choke back the added emotion of having been gifted with both a daughter and a son all those years ago -- a fact that had made my life even sweeter. Abby knew what I was feeling. Smiling up at me she mouthed, "You'll be fine," and then started to play.

I'd been practicing for months and held nothing back. I wasn't prepared for the faces staring back at me, some a bit shocked, some looking expectant, and all fully involved in the moment. Abby added her own emotions as she played "When I Said I Do" by Clint Black, joining in with me and singing the part that Lisa Hartman-Black once sang with her husband. When I finished the last chorus, there wasn't a dry eye in the place -- and that included Vicky. She couldn't contain herself as she ran to hug me before I could make my way back to the altar. She kissed me passionately and the whole room erupted in applause.

She whispered into my ear, "I love you with all my heart. You have made my world more special than you will ever know."

I held her tightly and it took all of my willpower to end our embrace and escort her back to the altar. But, I wasn't quite done yet. Pastor Hennessey picked up where he had left off and when the moment came and he asked for the ring, I couldn't stop the childish grin from spreading across my face. Vicky looked at him and then at me before arching her right eyebrow.

Trent reached into his pocket and handed me the ring. The only person to have a smile bigger than mine was Abby. She leaned into her mother and told her to take off her old ring and put it on the other hand. I caught what Vicky said as she whispered back to Abigail, "I'll get you for not telling me," which only made Abigail chuckle.

Pastor Hennessey addressed the group saying, "It was my privilege twenty-nine years ago to marry these two wonderful individuals. I can think of no one that has exemplified the meaning of marriage more than Simpson and Vicky. Simpson has his own vows that he would like to share with his bride." The pastor nodded to me, smiled at Vicky, and stepped back a few feet. The expression on Vicky's face just then might best be defined as *devilish*. Her eyes twinkled with an "I'm going to get you" look, and her smile said she was both thrilled and expectant.

I took her left hand in mine, the new wedding ring tightly secured in my right hand. My heart skipped a beat and I worried about being able to say my vows. I had to swallow hard a couple of times to regain my composure. But Vicky was glowing as she stood beside me and I knew she loved me with all of her heart. The world relaxed and I began.

"I once promised to love you in sickness and in health, for better or for worse, until death do us part. What I didn't know then was that in order to love someone deeply, you have to be willing to trust them with everything you are -- and I have -- because

Isolation

only then can you be a part of a future that binds you together until death. True love is a need that can never be satisfied. There is no obstacle too large or any distance too great to overcome. I was lucky enough to have found you, a woman so unique and perfectly special to me. I will never be able to show you how much you truly mean to me because every day we're together presents me with more reasons to love you. Vicky Rustad Jennings, you have graced my life for the last twenty-nine years and I will never get tired of showing how much I love you, how much I need you, and how much better I am because of you."

When I looked down into my now-open hand, the one displaying the gold and diamond wedding ring, so did Vicky. Her eyes were already welled up with tears, touched by my words -- but seeing the beautiful ring in the palm of my hand was more than she could handle. Vicky could only stare in disbelief at the ring, gasping for breath as her emotions got the better of her. I released her hand to reposition the ring in my right hand. Vicky's hand began to tremble and I worried that her legs were going to give out in a silly-girl swoon. She smiled up at me, her cheeks a warm red.

Calmness surrounded us and in that moment – for the space of one breath -- it was only the two us standing there. The stars had aligned perfectly. I wiggled the ring around on her finger so it could slide over her knuckle and when it nestled into its resting spot, Pastor Hennessey stepped forward.

He handed Vicky a tissue, which she gladly took. The sounds of music and laughter could be heard coming from the main area of the bar. It added a human element to the spirituality of the moment. The pastor began, "Do you Simpson take Vicky to be your wife?"

"I do."

"Do you Vicky take Simpson to be your husband?"

"I do"

"Then by the power invested in me, I pronounce you Husband and Wife…again. You may kiss your bride."

There have been several meaningful and tender kisses in my life. The first was after I proposed, the one I remember as being the most emotional was after Trent had been born, but neither of those compared to that day's kiss with Vicky. It was truly the kiss of "until death do us part."

The rest of the evening was as magical as the wedding had been. Family members and guests alike reveled in the celebration. Many times during the night, I caught Vicky admiring her new ring and every time she did that, she sought me out. Often it was just to give me a sweet smile or to silently mouth, "I love you." But on several occasions, she felt that she had to come and embrace me and I completely understood that need to express her love in such an overt way.

I was on the top of the world and couldn't think of anything that could possibly make me any happier. The party lasted until nearly one am. Considering myself a role model for my students, I made certain that I monitored my drinking during the night and took my last drink at ten-thirty. Still, I knew I'd consumed more than usual, and being a 'glass of wine with supper' sort of person, I made sure to eat plenty of food throughout the night.

When it came time to leave, I didn't have any worries about my capacity to drive. The last thing I wanted to do was to push the legal limit for driving under the influence. Yet, when we were nearly halfway home, we were both startled when three deer sprang out of the ditch on the left side. I tapped the brakes and slowed down in plenty of time to avoid them, took the car off cruise-control, and reduced my speed to have better control of

Isolation

the overall situation. If there were any more deer around, it would be in that stretch of the highway running through the valley.

Vicky had become silent, watching the roadway and ditches as well. Our hands were laced together and she stroked the back of my hand with her thumb. I could feel the size difference of the new ring, larger than her old one, but worth every penny. The caring in her caress and our closeness to each other have always been calming influences, even on my most stressful days.

The crest at the top of a long hill marked the line where the timber gave way to farm ground. I reengaged the cruise control and turned the radio up so we could enjoy the music for the rest of our drive home. With Vicksburg behind us, there were only ten miles left. Vicky's hand relaxed and I knew she had fallen asleep. I had carried her over the threshold twenty-nine years ago. I was betting I could still do it.

The lights from our town burned away at the edges of the night, giving off a welcoming beacon to guide us home. Lights suddenly shone across the highway from a crossroad to my left, possibly from another lovelorn traveler heading home. I gently squeezed Vicky's hand and softly hummed along with the song on the radio.

I was lost in love as the lights brightly illuminated the inside of our car, but somewhere deep in my subconscious I heard a questioning voice saying, "*They didn't stop.*"

There was no time to react, no time to pray, no time to say I'm sorry before the explosive noise and inertia tossed our car in the worst-ever simulation of a fairground ride. The lights of our hometown flickered out -- and so did I.

CHAPTER 3:
The Hospital

Simpson stood at the foot of Vicky's hospital bed. He couldn't recall how long he'd been standing there staring down at her. She was completely immobilized with casts covering both arms and one of her legs. The blanket was tucked around her shoulders, her head was completely wrapped with white bandages, and even her eyes were partially covered. Only her lips protruded slightly from within that mummified look and they were swollen and purplish colored.

Abigail and Trent sat by her, each on opposite sides, just as they had for the last two days -- *two days that felt like an eternity in hell*. His kids rarely moved from their mother's side, guarding and protecting her, something Simpson hadn't been able to do. Abigail's light brown hair fell across her face as it haphazardly escaped from the dull-yellow scrunchie containing her ponytail. She was sitting in one chair, holding her mother's hand, and resting her head on the bed. Her eyes followed the rise and fall of Vicky's chest. Trent was dozing uncomfortably in the chair on the other side of the bed. His head would occasionally slump forward, waking him. One blurry eye would open for a moment as he rearranged his head on the back of the chair before falling into a shallow sleep once more.

As far as Simpson was concerned, it had been either pure luck or why-wasn't-it-me luck, but he had survived the crash relatively unscathed. He had no broken bones and other than an insistent pounding in his head, he felt fine. How could two people, separated by mere inches, end up with such completely different outcomes from the same accident? It haunted his every thought and when he attempted to close his eyes, it tormented him in his dreams. More than the unjust feeling that it should have been him, seeing Vicky in such a broken state weighed on him. With each hour the weight kept increasing. He would gladly trade places with her and silently, he cursed God for being the person left standing by the bed instead of being the person in it.

Repeatedly in his mind, Simpson replayed the moment of the accident. He struggled to find anything that would absolve him from his failure to protect his wife. His growing agitation was all about the timing. A mere fraction of a second later and his Camry would have been past the collision point -- a few seconds earlier and the truck would have crossed in front of him – and had the deer not been on the road at all, then they would have been past the point where the accident happened.

The biggest and most unbearable question for Simpson concerned his consumption of alcohol at the wedding. Did it have an effect on his driving ability and could he have avoided the accident altogether if he had not had that one last drink? He had no excuses to offer and no one to pardon him for the guilt he felt. His wife was now fighting for her life -- and he felt responsible. Perhaps if he had noticed the truck, he could have reacted quickly, accordingly, but he didn't -- and now he would never be able to forgive himself.

Abigail and Trent were withdrawn and they both chose to ignore him and only converse with the specialist or the nurses that frequently came to check on Vicky's vitals. It hurt, but he didn't blame them at all because no amount of hate that they might have for him was equal to what he felt towards himself.

Dr. Morris, one of the trauma physicians at Decorah Memorial Hospital, had told all of them that it was a very bleak outlook. Vicky had suffered a problematic head injury, which in turn was exacerbated by a series of seizures, which was keeping the trauma team from performing necessary procedures. If the swelling within her skull didn't lessen, she would need to have surgery to relieve the pressure or risk permanent brain damage -- if not death. This was in addition to all the physical damage her body had sustained—a broken femur in the right leg, multiple breaks in both arms, and a dislocated and cracked hip. The medical staff was able to take care of those aspects of her body, but there was a strong chance that she might not be strong enough to make it through surgery. Her body was in shambles and Dr. Morris worried about her ability to fight the trauma she had endured, especially during a lengthy surgery.

When Trent asked him about the odds for recovery, Simpson noted that Dr. Morris' facial expressions wavered between professionalism and concern. He also saw the doctor's sideward glance and the slight furl of his brow. Morris truly wanted to offer them hope, but he also felt obliged, to be honest – and in the end, honesty won out.

Vicky's chances were going to be minimal at best and Dr. Morris made that clear. Her vital signs had stabilized and that made Simpson hopeful that the medication alone would ease the brain swelling and end the seizures. The expressions on his children's faces would forever be etched on his heart though.

The air in the room had a different scent one afternoon. It was a smell that he couldn't quite place -- but he remembered it from some distant experience in his own past. It wasn't a burnt-fur smell, but more like a wet-fur odor. He walked around the inside of the room, taking a few tentative steps, not wanting to draw the kids' attention, and searching for the origin of the smell. He couldn't stand to have his children look at him—their silent questions radiating from their eyes and stabbing him as sharply as any knife, "*Why?*"

Simpson could not bring himself to ask any questions about Vicky's condition – and he was in no shape mentally to even know what type of questions he should be asking. His anger and self-loathing were an unhealthy cocktail mixture that he couldn't stop drinking and he was actually thankful that both Trent and Abigail had taken charge.

As each day went by without any change, he slid more deeply within himself. When was the last time he'd eaten? He couldn't remember. He was still wearing his jeans and long-sleeved blue and grey striped shirt. His mind was a jumbled mess, so much so that he couldn't recall when he had changed out of his suit after the accident.

His life seemed to be anchored to the small hospital room. When Abby or Trent took a break, which they did quite often during the day -- sometimes together and sometimes alone -- he would sit in their vacated chairs. At night's end, the two of them would reluctantly leave their mother's room for a few hours to take a shower and grab some tormented sleep of their own. He would then stand a watchful vigil over Vicky in their absence, talking to her, begging for her forgiveness, and imploring God on her behalf to let her make it.

Simpson knew he was slowly losing his rational thought processes. Often he would take a stroll through the halls of Decorah Municipal Hospital. It was his way of trying to right his bearings. Occasionally, he stepped outside the confines of the hospital and into the warmth of the sun and during these brief escapes, he would find a secluded place to sit and openly weep for Vicky. God wasn't listening to his prayers and Simpson took it as a further condemning sign of his guilt.

His world suffered a devastating crash on Tuesday afternoon. Abigail was dozing in one chair and Simpson was in the other chair, watching some talk show on the television. More truthfully, he was blankly absorbing the light from the television set and ignoring the chatter of the guests as they debated some mindless topic. He couldn't have told you afterward who or what they were talking about.

The normal beeping of the monitoring equipment had once seemed accusatory, but now it chirped out metallic notes of hopefulness. Without warning, the blood pressure monitor began to beep dangerously and Simpson could only stare dumbfounded as Vicky's encumbered body began to thrash around on the bed. The pole supporting her IV bag dipped dangerously sideways, pulled by the whipping movement of her arm. Simpson didn't even have time to call out as a nurse burst into the room and raced to the bedside—righting the IV pole. She took one look at Vicky and pushed the emergency call button on the bedside to activate the response team. Simpson felt hopeless as his wife began to vomit blood all over the nurse who was trying to immobilize his wife's arms and protect her from further injury. The nurse didn't back away, stoic in her quest to help, but he did, horrified at the paralyzing thoughts in his head.

Simpson moved back from the bed as a team of specialists raced into the room. Abby stood by the window in the far corner of the room, mouth hanging open and both hands raised in front of her. She was frozen by panic, dread, and the realization that her mother might be dying. Her hands perfectly reflected those feelings of utter hopelessness—useless to reach out and help her mother and stuck midway from covering eyes that didn't want to see and the ears that couldn't bear to hear the sounds of death.

The emergency personnel diligently went to work saving Vicky's life. At one point, the pulse monitor flat-lined, and Simpson couldn't breathe as he listened to the long, drawn-out tone of nothingness. His vision began to cloud—he knew he was close to passing out. The voices in the room had an odd muffled sound as if they were seeping out from inside a sealed tin can. He tried to pray to God for his wife's life, but no sound would escape his air-starved lungs. Simpson knew that if she died, he would, for all intents and purposes, be as dead as she was. He might continue to walk among the living, but he would be nothing more than a ghost without her.

After multiple resuscitation attempts, Vicky's heartbeat finally pinged loudly as it registered once again on the monitor. Simpson was devoid of emotion—feeling neither hope nor sorrow. He was being sucked down into a quicksand of all-encompassing guilt. He tried to listen to, but he couldn't understand much of the emergency crew's conversation and the doctor had an accent that made it difficult for Simpson to follow.

He was so exhausted that he believed he had only closed his eyes for a second – but when Simpson looked up again, the room had been cleared of the staff. Abby sat in the chair again, holding onto Vicky's hand, until Trent burst through the door and went straight to Abigail -- his face pale white with shock. Abby rose from her chair and buried her face in his chest, her smaller body vibrating harshly from nonstop sobbing when she could no longer control her emotions. Simpson quietly walked forward until he stood behind both of them, placing his hand on Trent's shoulder. A doctor that Simpson hadn't seen previously came into the room carrying a clipboard and flipping pages as he walked. He checked the monitors and adjusted the IV drip before turning to face them.

"We have it under control for the moment," he said, though his voice hinted at more urgency, "We need to relieve the pressure in the skull or the next time we will not be as lucky. The surgical team is being assembled and we should be able to start operating within the next ninety minutes. We've reached a point where our options are limited and we can no longer wait for the ideal situation. Dr. Pandgoria and Dr. Parson will be the lead surgeons and one of them will meet with you in the waiting lounge before they proceed. The surgical prep team will be here shortly."

The doctor didn't wait for any questions and instead started giving directions to the nurses who had returned to the room. Simpson followed behind his children as they were hustled out of the room to make way for the prep team. A nurse escorted them down the hallway to a waiting room outside of two environmentally-sealed doors that led into the surgical wing.

Simpson felt emotionally numb and without direction. Trent, with his normally bright and inquisitive brown eyes, sat on the couch with his arm around Abby, a dull look on his face. He looked like the little ten-year-old boy who had thought it would be neat to chase after a rabbit with his bike until the rabbit tried to force its way through a fence and got stuck. Fur striped away and blood dripping from self-inflicted wounds, the poor creature squealed mercilessly, trying to force its way through the too small hole. The looks on their faces crushed what remaining spirit he had left. He was at a loss for words, at a loss period. If he could find some deep, dark hole to crawl into he would gladly do so and without prodding. He had no words of comfort to offer either of them. Simpson knew he should be trying to console them, but he was totally consumed by his own haunted feelings of doubt and hopelessness.

Dr. Parson met them in the waiting room on his way into surgery. Simpson noted Dr. Parson's overall appearance right away. He exuded an air of confidence in his mannerisms and appearance. He was over-weight with jowls forming under his chin, but his hospital scrubs were pristine and pressed, his fingernails professionally manicured. The doctor's baby blue eyes were in sharp contrast to his thick head of dark brown hair. Simpson smiled. *This man likes the finer things in life—including his food.*

Dr. Parson gave them some quick medical assurances and an explanation of what they were going to try to accomplish in surgery. What Simpson heard beneath the doctor's explanation was something altogether different though – "*Pray.*"

The waiting room had begun to feel claustrophobic, even though the three of them were alone – a fact for which Simpson was glad. Eventually, Trent got up from the couch to get Abby and himself something to drink. He couldn't hide the disdain for his father as he never bothered to ask him if he wanted anything or looked him in the eyes when he left. Simpson didn't think he would be able to bear those sorts of disdainful looks from any other people he knew -- the silent accusations of his transgressions. He was sure his guilt in the matter was stamped on his forehead in large words, "My Fault." Not long after Trent left, Abigail too wandered away from the waiting room. He supposed that she had needed some time alone and he could sympathize with her feelings.

It bothered Simpson that his two children had withdrawn from him rather than seeking him out for comfort. Since a couple of days had passed, he had thought that perhaps they might begin to show him some compassion, but they continued to avoid him and completely ignore him -- as if he wasn't even in the room. He only hoped that he would be able to repair the rift between them at some point in the future.

Trent returned before Abby did, putting a Styrofoam cup of coffee down on the only table in the room. He plopped onto the couch and used the remote to tune the television to ESPN. Abby returned just before a nurse arrived to talk to them.

It had only been three hours since Vicky had gone into surgery and they had expected the surgery to last for at least five hours, as Dr. Parson had indicated it should. Seeing the nurse standing there in her surgical attire could only be bad news.

Simpson physically shrunk back into the armchair he was sitting in. His mouth went dry in an instant and his heart began to beat faster. He waited for the news he didn't want to hear -- Vicky hadn't made it. It was difficult to read anything on the nurse's face since she had been around long enough to know how to hide her emotions and do what she was there to do. The only thing she said was that the patient would be out of surgery soon and moved to a recovery room. Then Dr. Parson would come to speak with them once he was out of surgery. It wasn't good news and all of them knew that as Abigail began to cry again and Trent tried his best to be strong -- but even he couldn't hold back his tears.

When Trent looked in his direction, Simpson finally said what his heart felt, "I'm so sorry." He could barely manage to say it louder than a whisper. Trent continued to look at him, his face contorted by the agony he felt. Trent didn't say a word in response and instead just stared at him. Simpson felt that he wasn't really looking at him but looking past him into the hallway. He didn't see hate in his son's eyes -- he saw loss and hopelessness. Simpson stood up, thought about saying something else to Trent, but instead chose to walk out of the waiting room and head to the one place where he felt that he needed to be -- the hospital chapel.

The little chapel was conveniently located near the surgical wing of the hospital. People most often prayed and sought guidance during their darkest hours. His own hours weren't just dark, they felt shrouded in unrelenting blackness. There were prayer candles on one side of the chapel and a small altar at the rear. A large and simple wooden cross, tilted slightly from the top forward, stood guard behind the altar. A beautiful stained glass window cast a comforting light into the chapel. It wasn't lit by sunshine but by an artificial light designed to create an appropriate atmosphere for peaceful reflection. Simpson believed the woman depicted in the scene on the stained glass window must be Mary, the mother of Jesus. Simpson considered himself spiritual, but not particularly religious. He walked up the center aisle and took a seat in one of the middle pews to his right. An elderly woman sat in the adjacent pew on the left side of the aisle.

Each pew had several Bibles stored in wooden pockets, evenly spaced on the back of the pew in front. Simpson noted that of the four he could see, three were well worn and only one looked like it was new. He didn't know why, but seeing the worn Bibles gave him some much-needed comfort.

The woman across from him was staring up at the cross, her hands together in prayer and her head slightly bent. Simpson couldn't tell if she knew he was there or not. Her lips moved in silent words and he suddenly felt like an intruder spying on her as she held a personal conversation with God.

Simpson turned away from her and studied the cross above the altar. He noted the gouges and worn spots, embellishing the wood, making it look all too real. Every Sunday school story about Jesus and his sufferings on the cross began to dance around the fringes of Simpson's mind. He could see the three crosses on Calvary Hill and images of Christ suffering on the cross. It made him feel small and insignificant.

He gently retrieved the Bible closest to him – but touching it made his heart ache and caused him to doubt the sincerity of his presence in the chapel. It might be better to simply leave and keep his guilt to himself. All of the questions and accusations he'd been throwing at God made him feel even worse.

He knew that he needed some sort of help before he was too far-gone. So, following the lead of the woman across from him, Simpson folded his hands together and rested them on the pew in front of him, closed his eyes, and took slow, deep breaths. When he felt calmer and slightly more peaceful, he prayed for forgiveness and he implored God for Vicky's recovery, knowing that one would not come without the other.

Simpson felt better. It didn't mean he felt good, only better. Abby and Trent were still on the small couch in the waiting room when he returned. Abby had her head resting on Trent's leg and her body tucked tightly into a fetal position. Trent was wedged into the corner, one arm around Abby's shoulder and the other propping up his own head. His eyes were closed and Simpson couldn't tell if he was actually asleep or not. He loved both of them and his heart ached for each of them. Unlike most brothers and sisters, the two of them had always gotten along well, one always protecting the other. He was thankful to have them and humbled by the adults they had become. He could not have been more proud. Looking at them in that moment, he could go back in time and see them as they had been as young children -- Abby curled up next to Trent as they watched a movie together on television. Along with their mother, they were everything he'd ever wanted.

Simpson was thinking about searching for a pillow and a blanket for them when Dr. Parson entered the waiting room. He stepped quietly towards Abigail and Trent. He touched Abby lightly on her shoulder, but she still awakened with a start. Her sudden movement was enough to make Trent bolt straight upright. Worry was etched on both of their faces and Simpson could only hope that the doctor had some sort of good news.

Their visible distress had no impact on the doctor who was accustomed to seeing anguished faces. Seeing that he had their full attention Dr. Parson began, "The surgery went better than I anticipated. I was able to reduce the pressure inside her skull, but we don't know what damage there is to the brain and what long-term effects the heart attack may have caused. I wish I had better news, but at this point, I just don't have enough information to make firm statements about her prognosis. The patient is in a coma and the vital signs are not good. Lessening the brain pressure should help ease the chance of another posttraumatic seizure, but that is still a possibility. I'm not sure that she is strong enough to survive another one like the last one. The next twenty-four to thirty-six hours are going to be the most critical."

"What are her chances for recovery?" Trent asked hesitantly.

Dr. Parson responded, "To be honest with you, less than fair." He kept his gaze fixated on Trent. "If we can manage to make it a few days without further episodes, then I truly believe we might have a fighting chance."

"What should we do?" Abigail asked. Her voice sounded more like a small child's than an adult.

Dr. Parson sighed softly. He was tired and hated to make the situation seem either better or worse than it really was. Long ago, he had determined that being as upfront as possible was always the best approach, even if it was sometimes the hardest way to discuss things with the loved ones of a damaged or injured person. It would always be easier to be optimistic, but the added pain always made it worse in the end for all involved. "I think you should hope for the best and prepare for the strong possibility that she might not make it."

Simpson could only stare at the doctor. He appreciated his candor, but it didn't make it any easier to hear the prognosis. The doctor's rather to-the-point message was that Vicky's chances weren't at all good and they should prepare for what might come next.

Simpson found it hard to breathe as he briefly allowed himself to contemplate a life without Vicky. It was a real possibility and one he didn't know if he could face. He opened his mouth to ask Dr. Parson a question, but the words just wouldn't come. His head was really starting to hurt and his body was exhibiting the after-effects of the accident. Along with all the stress and anxiety he had been through, all he could do was blame himself. He needed to be at Vicky's side, holding her in his loving embrace

"Doctor Parson, what should we be the most concerned about? I mean outside of death," Trent queried.

"Debilitating functions due to the head trauma and heart attacks," Dr. Parson responded without pause. It was apparently what worried him the most. "The brain is unpredictable, no matter what the professionals claim. It goes both ways and either way, it can rarely be explained. During surgery, I noticed the damage up close. It was bad, but I have seen worse. More than once, I had the belief that my patient wouldn't ever function again at a normal level. I'm happy to say that I was wrong in several of those cases. I can also attest to the fact that it sometimes goes the other way. Recently, a young boy underwent surgery for a brain tumor. I would have bet on the odds for total recovery, but I'd be a pauper if I had done that. The surgery went fine, but the boy was left without any form of emotion. He has the personality of a robot. It's as if I removed his soul. I can think of no other way to put it."

"Oh my God," Abigail muttered. She was visibly shaken by the doctor's words and by his perception of what it might mean for their mother's own recovery.

Simpson watched as Trent pulled her close to his side. Abby was close to a breaking point and the doctor noticed her reaction as well. He didn't offer any inflated clichés or optimistic words. He spoke only what he knew and did so with compassion. Simpson was impressed with Dr. Parson and he believed that Vicky was under the best possible care. Abby and Trent began to nod along as Dr. Parson finished discussing all the possible outcomes. Just as he was finishing the discussion, Simpson could tell the doctor had something else on his mind.

"There are times when I wish I could use my stunt double." The doctor gave a half-grin as he said it. Dr. Parson then cleared his throat and looked each of them in the eyes before continuing. "I have to bring this up because it is a possibility. In the case of brain death, there is a healthcare directive on file that no life support be used to sustain or resuscitate. There's also the matter of her being an organ donor."

Simpson's heart sank. He remembered his and Vicky's discussion on the matter. They had met with their attorney to update their wills. In the end, they both had agreed to take some of the hard decisions out of the hands of each other and the children. Neither of them wished to be kept alive by a machine, and Vicky especially wanted to help others if her organs could be used. Simpson understood why, but now he wished he didn't. It was exactly for this reason that they had signed the papers. In this case, it was easy being the one under the knife and unaware, but not the one worrying while someone was performing surgery on their loved one. It was a poor analogy, but it fit—maybe too well. He would respect their previous decision.

The silence in the small room was suffocating. Simpson wanted to escape. He felt pulled towards the recovery room. He wanted to see Vicky, to tell her they made a mistake and he would never give up fighting for her. Abigail was crying and Trent was doing his best to calm her, though he looked about ready to pack it in himself. Dr. Parson looked like he wanted nothing more than to leave, but he stood his ground, waiting a moment before he spoke again.

"I understand how difficult the notion is, but it is the legally written request on record. You have to understand that the hospital and I will do everything within our power, first and last, when it comes to that point. I have to bring it up because it is a possible outcome. As I said before, the next few days will tell us more."

"I understand Dr. Parson. I appreciate everything you are doing and your candor," Trent acknowledged.

"I'll send the nurse down when you can go back to the room. Go down to the cafeteria and try to eat something. It will be a while before you can go back up." The doctor rested his hand on Abby's shoulder. "Never give up hope." He let his hand rest a moment longer before turning and exiting the waiting room. Simpson was about to say something to Dr. Parson, but then thought it might be better to keep silent.

Isolation

Taking the doctor's words to heart, Trent guided Abigail out of the waiting room. Simpson watched them walk down the hallway to his left, the direction of the cafeteria. He wrestled with the idea of following them. His children were as traumatized as he was. Right now, they blamed him and that was okay since he felt that he deserved the blame.

Someday, God willing, they would all have a chance to heal. It would be easier on all of them if Vicky was a part of the healing process. He didn't want to think about it any other way – he simply couldn't at that moment. Simpson walked down the hall in the opposite direction of his children. He needed something positive, something happy to grasp onto. At the end of the long hallway, he turned left and entered the wing of the hospital reserved for pediatrics.

The moment he walked through the double doors, the atmosphere changed. It was as if someone had turned a light switch on to illuminate the dark. The nurses were bubbly and the tone of their conversation was definitely more upbeat. Simpson was suddenly very aware of his appearance. He didn't want to intrude on anyone and was worried that the sight of him would be enough to cause concern. But he'd come too far to turn around and he wanted what he sought.

Simpson walked right past the nurses' station. Thankfully, the two nurses at the desk were deep in conversation and neither of them looked up or tried to stop him. He gazed into an open door off the hallway. A young couple was huddled around the bed. The mother had an angelic look on her face as she held her newborn child.

"It must be a girl," Simpson said quietly as he noticed the pink stocking cap on the infant's head. The young father had that look—one that Simpson knew well. It was the look of pride mixed with "what the hell do I do now." Simpson began to smile in spite of himself, even as he contemplated the horrible situation that awaited him on the other side of the hospital.

Simpson continued walking towards the destination he'd specifically come to see. There was a "T" intersection ahead and he'd spent many hours there, though not for over twenty years. Back then, looking in the window at all of the newborn babies, sweet baby Abigail had been the one that stole his gaze and captured his heart. Decorah Municipal Hospital had undergone many renovations over the last twenty years, but the baby room was pretty much the same as Simpson remembered.

The room colors were now in pastels instead of bright whites and the cribs were glass instead of wood. Simpson's face was pressed against the window when an attending nurse happened to look his way. She held his gaze and had an inquisitive look on her face, but after only a few seconds, she lowered her eyes back to her chart and continued to write notes. Simpson sighed as he released his breath, glad she didn't feel the need to shoo him away.

Simpson counted the number of newborns. He added one girl for the one in the room he'd passed and he came up with three girls and two boys. Some of his fears slipped away as he basked in the innocence of newborns. Life was a cycle -- birth, living, and death. You couldn't have one without the others. Watching the sleeping babies gave him comfort. He vividly recalled what it had felt like to hold Trent and Abigail in his arms in this very place. Simpson's eyes began to tear-up as he lost himself in the memory of his sweet-faced baby girl. All those years ago, he'd promised to take care of her -- and now he prayed for the strength to do so.

 He stayed a few moments longer, staring through the window at the babies. He wasn't sure it had been the best idea to come here since his emotions were like a mixed bag of sweet and sour

Isolation

candy. There wasn't any middle ground to settle on. His actions had resulted in a ripple effect that could never be set right. It was mostly the negativity talking, but his heart and mind told him that Vicky wasn't going to be all right. He desperately tried shaking away those bad thoughts and grasping onto hope. It was why he came to this part of the hospital in the first place. He wanted to fill himself up with hope, but instead, it had caused him to feel an even greater sense of remorse.

Simpson felt old and very tired just then. The nurse looked up from her clipboard and seemed to study his face. She had a quizzical look on her face as if she was seeing him for the first time and not knowing whether he represented a friend or foe. She made no gestures or movements, stayed where she was, and stared at him with a concerned look unfolding across her face. Simpson took that as his cue to leave.

He left the pediatrics wing and headed back down the hall to the little waiting room. Trent and Abby weren't there, leaving an empty room for him to be alone. He sat down in the chair and stretched out his legs, resting his head on the back of the chair. It was quite uncomfortable, but he still drifted off, unable to fight the tremendous exhaustion pulling at him.

In his dream state, Simpson relived the moment of the crash. It seemed as if every time he closed his eyes he snapped back to that ill-fated moment. The radio was playing "When a Man Loves a Woman," and Simpson was thinking just that -- how he was going to love Vicky when they got home. He was alternately watching the highway, keeping an eye out for deer, and gazing at his beautiful bride in the glow of the dashboard lights. His last thought before the crash was of how lucky he was to have Vicky. Then she began to glow brighter in perfect correlation with his thoughts and the music. Simpson felt and heard the impact at the same time. His head slammed into the side of the car caused by the whiplash effect of the collision. He mercifully fell into unconsciousness and couldn't remember the crash itself.

When he did regain consciousness, he was lying on the shoulder of the highway and there was blood in his eyes, making it difficult to focus. With great effort, he managed to sit up. His heart sank while staring at the scene before him. What was left of his Camry, broken glass and mangled auto parts, littered the road. The car was on its roof with the back-end down in the ditch – and it was more than two-hundred feet away from where he was. Through his blurry vision, he saw someone he took to be a man trying to reach inside the car and Simpson could only assume he was trying to help Vicky. The other vehicle, a large truck, was on its side, still on the shoulder of the road immediately behind him. The driver's door was standing open to the sky. With the brightness of the moonlight, he was able to see most of the surrounding area. It was unbelievably bright, and when Simpson gazed directly at the moon, he had to look away as dizziness engulfed him.

The dullness in his mind found a sudden sharpness as Simpson panicked at the thought of Vicky being in the car and seriously injured. He stood and began to yell out her name, staggering toward the car. He made it several steps when he lost his balance and collapsed on the pavement. The pain in his head was excruciating and the pounding behind his eyes blurred his vision and made them water. He lifted his head toward the car and screamed out Vicky's name. He fought against the pain and tried to rise to his feet again. He had one foot planted and was trying to push off the road with his hands to stand when the lights went out for good. The last thing he saw before blacking out was the moon staring down at him.

Isolation

Simpson couldn't recall what had happened after that. Everything came in bits and pieces. He was obviously dealing with the aftermath of a concussion and his first coherent memory was lying in the hospital emergency room and listening to bits and pieces of conversations coming from people talking near him. The next time he woke up, he was sitting in the chair next to Vicky's bed. How he'd gotten there from the emergency room was vague. Simpson remembered yelling at the doctor, telling him he was all right and demanding that he be allowed to be at Vicky's side and not lying in a bed. "Yes, my head hurts, damn it -- but just give me some aspirin for the pain."

The doctor must have relented because he was sitting next to her bed when he awakened. His memory was clearly being affected by the blow he had sustained to his head, causing him to lose track of time, his movements, and pieces of his memory. He was probably hurt more than he wanted to admit, but he would die first before leaving Vicky's side. As long as he could move, he would manage somehow.

While in his slumbering state, Simpson was somehow still cognizant of the hospital sounds around him. He didn't know why this was so and he again wondered if his head injury was causing more damage than he was willing to admit. He was asleep and in the midst of a vivid dream, but he also noticed that he was also able to listen to a conversation between two nurses outside of the waiting room.

In his dream, he was waiting for Vicky to walk down the aisle and two of her bridesmaids were carrying on the same conversation that he was hearing the nurses engage in. The fact that he was aware of this in his dream, and that it was happening in real time, brought him out of his deep slumber, though he chose to keep his eyes closed. He begrudgingly admitted that he probably had some major injuries and should seek help. He made a mental note to talk to a doctor and get his opinion.

Simpson felt a slight breeze tickle his face and knew that someone had just walked past him. He opened his left eye tiny bit and in his peripheral vision, he watched as Abby sat down on the couch. She looked exhausted and worn -- her clothes were rumpled and her nose was bright red from being rubbed against too many tissues. She scrunched up a pillow and made an attempt to lie down and get comfortable. Simpson closed his eye and instantly dropped back into his dreams. Sometime later, he bolted upright when he heard Trent calling out, "Abby, wake up. The nurse is here."

"You can go back up to her room now," the nurse spoke. "If you follow me, I'll walk you back there. Dr. Pandgoria is waiting for you in the room and he'll fill you in on all of the details."

The three of them fell into line, hustling to keep up with the quick-paced nurse. She stopped at a security access panel and swiped the key-badge hanging around her neck. The big set of doors leading into the intensive care ward emitted a reverberating metallic click and an accompanying hum before swinging open with a sucking sound as the airtight seals separated. Simpson suddenly felt chilled. Some of that sensation was due to the noticeable temperature drop rolling outward from the interior of the intensive care ward -- and the remaining chill was due to his surroundings. This part of the hospital might be where countless lives were saved, but it was where many perished as well.

A bad taste worked its way up into the back of his mouth and he had to fight the fear rising inside. He swallowed hard a couple of times, but couldn't rid himself of the taste of plastic. His throat felt raw and he hoped he wasn't catching the flu on top of everything else.

The nurse took the first left and then the next right. She stopped in front of a door with IRR 4 labeled on it, gave a soft knock, and opened the door. Trent and Abby went in next, followed by Simpson. The only thing different about Vicky, outside of the change of room, was the oxygen tube inserted into her mouth. It made her even more unrecognizable. It could have been anyone lying in that bed with all those bandages wrapped around their head. Simpson swallowed hard again and the plastic taste was now coated with an awful acidic tang. This room had none of the pleasantries of the other room. There were no chairs for visitors to sit in, no television, and no fresh flowers sitting on the windowsill. Instead, there were even more monitors and equipment and more reasons to worry. The room was significantly smaller than the last one, could barely fit a half dozen people into it, and felt completely devoid of all hope.

A tan man wearing hospital scrubs with a crown of salt and pepper hair approached them. He stopped in front of Abby and Trent. Simpson stood behind them, his hand resting gently on each of their shoulders. It was a good feeling knowing that he could at least offer a little support to them without them pulling away from his touch. It wasn't much, but maybe it was a small step forward.

"Hello, I'm Nauhar Pandgoria," the doctor said with barely a trace of his native accent.

Simpson wanted to brush past the doctor and go straight to Vicky's side. He wanted the comfort of her hand in his. A strong antiseptic smell in the room made him feel queasy, but avoiding the issue wasn't going to make it go away. He searched the eyes of Dr. Pandgoria to try to get a feel for the man. The doctor was shorter than he was but easily thirty-pounds heavier. It was difficult to peg his age. Simpson also didn't sense the same level of sincerity in Pandgoria's eyes as he'd noticed earlier in Dr. Parson's eyes.

"I'm aware that Dr. Parson has already told you about the surgery," Dr. Pandgoria commented. "I was just checking the vitals and for the moment they are in acceptable ranges. There will be continued surveillance throughout the next twelve to twenty-four hours. After that, if things are progressing, we'll move the patient to the other side of the Intensive Care wing where visitors are allowed to stay for longer periods. I'll give you five minutes now, and then you'll have to wait in the waiting room. It would be a good time to go home, take a hot shower, and get some rest – perhaps take turns waiting in shifts for the next day or so. I'll make sure a nurse gives you frequent updates and she'll let you know at that time if you can come back for a few minutes."

"How soon do think it will be before you'll be able to tell if there is any lasting brain damage?" Trent asked the doctor.

"That's a very difficult question," Dr. Pandgoria began. Simpson studied the thoughtful look on the doctor's face, quickly deciding that he wasn't going to like his answer.

Continuing, the doctor said, "The symptoms can manifest themselves in various ways. Sometimes, they are easy to recognize, such as speech impediments or lack of physical dexterity. Other times, it might take months or longer for symptoms to appear. At this point, it really is too early to speculate. The more concerning question is the patient's ability to bounce back from the trauma and the effects of the surgery. I'm sure Dr. Parson has discussed the possibility of future attacks." "He did," Abby whispered, childlike.

Simpson's own heart was hurting as he noticed how small Abby suddenly appeared to be. She looked as if she'd physically regressed in age -- no longer a woman, but the little girl who still struggled to find her inner-confidence at times.

Dr. Pandgoria must have sensed that Abby was close to a breaking point because he tried saying something positive to curb the heaviness in the room. It was at least something, an attempt, and Simpson gave him credit for trying. Trent asked a couple of other general questions about visitation rules and who would be allowed into the room, but none of them really wanted to ask the doctor any tough questions. Sensing no further queries or requests, the doctor moved past them, leaving them alone in the room.

Simpson walked to the far side of the bed. The only illumination in the room came from the overhead fluorescent lights. Two lights attached to the wall on either side of the bed were off -- *rarely used*, thought Simpson. The monitor hanging on the wall directly over the bed beeped steadily. Simpson couldn't help the thought that permeated his brain. It made a sound that sounded like a ticking bomb counting down and that wasn't a promising sound. He recognized that his mood had deteriorated to the point of numbness. He loved Vicky with all of his heart, but as he stood over her, he felt ashamed and lost and hopeless. He had caused this and he was going to pay for the damage for the rest of his life. Trent and Abby stood on the other side of the bed. Abby was holding her mother's hand and Trent had his head bowed in silent prayer.

Abby began to cry and Trent slipped an arm around her shoulders. Simpson dropped a notch lower into his own well of self-hatred. He was ashamed but thankful when the nurse opened the door and politely informed them all that it was time to leave. He followed the kids out of the room and down the long hallway to the waiting room on the other side of the intensive care wing.

Simpson noticed that Abby walked as if she was trying to move against the current of a fast flowing stream. Trent was staring off into space, walking right past the nurse as she pointed out the entrance to the waiting room. Neither Simpson nor Abigail said anything to Trent, letting him keep on going to wherever he was bound. They entered the waiting room where a mother and her infant son were sitting on the lone couch.

The mother had a thunderstruck look and it made Simpson wonder if that was how he appeared to others. She couldn't have been much older than Abby, but her eyes were hollow and her face drawn into a mask that was a blend of grimace and forced smile. She looked aged and haggard. Her hand kept patting the infants back as he lay sleeping on her shoulder. He barely heard what she was mumbling, something along the lines of, "There, there, it will be alright." They were the words of someone trying to fight back against overwhelming odds that everything wasn't going to be all right and never would be again. Her pain, in a strange way, made him feel worse. He didn't want to think about anyone else's misery but his own.

Abby sat in the wingback chair in the corner, leaving him to choose either the spot next to the mother or one of the three straight chairs facing the television. He chose the nearest straight back chair. The television was on but muted and closed-captioning for the hearing impaired ran at the bottom. Abby had her eyes closed, head resting on the back of the chair. One leg was crossed over the other and her hands were folded in her lap. Her lips barely moved and Simpson knew she was praying. He watched the sparkle-effect of her tears as light from the lamp on the end table reflected off them. A picture hanging above the haggard mother showed a cabin shrouded in snow, nestled under two large pine trees in a winter scene. The artist made the light shining in the cabin's window appear warm and inviting to wayward travelers. Smoke rose from the chimney and Simpson could almost hear the sounds of the fire crackling inside with warmth.

Simpson felt a strong desire to walk out of that room and walk into the snow portrayed in the painting. He felt feverish and it was hard for him to breathe, probably another sign of his cumulative fatigue. There was an incessant pounding at his temples and he wondered if he was on the verge of a heart attack – but just as quickly as the pain came it dissipated. He knew before the nurse stood at the entrance to the waiting room that Vicky had just suffered another seizure. His own symptoms had been a premonition of what had taken place.

The nurse's nametag read, "Amelia." Her face was ashen and her right hand nervously played with the hem of her frock. Both Abigail and the young mother sat upright, their eyes boring into the nurse, which didn't help her nervousness. Amelia took several controlled breaths and then said, "There's been a major seizure and you need to come with me now -- right now."

The mother began sobbing loudly, patting the infant faster and chanting, "It will be alright," in-between her sobs and gasps for air. Abigail openly wept as she tried to stand, fell back on the couch, and then managed to claw her way to a standing position. Before he turned to follow the nurse, Simpson wanted to say something to the mother, give her some sort of reassurance, but he had none to give. He looked down the hall in the direction that Trent had gone. He was running towards them with a look of utter desperation on his face. Trent raced past him and grasped Abby's hand tightly.

Simpson knew without a doubt that he was losing the precious hold on his emotions. Vicky was going to die. He would gladly have given her his own heart if it meant saving her. As he entered her room, his thoughts turned to the painting of the cabin, and he thought, "That's where I belong."

CHAPTER 4:
Finality

SIMPSON COULD BARELY STAND UPRIGHT. HIS LEGS were trembling as his heart was breaking. It had come to a moment of decision. The three of them gathered around the bed. Vicky lay silently -- her face covered by an oxygen mask and her arms covered with dangling intravenous tubes and monitor-probes.

Outside in the hallway, Doctor Parson had been extremely compassionate with them, laying it all out in simple terms. She was being kept alive by hope and medical intervention. Her brain waves had slowed to a point of barely-existent levels, and the prognosis was now less than ten-percent for any brain function, even if there was a recovery. The heart had sustained major damage that only surgery could repair yes there couldn't be any surgery because of her diminished brain capacity.

It was time to say their goodbyes. But -- Dr. Parson, a man that Simpson appreciated for his kindness, also purposely reminded them of the health care directive, twice.

For the first time in days, Simpson attempted to talk to his children. "Abby, Trent, I'm so sorry for what I've done to your mother. I wish it was me…" -- and he couldn't finish the sentence, the grief choking his words. He slowly slid to his knees at the side of the bed. His vision blurred as the tears came freely.

He looked up at Abigail and Trent. Neither of them would look at him, their eyes fixated on their mother's face and arms wrapped around each other for comfort. It hurt to see them both in so much pain when he should be the one giving them comfort.

Simpson folded his hands under his forehead, closing his eyes and taking several calming breaths. Quietly he prayed, "Lord, please forgive me for my sins. I ask for your guidance and your spirit to comfort my children. I pray that Vicky finds peace in your loving arms. Lord, in your glory, Amen."

Opening his eyes, he looked across the bed and saw that Abigail and Trent were also on their knees and praying. It gave him a moment of comfort before he looked across the bed, just as Abigail lifted her head and opened her eyes. At first, Simpson saw a sadness in her eyes and then the sadness was rapidly replaced by shock and confusion. She stared intensely at him and he was uncertain how to interpret her look. He said what was in his heart, "I love you, Abby."

Abigail blinked and then her eyes closed as she crumbled to the floor in a faint. Trent responded quickly enough to catch her head before it hit the floor. "Abby, are you ok? Come on, Sis, wake up!"

Simpson was on his feet and moving around the bed. Two nurses raced by him as they stooped down to check on Abigail. Trent had her head cradled in his lap and from where Simpson was standing, he could see how pale she looked. The older of the two nurses was taking her pulse and the other was checking her eyes. After a few seconds, Abigail began to stir.

The nurses helped her to sit upright. Nurse Angela, by her nametag, was asking her questions and then directing her to watch her finger as she moved it side-to-side and up and down. Simpson couldn't read her nametag, but the older nurse went to the sink in the bathroom and came back with a glass of water. Abigail took it from her outstretched hand and began sipping it.

As soon as Abby was able to stand, she suddenly remembered what had caused her to faint. Her eyes darted to the bed, and then to where he had been kneeling. Her visible distress made Simpson believe she was going to pass out again. She was in a white-faced and panicky state as she scanned the room from side to side.

Simpson looked over at the wall behind where he had been kneeling on the floor – but outside of a cabinet, there was only a poster with patient procedures hanging on the wall -- nothing that should have spooked her. Abigail turned to Trent, buried her head in his shoulder, and he rubbed her back as she sobbed.

Simpson swung his own eyes back and forth across the room and noticed an empty wheelchair sitting next to the bedside. Why hadn't he seen it before? Why was it there and who was it for? It seemed strangely out of place – but in the midst of his personal agony, Simpson noticed that he felt physically better. His head didn't hurt and his body felt oddly free from the stiffness he'd been feeling.

Dr. Parson entered the room, took in the scene, and then waited patiently until the nurses maneuvered around to stand on either side of the children. Simpson took the only open spot and stood next to Angela. Simpson leaned slightly forward to get a better look at Abby. Her face was regaining some of its color, but her eyes had a haunted look. Simpson turned back to Dr. Parson as he cleared his throat.

"I was truly hoping that we wouldn't be in this situation." The doctor glanced at Trent and then at Abigail. Simpson was glad it was Dr. Parson and not Dr. Pandgoria. The doctor continued, "I'm very sorry, but if there is any sort of bright-side to be gleaned from this, then you need to know and believe that her sacrifice will save someone else's life. I have the hospital chaplain waiting outside. It's your choice if you want him to be present."

"Are you positive that there is nothing else that can be done?" Trent asked, but Simpson noted the tone of defeat in his voice as he spoke. It was just a question to be asked – not a demand or a statement of expectation.

"Are you a religious man?" Dr. Parson asked with sincerity.

"Yes."

"There is always hope for a miracle, but it is up to God now."

Simpson appreciated the approach Dr. Parson was taking with them – professional but still caring. The doctor's statement said it all. He was telling them that they had come to the end of the line as far as medical intervention was concerned.

The air in the room was chilly, yet Simpson felt warm. Every sound had a sharp edge and the room felt suddenly claustrophobic and closed-in. The non-stop sound of the heart-monitoring machine seemed to increase slightly in volume and that sound pounded away inside his head. Simpson felt close to fainting and he just wanted it all to be over.

"We will take off life-support, but should there be another arrest, we will not resuscitate this time. We'll keep watch and make the end comfortable. As I said before, and I believe this with all my soul -- it's in God's hands and if it isn't time, then he will provide the miracle."

"Are we allowed to stay here?" Abby asked in her quiet, little girl voice.

"Yes, of course," Dr. Parson responded. There will be a nurse in here with you at all times as well. I just need your consent to proceed. Would you like me to have Father Jacobson come in?"

Simpson was about to speak up and give his consent to the doctor when Trent spoke first, "Please have the Father come in." Simpson was proud of the man Trent had become. In this most difficult time, he had the presence to stand tall for all of them. Trent had a purposeful look, not quite defiance, but the determination to conquer the hard road at all cost. The doctor nodded his head and backed out of the room. The door remained slightly ajar, held in place by the doctor's foot. When Dr. Parson stepped back into the room, he was followed closely behind by Father Jacobson.

The Father was gaunt with a colorless face beneath his large, round, and balding head. The baggy pants of his "blacks" hung loosely on his rail-thin frame and made him look like a survivor of some serious illness. In spite of his awkwardly skeletal appearance, his blue eyes still had a sparkle and his smile was the perfect blend of compassion and comfort. As he moved forward, Simpson noticed that he had a slight limp and his left arm was tucked in close to his side instead of hanging freely.

"God be with you," the priest said with genuine compassion as he walked forward to stand at the foot of the bed.

Simpson instantly liked Father Jacobson, admiring anyone who had the fortitude to live in the world of darkness and provide what little light they could to others. Simpson searched for the word that described him. It came to him instantly -- credible. In a world where everything and everyone seemed to be tainted by something, Father Jacobson had an aura of purity about him.

The Father embraced both Trent and Abigail, then looked in Simpson's direction. Much like Abigail earlier, his face registered surprise to see him standing next to Abigail. The look was there -- and then gone. Raising one bushy eyebrow, the Father smiled directly at him and Simpson couldn't say why, but it gave him a feeling of discomfort -- completely the opposite of what he had expected to feel.

Simpson bowed his head as Father Jacobson prayed for his wife's soul and for her to be free of her earthly sufferings. Abigail had begun to sniffle, trying and failing to fight back her tears. The nurse reached past him and offered her a tissue, which she thankfully took. Simpson couldn't look at her. Doing so would cause him to lose what little grasp he had left on his sanity. His heart was breaking and his grief was becoming too much for him to fight. When the Father finished his prayer, Dr. Parson motioned for Trent and Abigail to follow him out into the hallway and Simpson overheard him saying that they needed to sign the release forms.

Father Jacobson used the moment to move around the bed to where Simpson stood. The nurses were busy checking Vicky's vital signs and making notations on an iPad they used to record data. The Priest didn't say anything to Simpson—just bowed his head and whispered another prayer just loud enough for Simpson to hear.

"Lord in your grace, grant your lost lamb the wisdom to find the answers for which he seeks. Guide him and comfort him on his journey. Ease his troubled heart and grant him peace. Amen."

Simpson was going to say something to the Priest when the older nurse stepped around the side of the bed and said, "Excuse me, Father." Father Jacobson stepped back and moved toward the foot of the bed. Simpson packed himself into the corner so the nurse could check on the machines at the head of the bed. When he looked over at the Priest, the Father was making the sign of the cross and talking in silent words. When he finished he looked over at Simpson, gave him that same reassuring smile, and nodded his head just once.

The Father's actions and his prayer were confusing to Simpson. That prayer had definitely been directed at him. Though he needed the Lord's guidance now more than ever, the part about him being on a journey and granting peace didn't make any sense. Simpson moved past the nurse toward the Father. Before he had taken two steps, the door opened as Trent and Abigail came back in with the doctor.

"If you need it, I can have the nurse give you a pill to help calm your anxiety," Dr. Parson offered to Abigail. "It's quite natural in high-stress circumstances," he added.

"I'll be okay, but thanks."

"Nurse," the doctor said as he motioned toward the younger one, "be so kind and stand with Abigail."

"Yes, doctor," she said compassionately and moved next to Abigail. Abby took her hand. Trent stood close to Abigail, his hands buried deep inside of his pockets. Simpson could hear him playing with the change in his pocket. The air in the room was getting heavier by the second. The Father had squeezed in behind Trent, Abigail, and the younger nurse. Dr. Parson stood next to the older nurse at the head of the bed and Simpson stood alone at the foot of the bed. His hand felt constricted as if someone were squeezing it tight. The wheelchair, on the opposite side of the bed, had moved slightly and was resting at a different angle, even though he had not seen anyone touch it.

The nurse helped the doctor to remove two of the plastic tubes feeding Vicky necessary, life-sustaining drugs. Then Dr. Parson carefully removed the oxygen mask from her face. Simpson's hands ached and his wrists hurt in sympathy with the imagined pain he knew Vicky might be feeling and he tightly clutched the bar at the foot of the bed. If he let go or stopped squeezing, he was afraid that he would succumb to his fears.

He listened to the heart monitor beeping out the final sounds of her life, his own heartbeat in perfect sync with hers. Vicky's body convulsed once and her heartbeat sped up, accurately and mechanically measured by the monitor. It slowed back down again and regained a normal beat. Simpson held his breath and almost allowed himself to believe in that miracle -- but then the monitor's harsh beeping began to slow.

He knew it was wrong, knew it was purely selfish, but when you lose someone that you have shared your life with, you don't care about anyone or anything else in that instant. The moment that the beep became a single, shrill cry of finality, Simpson snapped off his attached-to-reality switch and walked briskly out of the room.

His head hurt and he felt as if the life had been sucked out of him. He loved his children and hoped that they would understand – but he also sensed that forgiveness would not be easily given. There wasn't a rational reason to walk away, especially in the moment of that profound sorrow that surrounded them all. But he needed solitude, a place to grieve and collect his thoughts. He would call the children later to let them know where he was and when he'd be back – and there was so much that needed to be done. A bad taste in his mouth made him long for a stiff shot of whiskey, the first of what might be many upcoming excuses to drink himself into the comforting arms of oblivion.

Outside of the room, the familiar sounds of the hospital sounded dull, flattened, much the same as he physically felt – numb was an appropriate way to describe the way he felt at that moment. At the T-intersection, he could turn left and go to the chapel or right toward the elevators. Something was off-kilter in the direction of the chapel though -- it didn't feel right and was too bright. He supposed it was his anger towards God, so Simpson turned right, away from salvation and towards self-loathing.

He walked down the hall toward the open elevator and entered it. Without remorse, Simpson pushed the button for the ground floor. With the pinging of the doors, they opened out on the ground floor. Simpson walked out the front door of the hospital and across the parking lot. At the corner of Vinton and Merrimac, he got on the city bus and rode it to Fifth Street. Then he walked three blocks further to the Greyhound bus terminal. The next bus north to the Twin Cities left in ten minutes and from there he could catch another bus to Krofton in northern Minnesota. With any luck, he would make Switchback Lake and be at his father's old cabin by four that afternoon.

He would never be able to explain to his children why he had to leave -- why the pull to go to the cabin was so compellingly strong in the face of the duties and responsibilities he was neglecting. Worse, why he didn't care that what he was doing was wrong? He had no answers, but it felt right – as if it had a purpose. Simpson silently promised that he would call them the instant he arrived in Krofton to let them know he'd be back in two days. That should be enough time.

CHAPTER 5:
The Cabin

Krofton was bustling with tourist activity, which surprised Simpson because the town wasn't nearly the hub that Brainerd and Ely, Minnesota were. Krofton was the ugly stepsister compared to those two, but it had a fierce loyalty among its regulars. From late April to early October, the town tripled in population and the nearby resorts were mostly full. This late in the season, it would normally have less traffic, so with the downturn in the economy and higher gas prices taking their toll, Krofton should have been quiet. From Krofton it was 75 miles of twisting back roads and highway to get to Ely where the entrance to the Boundary Waters officially began.

What Krofton offered in abundance was good fishing and more privacy. Switchback Lake, Ridge Lake, Bottle Lake, and Twin Lake were most people's destination out of Krofton. Twin Lake was the largest and boasted two large lodges and a dozen cabins spread out around the lake. In comparison, Switchback Lake was the hardest to get to and only had four cabins on the entire lake. It was larger than either Bottle or Ridge lakes, but both of the others were where the majority of tourists headed since they were both accessible by the main roads and the closest lakes to Krofton. People who stayed there spent a fair amount of their time hanging out in town and joining in the local festivities.

In most springtime seasons, the cabin on Switchback Lake was unreachable. The old logging road that gave access to the cabin was nearly always underwater during the melting snow runoff. Sustained or heavy rains in the summer could also make the road dangerous to drive on. Due to the layout of the lake, another access road would have been costly to build.

Logging had long since moved out of the area and the lake wasn't currently on the state's radar for an increase in the number of occupancies or development. But the beauty of Switchback more than made up for the difficulties in getting there. Before his father passed away, he'd cleared a small patch of land on either side of the washout. Carl managed to purchase a leeway right so he could build a two-car garage on the town side. It also granted him the right to build a small shed to store a couple of Jon-boats and motors on the cabin side. In fast-moving water, it was borderline-suicidal to cross the fast water, but it beat getting wet when the entire lake was sitting high and it was safe to cross.

It was nearing the end of fishing season for the majority of cabin owners and only a few had hung around for hunting season. All that was left to do was winterize the cabins. School had started nine weeks earlier and the nights were already beginning to dip below freezing. Most of the tourists staying at the lodges were enjoying a last "back to nature" trip before the snow started to fly. They were the ones who really got it. Simpson had to give them credit for that -- nothing was as romantic as snuggling underneath a huge quilt on the deck while overlooking the lake, sitting in the crisp and clean air as you sipped a cup of hot and generously-spiked cocoa. When the evening chill was too much, the warmth of the fire heated up more than chilled bones.

Isaiah Jennings, Simpson's grandfather, had bought the cabin on the far north side of Switchback Lake from Ernst Steinbraun, a poor logger, and an even worse cabin builder. Steinbraun worked for Pinehurst Logging Company at the turn of the century and they originally excavated the road around the lake. At that time, Krofton had been nothing more than a mill and small logging settlement.

Steinbraun was taken with the beauty of the lake and with the logging owners' help, he procured a deed for the thirty acres where the cabin now stood. Isaiah encountered Steinbraun in 1946 while staying at Eagle's view lodge on Twin Lake. Isaiah was fresh out of the army and staying with his best friend, Thomas Hastings, whose father owned Eagle's View. Steinbraun was thirty years older than Isaiah, but they struck up a close relationship, much like a favorite uncle and nephew. Isaiah spent the summer working for Tom's father and on his days off, he would hitch a ride as far as the road would take him, hike the three miles back to the cabin, and spend the day fishing with Ernst or helping him clear the land. Together, they built the foundation for the dock that was still in place today -- only a few repairs having been done over the years to maintain it.

Ernst had caught a nasty bout of pneumonia in 1951 and was never the same after that. His health failing and the bills mounting, he turned to Isaiah. They worked out a deal that allowed Ernst the use of the cabin until he died, or until Isaiah paid the purchase-price debt off and kicked him out. A secondary clause exonerated Isaiah of all remaining debt if Ernst died before the final payment. Grandpa Jennings came out on the plus side as

Ernst died in the spring of 1954. The original cabin was torn down and the wood that was salvageable became part of the new cabin that Isaiah built with the help of Simpson's father, Carl, during the summer of 1961.

Carl and Isaiah were more like uncle and nephew than father and son. Isaiah's wife Mary had died in childbirth during the depression, not a surprising event given the deprivation of the times -- but it left a hole in Isaiah's heart that no one else ever filled. Needing to travel around to find work, Isaiah had little choice but to ask his sister Peggy to raise Carl. Isaiah tried to do his best by Carl, but Peggy's husband Stephen was the one who filled the role of father.

When the war broke out, Isaiah had enlisted immediately -- more to get away from the haunting memories than because of patriotism, even though he was fiercely patriotic. During the war, Isaiah would prove himself repeatedly, serving with distinction and claiming many a medal for his bravery. Like most servicemen of the time, Isaiah never talked about those moments of combat or how the war reshaped the rest of his life. Isaiah did his best during the latter part of his life to be a good influence and a responsible part of Carl's life.

Simpson first saw the cabin in 1969 when his grandfather invited him and Carl to come up for a couple of weeks of fishing. To a seven-year-old, the secluded cabin and gorgeous lake left a strong impression that altered his psyche forever-after. Sitting on the dock and watching the sunset, with the magical sound of loons calling down the sun echoing across the lake, were some of the most peaceful times Simpson ever enjoyed and could never duplicate anywhere else. He carried those impressions with him and they became an integral part of his internal makeup. Whenever he needed to step back and regain his center, he would search his memories no further than to the wonderment of his first moments at the cabin. It would be his "happy thought" if Peter Pan ever allowed Tinkerbelle to sprinkle fairy dust on him so he could fly.

Simpson was the next to last one off the bus. He was in a heated internal debate with himself about getting off the bus or riding it back to Decorah. The other remaining passenger at the front of the bus was sound asleep. With a last deep breath, Simpson stood and purposely walked forward, past the driver who didn't even bother to say, "Thanks for riding with us" the way he had done to all the others.

The sidewalk in the front of the bus station led down the block to the intersection of Oak and Main Street or up the street to a residential neighborhood. Simpson headed towards Main Street. With nothing but the clothes he was wearing, he thought it might be prudent to stop and pick up a few necessities for his stay at the cabin. His father, like his grandfather, always kept the cabin stocked with both food and clothes -- just in case -- so when he'd inherited the cabin, he too kept it stocked, even if he wasn't using the cabin on a regular basis. Simpson paid Irv Waldbusher, a lifer of northern Minnesota, to keep adding to the inventory on hand and to monitor any rodent problems and deal with them accordingly.

At the corner, Simpson headed right on Main St. He wouldn't call the town busy, and it didn't have the usual spark so notable during the height of summer, but the town still felt well-occupied. That was a good way to put it. The economy might not be booming, but money was still coming in and the town was becoming more comfortable once again.

Grothman's hardware and grocery were two blocks ahead on the right. Simpson was shocked to see the doors closed and chained with a big "For Lease" sign in the window. He remembered old man Grothman and his wife Erma, fixtures of the store forever. It saddened him to think that bad times, most likely down to health issues as they aged, had anything to do with them closing. They were the archetype of small-town storeowners -- courteous, knowledgeable, and honest to a fault. Under better circumstances, he would like to ask around, find out what happened, and offer his condolences, if need be -- but today, he just wanted to get to the cabin.

If he turned around and walked all the way through town, there was another grocery store on the south side -- but Simpson wasn't in the mood for that -- so he headed north toward the outskirts of town and Mike Phisler's small gas station. Mike's sold bait and had a modest amount of fishing tackle. Both Carl and Isaiah swore by Mike's claim to the "best damn crawlers in the state." Simpson's grandfather would have said that every time he hooked a big Walleye Pike. Walking down the hill, he noticed two men engaged in earnest conversation. Neither of them looked up or paid any attention to him as he walked over and then stood off to the side, waiting for an opportunity to ask about catching a ride.

As he stood waiting, Simpson overheard the driver talking with the employee of the filing station -- discussing recent fishing adventures and some new waitress in town that had most of the eligible and not-so-eligible men turning their heads in her direction. Simpson had heard the driver's name during the conversation – Tad – and when he mentioned that he was heading out to Pete's cabin on Switchback Lake to drop off some supplies, Simpson approached him and asked to ride along. He barely acknowledged Simpson, acted as if he hadn't even heard him, and just as Simpson was about to ask again, Tad cocked his head toward the rear of the truck, giving a barely perceptible nod -- or something like it. Simpson took that as his cue and he crawled up into the truck's bed. When Tad didn't yell at him to leave, he figured he'd read him right.

The truck bumped along at a good clip, jostling Simpson from side-to-side, nearly tossing him out the back after Tad swerved to miss a pothole. The gravel road heading toward the lake was rough from constant overuse and the effects of heat and settling. Thankfully, Tad gave Simpson's back and rear-end a break as he slowed down a bit and navigated the road more cautiously. At the junction where the Switchback Lake road split into two directions around the lake, Tad slowed – but hardly stopped long enough for Simpson to jump out of the back of the truck.

Simpson watched Tad drive off to the south toward the three cabins that the south fork of the road serviced. He thought about waving, but then decided it wasn't worth his effort. Rubbing the kinks out of his lower back, he started walking up the north fork of the road. When Simpson patted his front pocket, the phone that had once been there was now gone. Instead of feeling angry about losing it, he felt relieved. His intention to call both of the kids wouldn't happen today -- and even if he had decided to do that, it should have been back in the town where he had a passable signal. When you're already waist high in the muck, you might as well hold your breath and dive in.

The first thing that Simpson noticed as he walked was the lack of tire tracks on the old gravel road -- if you could even call it gravel. In some spots, the grass was thick and tufty. Simpson tried to remember when he'd last been to the cabin. His father had inherited the cabin from his grandfather in 1977 and for a while, he'd spent at least one month every summer on the lake. After his own kids were born, the number of trips diminished. The rest of the family enjoyed their time at the cabin, but for him, there was always somewhere new to go and something new to see. He didn't – or couldn't -- come up after his father passed away two years ago.

Simpson found it hard to pinpoint that last trip. It had to have been at least eight if not ten years since he'd been here. That realization suddenly made him feel guiltier about not coming to the cabin than he did about leaving his children to deal with the death of their mother and his irresponsibility.

After inheriting the cabin, he hadn't made any effort to keep tabs on it and even though he'd kept in touch with Irv Waldbusher, he didn't' have a clue about what was in store for him. It was possible that the cabin had been vandalized, was falling apart, or had been invaded by an infestation of raccoons or squirrels. The real truth for not coming here had been avoided long enough -- shoved to the back of his memories. He had spent many happy times with his father here and coming back now meant that he would have to say goodbye to him all over again.

It was both a good and bad sign when he came to the runoff area. A large pine tree had fallen across the road, barely missing the large shed on that side by less than six feet. He would need to spend a day cutting and hauling away the portion blocking the road. It was good that the low spot was dry and by all appearances had been for a long time since the weeds all around were quite tall and already turning to an autumn brown. By the runoff, the gravel road had been overtaken by patches of thick weeds. If vandals had attacked the cabin, they would have needed to come by boat or on foot.

Simpson walked around the base of the fallen pine tree. The exposed roots were still encased within a mound of dirt and easily reached a couple feet over his head. It must have been a prolonged and intense wind to knock over such a tall pine tree.

Simpson used the palm of his hand in an attempt to clean a spot off the dirty eastside window of the large shed. Looking inside through the somewhat cleared glass pane, he spied the old boat trailer and the ancient Mercury motor propped up on a sawhorse. The old jeep that they kept housed there for emergencies wasn't in the far stall and not seeing it gave Simpson a momentary pause. Unless it had been stolen and he was never notified, there wasn't any reason for it not to be there. He also couldn't remember his father ever selling it.

Again – his own fault for not coming up to check things out after his father died. Tugging at the lock on the door, he found it secure and the door showed no signs of being tampered with. He tried to raise the garage doors, but they too were tightly locked.

Simpson walked all around the exterior of the shed, carefully examining the windows, prodding each one to see if he could open them. Satisfied that something logical and explainable must have happened to the jeep, he stepped off the road and down into the low area. As he walked through the weeds, a mixture of dust and pollen floating in the slight breeze swirled around his nose and caused him to sneeze. He had to step around several dead branches, mounds of rocks and mud, and even a tangled mess of chicken wire with weeds growing through it -- a comical bear-like shape having a bad hair day. After a chuckle, he frowned at the mess of chicken wire. If it had washed down the runoff, then where it had originated from might be a reason for concern.

After several more minutes of self-chastising, Simpson considered that it might have been several years since anyone had made any effort to keep the low area cleaned out, so in reality, it didn't look too bad. Every year after the runoff, his father had spent hours prepping the ground so that a vehicle could drive safely through it without getting stuck or damaging the undercarriage of the vehicle. Most years, that meant hiring a road crew for a couple of hours to grate and smooth out the inclines and occasionally drop off some much-needed gravel. Simpson climbed up the short incline out of the low area, immediately noticing the raggedness and steep angle. Without some concentrated work to fix the road, just cutting the tree out of the way wouldn't accomplish much. Sighing at his negligence, he trekked up the road toward the cabin.

The breeze wove its way through the timber, bringing with it the rich smells of fall. There was a muskiness in the aroma that conveyed the cool moisture of dewy nights and leaves warmed by the sun during the days. The smell from the lake held the promise of fish for supper. Off to his left, the trees obscured the setting sun and cast dancing shadows along the road and an array of pastel-colored leaves had already begun to fall. It would only take one hard-killing frost and the last of the leaves would give up their grasp on the trees and the landscape would change from deep reds, yellows, and tans to earthly dark tones. The first sting of winter wouldn't be far behind. Simpson knew the cabin held special memories and he didn't doubt for one minute that it was going to be tough on him to overcome those lonely ghosts of memories past -- waiting there to haunt him.

The road climbed steadily, winding its way around the bluffs protecting the northern tip of the lake. The exertion of the climb felt good and Simpson managed a smile when he reached the top of the hill and was able to look out over the lake, seeing it in its beautiful depth of colors. From this high vantage point, it was a postcard-perfect view.

That peaceful feeling, however brief, comforted him and made him thankful to be there. But Simpson allowed one harsh thought to creep in, then another, then another. Just like the unexpected moment in a horror movie when evil attacks, he suddenly felt as if the imagery and atmosphere of peacefulness that he felt about the lake was somehow false, an illusion, just a lure cast to catch him and then propel him into the depths of hell. He didn't know why in the world that thought had inserted itself into his mind since he'd never felt that way about the lake before. Simpson shook his head to rid himself of the nasty thoughts.

A warm burst of air blew across his face and suddenly he thought of Vicky. She gripped his heart and held it tightly. God help him -- he missed her -- needed her. Simpson rounded the last bend in the road. The trees began to thin out and the waning sunlight expanded, instantly bringing back a feeling of warmth.

Simpson wasn't sure what to expect next. His mind raced with visions of the cabin vandalized and in utter destruction. A worse notion permeated his thoughts -- the cabin might be home to squatters, *with rifles and long knives*, waiting for him with traps set to snare the unsuspecting. Realistically though, when he could force his thoughts away from any horrific possibilities, he honestly believed that he would simply see a cabin left to the mercy of time and neglect awaiting him.

He sucked in his breath as the trees gave way and the side of the cabin came into view. It looked as if he might have been right to worry about squatters after all because the protective shutters were open on the windows, a sign that the cabin had been opened for use -- or else no one had remembered to close them in anticipation of the coming winter.

If option number two was the case, then *who* had opened them and *who* had been using the cabin? The only person who had any business being there was Waldbusher -- and he had his own cabin on Bottle Lake.

Simpson moved in closer. The cabin didn't look run down or vandalized. Instead, it looked inviting, *as if it had been waiting for him to show up.*

The yard was free of fallen branches and looked well cared-for. There was a large pile of freshly cut firewood stacked neatly alongside the back door and two larger stacks were carefully arranged between pairs of pine trees. There was no light coming from the cabin and no other signs that would suggest current occupation of the cabin – so the only plausible explanation was that Waldbusher or one of the other cabin owners on the lake had been taking care of the place for him.

At present, the only way to access the cabin was by boat or on foot since the road was now blocked by that fallen tree. No one could have arrived by car. He knew he'd have to make a stop at one of the other cabins when he was out on a fishing trip and ask if they knew who had been at his own cabin.

Still not quite willing to accept the simple answer, Simpson walked around the cabin toward the front door. Without climbing the steps, he could see that the heavy wooden door was padlocked and secure. If someone had been squatting at the cabin, it would have been unlocked. A wave of relief and a slight bit of relaxation washed over him.

The burn-barrel to the side of the cabin was empty and the valve on the propane tank fueling the cabin was turned off. He knocked on the side of the tank and Simpson was rewarded with a dull thud sound, thus indicating that the tank was full.

Simpson headed back to the storage shed behind the cabin. It had three enclosed steps rising to meet a small landing at the top. He stopped on the second step and bent over so he could maneuver the board that comprised the top step out of position. He stuck his finger in an empty knothole and slid the board to his left until he could see into the hollowed out gap underneath. Reaching inside, he pulled out a small plastic box containing the extra key to the shed's padlock. Then, after replacing the step, Simpson stood at the door and inserted the key. He had to twist it hard to one side to allow the locking mechanism to spring loose. As he flipped back the latch and turned the knob, the door gave out a long moaning creak as he pushed inward.

There were no windows in the shed and the only light that penetrated the darkness came from the open doorway and cracks along the roofline. The far corners remained untouched by the light. Simpson stood just inside the door. He reached his hand up and to the right until it found the shelf on the backside of the open door. Once he had found the box in its familiar place, Simpson undid the cardboard flaps and stepped to the side so the light from the door could illuminate the inside of the box containing three flashlights and a variety of batteries. He pulled out the largest of the flashlights and pushed the button. Nothing happened. He unscrewed the cap and was relieved to see it was empty and not full of corroded batteries. He rummaged through the box until he found two C-size batteries, inserted them into the flashlight, and tightened the cap. This time when he turned it on, a strong white light illuminated the interior of the shed.

Simpson shone the light around the shed, relieved to see that it was just as he had remembered it. Boat supplies lined one wall and tools hung on the other wall. A gas generator, old folding chairs, and a pile of discarded boat cushions protected the back wall. As soon as the beam of light touched the boat cushions, they began to move – but Simpson wasn't fazed by the movement of the cushions. He stepped to the back of the shed and kicked at the pile, figuring it had to be a mouse or a chipmunk. A second kick to the pile brought out a hissing sound and Simpson jumped back, thinking it was a snake and he needed to be more cautious. Squatting down, slowly and carefully, he used the flashlight beam to probe the gaps in the seat cushions. His beam suddenly reflected off two eyes that were set within a mottled face.

"A cat. Go figure!" Simpson said to himself.

In the past, there was only one way for a cat to have found its way into the shed and that was through a small gap where the sidewall met the ceiling at the back of the shed. Over the years, the footing at the back of the shed had settled enough to cause the gap, so this wasn't the first animal to seek shelter inside -- but it was the first cat. In fact, Simpson couldn't ever remember seeing a stray cat this far out in the wilderness. Now wasn't the time to make friends though since he needed to retrieve the key to the cabin and get inside.

"Sorry kitty, introductions will have to come some other time." Simpson backed away from the cat's hiding place and turned to face the open door. Hanging from a hook on the back of the door was a fishing vest. He shone the flashlight beam on the vest as he lifted the flap on the left breast pocket. From within the pocket, he pulled out the set of keys to the cabin. After turning off the flashlight, he stepped outside and closed the door behind him – but then he had a second thought -- it might be better to leave it open since it would give the cat a chance to escape.

The cabin was built on solid footings that raised the main floor a good three feet off the ground. Though the level of the lake had never risen high enough to come close to reaching the cabin, it was always smarter to play it safe. Simpson mounted the four steps to the front porch. There was a fine layer of dust covering the porch decking. Several of the boards showed wear and one had a distinctly mealy look to it. When he touched it with his toe, it proved to be spongy. There were several rodent tracks running along the wall – but what he didn't see were any human footprints in the dust.

The screen door was secured in place by two wood twist-latches. The simplest methods are sometimes the best. He put pressure on the door while at the same time turning the rectangular wood pieces vertically. As he swung the screen door open, it welcomed him with the familiar musical squeak of the hinges.

Letting the screen door rest against his back, Simpson pulled the knob on the heavy oak front door towards him. Without applying pressure, it would be nearly impossible to get the padlock unlocked, but the key turned easily and Simpson popped the latch so he could push the door open. Whoever had been keeping up the yard must have also kept an eye on the inside.

His parents had become friends with Bob and Emily Patterson, owners of the cabin in the lower part of the lake. Occasionally, they would all get together for meals or keep a watchful eye out on renters or friends using each other's cabins. It was a good way to make some extra money when you couldn't spend all of your time on the lake. Simpson was willing to bet that Bob was the one who had been keeping the place up.

The inside of the cabin had a musty smell, the true sign that it hadn't been open to the fresh air in a while. When Carl had built the cabin, he went for functionality rather than aesthetics. It was a large three-room cabin. The two bedrooms were at the back of the cabin and only large enough to hold a twin bed, nightstand, and a dresser. In between the two rooms was a wide hallway leading to the back door. Hooks lined the walls for coats, fishing poles, and other tools.

A large potbelly stove sat slightly off center in the main room to his left, where a couch and two padded chairs sat nearby. The kitchen was on the right along with a table and six chairs and it had plenty of cupboards for supplies and a deep closet for storing coats and extra gear. There was a small propane refrigerator with the door left ajar—another sign that the cabin hadn't been in use. Along the side wall next to the refrigerator were the double sink and a gas stove. There was sufficient counter space to accommodate all the necessary cooking supplies – as long as you weren't trying to be a gourmet chef or even a well-stocked one. Water from the lake could be drawn up and into the kitchen sink by a pump, but a bottled water dispenser also sat on the backside of the front wall. In the old days before bottled water dispensers became the norm, they had just treated the lake water for cooking and drinking and hoped that it was safe. Simpson was glad to look over and see three big blue water bottles sitting next to the dispenser and he quickly checked the expiration date on each of them. They were dated from the previous spring, so not too far past their optimum. Irv was supposed to make the cabin ready each spring -- just in case.

The bathroom, *really just an old outhouse,* was one modest step above being primitive. It was set a good fifty paces in back of the cabin and had a divider separating the toilet seat, mounted on a wooden box, from the small shower stall. A small propane water heater sat in the corner and the propane tank to run the water heater was enclosed within a protective cupboard attached to the outside of the outhouse.

Long ago, the shower had replaced the other toilet stall at the request of Simpson's mother, Patricia. She liked to come to the lake with Carl, but after a couple years of either bathing in the cold waters of the lake or using water that had been heated on the stove for a sponge bath, she insisted on having a warm and consistently available shower. At first, Carl grumbled about all the extra work it would take to build and maintain it, but his comments fell on deaf ears. Even when he tried to explain how it would take away from the so-called 'charm' of the cabin, all he received in response was a glowering stare from his wife. In the end, he built it – just for her -- and after the third year of using it, Carl completely redid it to make it even better. Pat said nothing – she simply smiled.

All of the other great memories came flooding back to Simpson as he looked in through the doorway. He was still deeply saddened by the loss of his father, just as he knew he would be. It had hit him hard. And it was funny, but the pain and sadness that he felt for his father was a step up from what he had been feeling inside while trying to deal with Vicky's death and his own selfish flight away from his children and into isolation. If he didn't deal with it – both of the its -- he knew he would be consumed by them. *Maybe that would be a good thing,* he thought to himself.

First-things-first though. He tossed the keys on the table and headed straight into the kitchen to check on the supplies that might be available. Over the next few days, he needed to let the process of grieving come first -- and he really didn't want to disturb that to make a trek back into town for groceries if he could get by with what might be there already. The first cupboard he opened was stocked full of assorted canned goods -- *a good sign.* He scanned the rest of the cupboards while making a mental inventory of what he had on hand. He wasn't a big eater, so if he caught a few fish along the way, he could probably make it for nearly two months with all that was stored at the cabin already – perhaps even longer if he wanted to eat mostly rice and beans.

Simpson was both hoping and dreading that he would find his father's personal stash of whiskey. The cupboard over the refrigerator held two unopened bottles and one that was half-full. There were also two bottles of wine and a small bottle of port. Part of him wanted to take them all out and dump them before their siren song called out to him. The pain was most assuredly going to come and he knew he wasn't strong enough to face it alone. Booze was never your friend though -- it only lied to you with false hope.

Simpson picked up one of the opened bottles of whiskey, held it up in a mock salute, and after twisting off the cap, he took a big slug and then gasped. It burned his throat and stabbed at his stomach. He smiled the smile of a madman.

Turning around to face the inside of the cabin he said aloud, "Here's to you, old friend. I've come a long way to seek refuge and reflection. I only ask that you take it easy on me." Simpson put the top back on the bottle and replaced it on the shelf. "I caused the pain that I feel and I need to deal with it. I will not give you the satisfaction of numbing my pain or adding to it when I am at my breaking point!"

Simpson closed the cupboard door knowing that he wouldn't want to give in to the easy way out -- yet equally understanding that the cupboard door would not remain closed for too long.

Simpson opened the door to the bedroom nearest the kitchen. The chill from inside the room washed across his face causing him to shiver at its touch. The sun had passed over the window and into the room many hours previously and any warmth had slipped away. He got down on his hands and knees to look under the bed. Three large sealed-plastic tubs of extra blankets and clothes were stashed beneath this bed and there would be others in the other room. He slid out the middle tub and found his favorite jacket resting on top. He tossed it on the bed along with a t-shirt, sweatshirt, and a pair of his old jeans. The top drawer of the dresser had toiletries and an assortment of medicines and bandages. Extra socks, underwear, and pajamas were in the next drawer down, towels and swimsuits in the middle drawer, and the fourth drawer down had sheets and pillowcases. The bottom drawer was empty.

He stripped out of the clothes he had been wearing for days and redressed more appropriately for the weather. The smell of his old clothes tickled his senses. It wasn't a musty smell. It was actually pleasing, a mixture of old campfires and fresh air was woven forever into the fabric. His favorite flannel shirt was hanging on a hook by the back door and Simpson had seen it the instant he walked into the cabin. It had once been an obnoxious bright purple but had faded into a moderately annoying purple with black and white lines forming the traditional square pattern. The collar was frayed and the shirttail had several small tears in it – but it was also his lucky fishing shirt. He grabbed it off the hook and rubbed his face in it as a smile crossed his lips. So many happy memories were contained within the feel and smell of his shirt.

Without bothering to unbutton it, he pulled the shirt straight over his head. He felt the bulge in his left breast pocket and after sliding his fingers inside, he extracted the familiar Iowa Hawkeye lighter. He ran his thumb across the igniter several times until it flared up. Then, instead of putting in back in the shirt pocket, he stuffed it into the front pocket of his jeans. Sitting by the back door was the pair of hiking boots that he'd left at the cabin during his last visit. Simpson slipped the long metal bar out of the slots securing the backdoor. He swung the door open and instantly the fragrance-filled outside breeze pushed its way into the cabin, scattering dust and rattling the fishing poles hanging on the wall.

Isolation

Simpson carried his boots as he stepped out on the landing, pulling the door closed behind him and securing it with a swivel block latch. Sitting on the top step, he put on the well-worn hiking boots that had taken him over miles of trails, just for fun, and in pursuit of hundreds of mushrooms over the years. The comfort they brought felt good as he headed towards the outhouse and the propane tank.

Simpson opened the protective enclosure and rapped his knuckles on the tank. Not much reverberation -- so it too must be nearly full. He twisted the nozzle to let the gas flow into the pipes, then he followed the water line across the ground to where the filter at the end of the hose was submerged in the ice-cold water of the brook that fed into the lake. He lifted the mesh-enclosed filter out of the water, unhinged the cage, and examined the filter. It looked all right -- but he shook it to dislodge the plastered on leaves and mulch -- pulling out what he could from the openings in the mesh. Stepping onto a large flat rock in the deeper part of the brook and squatting down, he swished the cage back and forth until it was mostly clean. It only took seconds for his hands to begin aching from being submerged in the cold water. Careful not to slip on the wet rock as he stood up, he jumped back onto the grass. If the water wouldn't pull, he'd have to check the tubing.

Inside the outhouse, he lit the pilot light on the water heater and opened the water flow valve. It would take at least five hours before the water would be moderately warm and seven or more hours before he could have a hot shower. In another month, even if he did have hot water, taking a shower in that outhouse would be a very cold experience -- like getting in and out of an outdoor hot tub in the wintertime.

Simpson stopped at the large propane tank at the back of the cabin. There were two other tanks next to the one currently hooked up to the gas line. They both should be full since any empty tanks were always kept next to the storage shed as a reminder to take them into town to be filled. The propane in one tank would last a good month or more with normal use and longer if he didn't overdo it. The biggest use of gas was from the refrigerator, but he didn't have anything to put in it at the moment.

When the snow began to fly and the temperatures turned brutally cold -- *it* suddenly *dawned on him that he was already thinking about staying out here through the winter months and it didn't bother him* -- the firewood would be his lifeblood. The cabin was sealed around all the doors and windows, but it was far from being a cozy little (*insulated*) cottage.

Simpson opened the valve on the propane tank, hearing the gas filling the pipe. He was opening the back door when a mewing sound caught his attention. He turned and had a good look at the cat that had been in the storage shed. She was a beautiful calico cat with white and black feet and soft browns mixed-in all along her body. Her nose was black except for a pink circle that was just off center. Seeing the cat caused Simpson to suck in his breath. It wasn't possible and he knew that, but the cat looked eerily like Sophie, his wife's cat. It was only a coincidence, but for some reason it made his heart race. It wasn't possible for it to be Sophie or even an offspring. She'd never been to the cabin and had died several years ago.

Simpson studied the cat as it sat watching him. Her muddy-gold eyes studied him, contemplated him. Simpson felt shaky all over, so he sat down on the top step. He'd always considered himself a rational person, but lately, irrationality had taken a firm root inside his control center. Simpson considered the possibility that it was Sophie. If you looked at it sideways, it made sense, albeit in an *otherworldly sign from Vicky* sort of way. When

Isolation

rational explanations won't fit, then the implausible ones have to be considered. Why else would a Sophie doppelganger be here to greet him?

Sophie, he'd decided to call her that regardless of whether she was or wasn't, zigzagged her way towards him. Her fur was clean and soft and she looked fit and healthy -- another reason to do away with the plausible. The cat stopped at the bottom of the steps and Simpson noticed a pink collar with decorative glass studs on it.

Finally, this was a rational clue and a welcome relief to his sanity because Vicky's Sophie wore a deep red collar without any decoration. Even if there wasn't a tag on the collar for identification, this cat had been, or still was someone's pet. There was probably a very normal explanation -- either someone from one of the other cabins lost her or they had purposely discarded her here. He hoped it was the former since he hated the thought of someone just abandoning her.

Simpson stood up and entered the cabin. He left the door open a crack, kicking a block wedge in place to stop the wind from pushing the door all the way open or the spring from closing it. Then he busied himself with other settling-in tasks, lighting the pilot light on the stove and priming the pump so that water would start to flow out of the faucet. He took down the canister of powdered milk from the shelf over the counter by the sink. Digging around in the miscellaneous cupboard under the counter he found an old plastic bowl that once might have been a prettier shade of green. The water had to run for several minutes before he decided it was clear enough for the cat. He mixed the powdered milk with the water and carried the bowl to the hallway. The cat's shadow stretched across the back stoop, so at least she had come up the steps. He hoped that Sophie would come in. He couldn't say why, but the thought of having a companion, even an *otherworldly cat,* gave him a tiny bit of cheer. She would, in fact, be a most-welcome bit of company.

Thoughts continued to roll over him in waves. The fact that he cared more about the cat than he did his own family wasn't lost on him. What could his children possibly think of him right now? Granted, they hadn't been at all supportive or even willing to communicate with him since the accident. Now that he was here, seven hours removed from the passing of the woman he loved more than anything, he inexplicably felt no remorse. Simpson had turned 180 degrees from his core personality. He had never been the type of person to care only about himself -- and yet by running away immediately after Vicki's death, he was doing exactly that. He couldn't say why, but that was where he was supposed to be. In his mind, the cat outside was his proof. Any thought of leaving that spot or returning to his children and his responsibilities had left the station the instant he stepped off the bus.

Simpson installed one of the blue water bottles on the dispenser stand, enjoying the gurgling sound of the water as it settled. He opened the potbelly stove and pulled the lever to open the damper. Rolling up a section of a newspaper, he lit the end, held it inside the stove, and was relieved to see the smoke and flame sucking strongly upward. Perfect, he wasn't looking forward to cleaning out the flue if it had been plugged. Simpson smiled at the sound of the cat lapping up milk. Looking over the potbelly stove, he watched Sophie as she attacked the milk like a man who was dying of thirst. He intentionally ignored her as he sat down on the couch to think through the list of other things he needed to get done. And he knew that with cats, it's always better if they make friends on their own terms and in their own time. After a brief rest, he went into the kitchen and stood by the sink, looking out the window at the boathouse.

Inside the boathouse was where his father's 1986 Alumacraft and 25-horsepower Mercury motor were stored. The boat was seventeen feet of fishing heaven. Carl bought it new and he babied it, building the boathouse especially for it. The boat had been ten years old before he finally let Simpson run it for the first time. Simpson smiled warmly at the thought, hearing his father's voice, "Bring 'er up slow -- and don't be gassing it. She cuts tight. Watch out for the rocks -- a broken prop and you'll be the one doing the paddling back to the cabin."

That had been a good day and it was a special memory. He'd never forget how he'd caught a big fish while trolling the lakeshore. He handled the motor just like his father did -- cutting the engine far enough out to allow the boat to gently drift and not end up on the shore while still keeping the line taut until he could wrestle the fish in.

It was the first time Simpson noticed that the relationship with his father had changed. They had talked to one another as adults, able to share stories on equal footing. Simpson listened to the sound of his father's voice in his head now, and when he said, "Looks like a storm coming," Simpson replied aloud, "Going to be a nasty one too."

The sky was especially dark over the western end of the lake. The sky in northern Minnesota during an autumn storm was a painting detailed by exquisite coloring and depth. Simpson didn't know if it was due to the lack of pollution or because there wasn't a massive population bombarding the sky with artificial light, but the skies over those lakes had a full, deep, and more colorful appearance. There wouldn't be a chance to go out and check on the boat or test it out on the lake due to the impending arrival of the storm.

It was going to hit soon, so with no time to waste, Simpson spun around and headed for the back door. Sophie was curled up on the couch, her puffy tail tucked delicately under her chin and her eyes closed in total ignorance of him. It made him feel good to see her comfortable – and more than that -- *it felt right*.

His hair fluttered as a cold burst of air shot down the hallway. The fishing poles banged loudly against the wall and the door would have slammed forcibly against the wall if it hadn't been for the rubber boot in the way, preventing that explosive sound.

Simpson hurried out the back door and across the yard to the storage shed. He raced up the steps and shut the door, securing it in place. He did a quick check of the outhouse to make certain that the door was closed and the propane cupboard was secure. When he climbed the steps to the cabin, a big raindrop hit him perfectly on the back of his neck, causing shivers as the wind blew and kissed the moist spot.

Simpson shut the back door and sped through the cabin to shut the front door as well. The temperature outside must have dropped ten degrees in a mere few minutes. Up here, storms could last for less than an hour or for the entire night. Either way, they weren't great to be caught in if you were unprepared.

There was plenty of wood inside for the next few days, if necessary. His biggest concern would be the roof and any spots that might leak. A small leak could be contained, but with a driving rain and wind, large leaks could quickly become disasters. The instant he grabbed the outer door, a wind gust nearly pulled it out of his hand. He closed the screen door and secured it with the two hook and eye latches. In high winds, a tree branch or falling tree could cause considerable damage to the cabin.

With the inner door finally closed, the cabin became noticeably darker. There were several kerosene lamps positioned strategically throughout the cabin -- but of course, he'd forgotten to bring in one of the gas containers from the storage shed. Thankfully, the lamp sitting on top of the refrigerator was nearly full of kerosene. He took it down and raised the glass -- turning the wick up and using his lighter to ignite it. The hot kerosene odor stung his nose and eyes as he carried the lamp to the table and set it down. The table had a double-lamp propane-fed hanging light over it. There were also propane-fed lights over the kitchen sink and in each of the bedrooms. His father had always told him that it was safer to use the lanterns in a storm.

Simpson collected some of the smaller kindling and carried it over to the potbelly stove. He walked by Sophie, who paid little attention to him, as she curled herself tighter into a ball. "Hold on kitty. Give me a few minutes and I'll have it nice and toasty in here."

Simpson layered bigger pieces of wood on top of the kindling and crumpled up a few sections of newspaper underneath the grate. He could have used a fire-starter stick, but he wanted to save them for future use. His eye caught the date on the newspaper as he balled it up -- *Duluth News Tribune, September 8, 2008*. Something about the date switched on a light in the back of his mind – but when whatever memory was back there didn't decide to immediately appear, he stuffed the newspaper under the grate instead. He lit the paper in several spots and watched as it ignited and then shot flames upward into the flue. The drier kindling began to snap and pop and then some of the larger pieces caught. The fire was soon crackling with heat and the richly fragrant smell of pine.

Simpson smiled when he saw Sophie lift her head and yawn, her pink tongue curling out and back in. She held his gaze for an instant and he was aware of great depth in those eyes, an eerie intelligence that animals sometimes seem to possess. Sophie shifted her position on the couch, walking from one end to the other as she turned her back to the heat for awhile and then moved closer to the fire. Simpson tossed a couple more logs on the fire and headed for the kitchen to find something for both of them to eat.

The provisions weren't going to last nearly as long if he shared them with Sophie. Cats were finicky at best and extremely fussy at worst, but he didn't much care since having her there would be worth sacrificing some of his food. There wasn't much in the way of cat favorites and five cans of tuna weren't going to go very far. Dried beef and beef jerky would be iffy at best.

Surprisingly, he wasn't hungry, even after his long journey to make it to the cabin and the lack of food consumption over the last week. Honestly, he couldn't recall what he had eaten – or when. He always had a coffee cup nearby, mostly full, but he didn't recall ever going to refill it. He did go with Trent and Abby to the hospital cafeteria one time, but he hadn't been hungry at the time, so he just sat silently with them as they ate their food. His stomach had decided that now was the time and it gurgled out an order to proceed.

 He took down a weathered-looking box of instant chicken soup, opened it up, and removed two of the packets from inside. Grabbing the soup pot from the rack above the stove, he filled it with water from the dispenser and set it on the burner after the flames had kicked into a deep blue hue. The fire made any sloshed droplets of water on the side of the pot sizzle until they evaporated away.

Simpson was lost in thought as he stirred the contents of the chicken noodle soup around in the pot. He couldn't understand why he didn't feel awful for leaving Trent and Abby to deal with the aftermath of their mother's passing, along with his unexplained flight from sanity -- he simply didn't understand how he could have done that. Instead, he felt calm -- as if he was where he was supposed to be. If someone had asked him to explain why he felt that way, he would have been at a loss to do so. Simpson also knew that he should stay there long enough to discover what it was he was supposed to learn.

He truly believed that very few things in life happened by chance and everything worked by cause and effect. Sometimes, it was by God's design -- and Simpson was a believer. To him, it felt as if the moments that he was living were being orchestrated by God. That sensation had begun when he first saw the painting of the cabin in the waiting room of the hospital -- and it was reinforced again the moment that Sophie walked out of the shed. If he had been of Native American descent, Simpson might have called Sophie a spirit guide. He had plainly been guided here to learn something and he had no illusions that what was coming was going to be good and uplifting. The storm outside, the one on his doorstep, was an ominous sign that he should prepare for the worst.

When it hit, the storm brought high winds and horizontal rain. The only one not worried by the pounding of the rain on the window was Sophie. She stretched one paw lazily towards the fire, flexing her claws. A quick lick between her toes, a large yawn, and then she curled herself into a ball, quite oblivious to the storm's commotion and Simpson's frantic pacing. The persistent thought that was racing through his mind was the potential for rising water that could block his way back to civilization and a humbly apologetic reunion with his family. In spite of knowing that he had been sent to the cabin for a reason, for some sort of lesson, he continued to feel intermittent periods of shame and guilt and the storm seemed to be acting as an exclamation point about his poor behavior.

The one thing he refused to do was to blame the storm outside for his predicament. Depending on which side of his body faced the fire, he too was like the cat -- either too hot or too cold. He began to feel frantic as he surmised that just like his life, there would be no middle ground, no peace, and no comfort.

The dampness seeped through the walls of the cabin, but the roof held without a leak. Outside, the darkness suddenly erupted with brilliant and rapidly repeating clusters of lightning -- and then as that energy took hold, thunder shook the cabin – again and again.

Simpson took a large gulp of whiskey and then quickly put the bottle away. It calmed his nerves before he even felt the alcohol have a chance to warm his insides.

"Mind over matter," he muttered to himself.

Grabbing the comforter off the back of the couch, he wrapped himself up tightly and snuggled into a corner. His last thought before drifting off to sleep, *"I should have stayed with Vicky."*

CHAPTER 6:
Settling In

It hit Simpson on his fourth day at the cabin --that *settled in* feeling he'd get when spending time at the lake. He would quit doing things by thinking and start doing them by a combination of routine and instinct. It was hard idea to explain to someone who had never experienced it. He had tried to convey those ideas to Vicky once, only once – and her face immediately communicated a mixture of disinterest and concern for his well-being if he thought that this was some sort of important philosophy to live by. What he was trying so hard to sell, she had no interest in buying.

To Simpson's way of thinking, the people who had the best vacations were the ones who easily adapted to the pace of their new environments -- the rest went home exhausted, needing another vacation to recover from their vacation. Eventually, to some degree, most settled in, but some never quite seemed to adjust and you could spot them from a mile away. They were the people you took one look at and shook your head in apologetic sadness -- miserable on the beach, upset over every little obstacle shaking up their perfectly planned schedule, relentlessly complaining about the food, weather, or price of things. They were also the ones with the ungrateful attitudes thrown at hard-working servers about at how much money they were spending and "By God," those restaurant or hotel staff should acknowledge it and be grateful for their patronage. A similar thing happened with a routine change of geographic setting – not just a holiday. You could take someone from the big city and put them on a farm and they were either going to settle in and adjust or be on the next bus back to the city. He'd already quit thinking about all of that by the morning though. Hell, he didn't even know what day it was and *didn't care*.

Sophie awakened him up by purring in his ear, her tail draped across his face and tickling his cheek. After the third time Simpson swatted the loud mosquito buzzing in his ear and dancing on his face, he finally figured out that it was the cat. If two creatures ever needed the company of one another, it was the two of them. She needed somebody to scratch behind her ears, talk nonsense to her, and generally be her sugar daddy.

Simpson was thankful for her companionship, even as he brushed her tail out of his face and spit out the cat hairs clinging to his lips. The area on his body where Sophie's tail had previously rested chilled suddenly in the morning air. It was at least six degrees colder that morning than it had been on the previous day. He wasn't thinking, *maybe I should start a fire*. He said aloud to the cat, "Fuzz-ball, today is going to be a long underwear day." That was when Simpson knew he had settled in.

Simpson's instincts were also kicking in and reacting to his surroundings without the need to think first. Starting a fire now meant feeling the chill too early and giving in too soon to the cold. Simpson couldn't say how long he would stay at the cabin. Common sense would dictate leaving before the incoming winter gave him no choice but to stay. That meant he had six weeks to come to grips with the state of his mental health. If not, then he had better prepare to rough it alone for four months longer. He scooted up and sat in bed. Sophie did her cat dance on his lap and then curled into a ball, wrapping her tail around her face. Simpson began to stroke her back and she started to purr again.

"Anything else I can get you Princess Sophie?" he said chuckling. Her response was the clutching and unclenching of her front claws. Simpson laughed and Sophie's rewarded him with her one-eye glare. The cat yawned and repositioned herself beside him, but still within his petting range. The temperature must be in the mid-thirties outside and low-fifties inside. It might come down to sleeping on the couch in order to keep warm and to keep the fire going – and suddenly, the supply of firewood outside didn't seem to be nearly enough.

The cat was still a puzzle to Simpson. He knew that surely it wasn't possible for her to be Sophie reincarnated, but then she'd do something *Sophie-like* and make his insides churn with supernatural uncertainty. He was drawn to her -- and unless she turned into a "were-cat" at the next full moon, it really didn't matter. He'd asked her once why she was there and she gave him a look that could easily be read -- "Silly man -- I am where I am supposed to be."

Simpson slept in the guest bedroom. Why? It was because the other room was where his father had once slept and from the moment he opened the door, it had a haunted feel to it. From that room, he took the extra woolen blankets and checked all the clothes underneath the bed and in the dresser.

It was a surprise to find the twelve-gauge shotgun and the 22-caliber rifle in their protective cases underneath the bed. His father wasn't a hunter, and he had never stayed there during the fall when it was bear and deer season. The rifle was understandable though. Occasionally, it was necessary to put down an undesirable critter. Skunks, raccoons, and rabid muskrats couldn't read the 'No Trespassing' sign his father had tacked to the side of the shed. The shotgun was different and it instantly gave him a bad vibe. While his eyes didn't roll back in his head and there weren't any prophetic visions filling his head, the mere touch of it sent inexplicable chills down his spine.

Twice Simpson heard noises coming from inside the room and he ventured in to investigate. Both times, when the door opened, the air felt heavier -- and the second time, he smelt his father's Old Spice cologne. That was when he'd seriously thought about nailing the door shut.

Simpson cautiously shifted out of the bed so he wouldn't disturb Sophie. Dressed in sweatpants, ankle socks, a *Journey* tee shirt from the eighties, and his old faded Hawkeye sweatshirt, he would have made a slightly humorous and mixed-era portrait if anyone had chosen to paint that. The icy-cold air attacked his body as it transitioned from the warmth of the bed to the colder, inside temperature. Over the ankle socks he'd slept in, Simpson added a pair of wool socks with leather pads on the bottom.

The cabin was slightly warmer as he approached the potbelly stove. Opening the door, a pleasant burst of heat escaped from inside. The large logs he had tossed in before going to bed were nearly gone, leaving only a few red flecks of amber on an ash log. Cleaning out the ashes, Simpson added some kindling on top of the smoldering piece of wood and blew gently on the last amber patch until a yellow flame danced up the side and the kindling caught. Once the flames were pulled up the chimney, he added several logs and left the door open, enjoying the warmth. Making a pot of coffee was the next important thing to do. Carl had done a good job of insulation when he built the cabin since it didn't take long for the heat from the fire and the burner on the stove to warm the cabin. Thirty degrees outside was still a long way off from zero or *forty below*.

    Simpson let the coffee perk for an extra couple of minutes to give it a stronger taste. With steaming mug in hand, Simpson sat down on the couch next to Sophie. They were already developing a morning ritual, Simpson and his first cup of coffee, Sophie getting her ears scratching as he drank it, and a second cup meant that it was time to find the cat something to eat. Sophie paid no attention to his third cup -- that is unless one of the doors to the outside suddenly opened. She would be nowhere in sight, hidden from human awareness in whatever place cats go, still watching, and the instant the screen door squeaked, she was right there, underfoot, and then racing around the cabin.

    Simpson spent several hours each day chopping stacks of firewood and collecting kindling. With each chop of the ax, a negative thought would slip away and the bantering voices from within weren't able to refill his well of internalized self-loathing quite as quickly as the day before. The previous day, he'd been stuck in the replay of the accident and the unholy sounds of hospital monitors counting down. Lost in his memory, Simpson chopped in rhythm to their incessant beeping, tears running down his face, with no means of avoiding the mental pain. As he failed to concentrate, one swing went wide and almost caught the inside of his ankle with the blade as the ax head veered off the tree stump. Nearly losing an ankle brought him back to reality with a crash. Afterward, and in spite of there being very little of it in reserve, Simpson used up all the remaining hot water as he stood in the shower, trying to massage the unforgiving knot of tension out of his neck.

    Simpson had begun to retreat into a semi-functional state of numbness once again and Vicky was never far from his thoughts. He saw her smile, felt her loving touch on his hand, and smelled the fragrance of her favorite cherry blossom body lotion. At the same time, he also moved through each day by doing what needed to be done, somehow making it to next day as the guilt lessened with each setting sun.

    Simpson had worked on the boat and motor, using the hoist to lower the boat onto the wheel runner, then winching the boat down the incline into the water and tying it to the dock. The wind was up, causing the lake to swell with white-capped waves, so going out on the lake was saved for another day.

    From where Simpson sat on the couch, one hand deep in Sophie's fur, the other holding an empty cup of coffee which he didn't recall drinking, let alone enjoying, he could see the calm lake outside the cabin window. He had planned the first foray out on the lake and an attempt at catching some fish for his furry friend and himself. Simpson hated the idea of wasting propane, but with enough fish caught, some would need to be frozen and that meant running the refrigerator. Sophie would be happy to have plenty of ready fish on hand to eat, especially after the way she had devoured the tuna the previous day.

    The sound of her purring was calming. There was a hypnotic rhythm to it and when he closed his eyes there was a warming ray of hope within his tortured mind and some needed peace seeped in. A log in the stove popped loudly, catching Simpson by surprise. Sophie yowled and arched her back as Simpson squeezed her too hard in response to the sound. After several times saying,

Isolation

"I'm sorry," Sophie settled back down. In her kitty-telepathy way, she had let Simpson know it was time to make breakfast.

Simpson filled his cup with hot coffee and mixed Sophie a bowl of milk. Once the can of Spam was opened, he cut up several small chunks for her. He cubed some if it and added it to his mixture of powdered eggs, pouring the whole conglomeration into a cast-iron frying pan. He wasn't actually hungry, but he ate because it was what he was supposed to do.

Ever since the accident, food hadn't tasted good and wasn't satisfying. Spraying the cast-iron skillet with a vegetable spray did little to stop the powdered eggs mixture from sticking, but after adding enough pepper, they almost tasted like eggs. The last few bites went to Sophie. He knew how badly she wanted it since he always had to stand up when he ate to keep her out of his food.

Simpson finished the dishes, shutting off the water in the sink. He heard the sound of a voice coming from inside his father's bedroom and Sophie heard it too. She took two steps towards the door and then stopped, looking back at Simpson in her usual charming way. Telepathically, she said, *"I don't have hands, so don't expect me to open the door."*

Simpson dried his hands on the towel, his head cocked sideways and his body leaning toward the closed door. His feet weren't moving and his mind was running through a mental checklist of all the possible explanations for the sound of a voice. An intruder had come in through the window, a radio was playing, neither of which was plausible. "*No, it's a ghost,*" responded the irrational part of Simpson.

"Okay," he stated aloud, "then it must be the wind blowing just right making it sound like someone talking."

"*Sorry friend, but what wind? You've already looked outside at the glassy-still lake. It's a ghost,*" the inner voice said.

Sophie took a couple of steps closer to the door and Simpson summoned up the ability to move, his concrete shoes no longer holding him in place. The scared part of him was thinking about crazed zombies or evil poltergeists and he feared that something would harm Sophie if she got too close. Breaking through his paralysis and racing forward, Simpson scooped Sophie up off the floor, shaking because he knew that something was going on that defied explanation.

Simpson backed away from the door, but the voice was louder, feminine, and familiar, which caused him to stop and listen. Though he couldn't make out the words and couldn't even be sure that they really were words, he knew that they were meant for him. Simpson put Sophie on the couch and gathering up his courage, he walked bravely to the door. Ignoring his dangerously beating heart and churning insides, as well as the cowardly inner voice pleading that the *"ghost leave now,"* Simpson didn't stop. To his dismay, he opened the door and boldly walked into the room.

The abrupt opening of the door created an air current fanning the window drapes and Simpson half-heartedly believed it was the wind. The sudden movement of the drapes gave false hope to the wind theory until his brain rationalized that their movement was due to the opening of the door. Standing in the center of the room, Simpson studied everything.

The female voice was no longer talking, the room was empty, and the drapes had stopped moving. Just to be sure, he slid the drapes apart and looked out the window. There was nothing of note to see other than trees -- no spectral forms floating away or beckoning him to follow. The room was ghostly cold, but that was easily explained and certainly not a sign of some supernatural presence. With the door closed, the heat from the fire was unable to penetrate into the room.

Simpson shivered again, more from fear than because it was cold and he couldn't explain why he was so frightened. As if on cue, a wolf howled far away in the distance. The sound carried dramatically over the waters of the lake, enhancing the richness of its tone. A new ripple of shivers ran down his spine and Simpson knew without understanding why that he needed to be concerned about the wolves.

A book on top of the dresser caught Simpson's eye. He could have sworn that it wasn't there when he first looked in the room. Maybe he'd just missed it before -- or it had materialized out of thin air. That wouldn't have surprised him, given the circumstances. His mind was racing with thoughts of the unexplained and seeing things through a skewed eye. The improbability of the book was what made it stand out -- it was one of Vicky's favorites and it hadn't been written until 2010 – long after his last visit to the cabin. There was no answer for how it came to be there and Simpson's hand was trembling as he picked up *Our Heart* by Brian L. MacLearn off the top of the dresser.

Opening the front cover, Simpson studied the author's autograph and inscription: "To Vicky and Simpson, Enjoy!"

He was a local author from Iowa who signed the book at the Better Read Bookstore. Without a doubt, this was Vicky's copy. She never got tired of loaning it out to friends, but always with a warning that they should keep *a large box of tissues* nearby.

Just like the sensation that ran through him when he touched the shotgun, the book also sent a perplexing wave of feelings through him. But unlike the evil he felt with the shotgun, the book warmed him with a sense of hope that was accompanied by loss and sadness. Tears began welling up in his eyes. Simpson's heartache for Vicky and the feelings that seeped into him as he held the book crushed his wall of resistance.

He tried putting the book back down on the dresser, but it didn't want to go there. His hand refused to let go and a sensation like a knife penetrated deeply into his heart as he attempted to release it. The feeling was so real that he actually grasped his chest and gasped for air at the pain that it caused.

Shaken, Simpson staggered out of the room, carrying the book and closing the door securely behind him. Simpson seriously thought again about nailing it closed -- picturing the boards nailed across it from the old stack underneath the shed. Sophie crisscrossed between his legs, rubbing her fur along the bottoms of his sweatpants. The cabin that once brought him hope now began to make him feel suffocated. He needed to get out of the cabin, find some space, breathe some cold air, and regain some much-needed tranquility out on the lake.

It felt fine when he put the book down on the table on the second attempt. It didn't suddenly fly open in an unexplained wind or levitate off the table as he laid it on top of two others he'd decided to read. Sophie was either completely unaware of Simpson's heightened emotional state or was uninterested. She sat stoically at the front door, tail curled around her front feet, her eyes conveying her impatience.

"I'm coming girl. Give me a second." He glanced back for one last look at the book. It was still a book -- only a book -- but there was also a gnawing sense that it was something more. Simpson closed the door on the potbelly stove and stopped at the kitchen sink to splash water on his face. The water was cold and stimulating, but not nearly enough so to douse his uneasiness. Simpson jumped at his own reflection in the sun-drenched window.

"Damn," he swore under his breath, throwing more water on his face and rubbing it into his eyes. Simpson's pulse was charged up and beating furiously as he glanced at the cupboard protecting the whiskey—*not yet, not this way.*

He banished the thought – temporarily -- and grabbed the fishing tackle from the hallway. Just holding on to the pole soothed his anxious feelings a bit. Sophie watched from her spot at the front door and when he grabbed the wide-brimmed fishing hat off the hook, a second ball cap fell to the floor -- Trent's old Hawkeye hat. Simpson remembered the day Trent couldn't find it. It was the start of football season and his son always wore it during the games while they watched them on television together. They had torn the house apart trying to find it -- but it had been here in the cabin the whole time. Picking it up gingerly, he hung it back on the hook. It would be going home with him when he left.

Simpson paused as he acknowledged the connection between his thoughts and a desired course of action—*he was going to leave.*

Simpson was almost at the door when he noticed that he wasn't wearing his fishing clothes. He leaned the fishing pole against the table and put the tackle box on the floor next to it. When the sun went down and the wind picked up, the air on the lake could turn bitterly cold, even in warmer temperatures. The moisture could cut right through you, so he added several layers, including long underwear. Simpson smiled as he donned his lucky fishing shirt and then grabbed a windbreaker off one of the hooks. Sophie hadn't moved from her spot at the front door, but her eyes were a stinging glare of impatience. Once the door opened, she was off like a shot, racing around to the back of the cabin. To satisfy inner voices that were persistently whispering about *ghosts*, Simpson walked around to the side of the cabin next to his father's bedroom window. It was a relief to see that there were no footprints beneath the window and no signs of anything that could have imitated the sound of voices. *I'm not crazy and the cabin is not haunted*—he told himself. What he heard must have had a rational explanation, but saying it and believing it were two completely different things.

Out of habit and hard lessons learned, Simpson checked the gas can for the motor and made sure that the paddles were in the boat. A slight breeze had picked up from out of the west, carrying a warming sensation with it. His grandfather used to say, "The fish bite the best with the wind in the west." Remembering him and his witticisms brought a genuine smile to Simpson's face. He whistled his grandfather's familiar tune as the motor turned over on the third pull. Then he let it idle as he untied the mooring line. The boat backed away from the dock and once it was brought around facing out to the lake, he increased the speed of the throttle until it was running full open. The boat skidded easily on top of the water and like the kid he once was, the bounce of the boat made him grin in anticipation of catching fish. The smell of the lake mixed with the scent of autumn crispness was nearly narcotic. Without sunglasses, the sting of the breeze made his eyes water, forcing him to squint. The hum of the motor and the vibration of the boat cutting through the water took Simpson back in time to happy memories at the lake. He didn't care if there weren't any night-crawlers or minnows to use -- he had his lucky shirt.

The morning haunting had been completely forgotten. He fixated on remembering the best fishing spots in the upper portion of the lake and the closest was Seagull Rock. The large flat rock stuck out of the water, beckoning the seagulls to flock to it. Around the submerged island, Walleyes, Northerns, and Bass frequented the deep holes. Which side of the island they were on changed with the direction of the wind and the time of the year. Simpson saw the seagulls first. There must have been nearly thirty of them, crammed together on the rock. He didn't expect them to be at the lake since they should have migrated south by that time.

Simpson throttled back the boat and put it in neutral, letting the current carry it toward the rock. The seagulls were agitated by the intrusiveness but held their ground. Digging through the tackle box, Simpson found a lure with a plastic worm and he rigged up the line and sprayed the worm with a fish attractant. In some places around Seagull rock, the water depth reached forty feet, other spots ten feet or less. With the luxury of polarized sunglasses, you could see several feet down.

Simpson tossed the line out behind the boat. The plopping sound of the sinker hitting the water was enough to scatter the seagulls away from the rock. Two of the largest seagulls landed in the water fifty yards away. They'd be keeping track of any fish caught, hoping that something was left behind. With the boat kicked into gear and the speed set slightly higher than at idle, it wasn't until the third circle around the rock that the first fish struck. Simpson reared back against the hit and set the hook. He put the motor in neutral and shut it off, but made sure to keep his line taut. By the pull on the line shortly afterward, Simpson could tell it was a good-sized fish and he wrestled with it, waiting for it to break the surface so he could get a closer look and ready the net. Then it hit him, no net. "Go to hell!" Simpson swore aloud.

The fish put up a monster fight, darting back and forth, forcing him to be careful against it snapping the line and after a long ten minutes, the fish surfaced -- a large Northern, easily over ten pounds. A certain cat back at the cabin was going to be well fed if Simpson could manage to get it into the boat without losing it. Simpson felt confident enough to attempt lifting it into the boat, even knowing that the teeth on a Northern were extremely sharp and the fish was extremely slippery and hard to hold on to.

"Alright buddy, let's do this the easy way," Simpson told the fish. He lifted the Northern's head out of the water slightly and brought it into the boat, squeezing the fish behind the head at the gills to render it motionless. So much for being docile, once in the boat, the fish jerked wildly, snapping the line and cutting Simpson's fingers with its gills. The fingers would heal and the tasty meal of fish would outweigh the loss of blood and sore fingertips.

In the distance, a loon called out. Simpson couldn't help himself and in celebration of the first fish caught, tried to do his best imitation, "Ahhwooohooo." The excitement of landing the fish and being out on the water had gotten the better of him.

Simpson's father had been the only one in the family who had the knack of calling like a loon. From his silly fishing hat to his uncanny ability to mimic a loon, he was never more in his element than when he had a fishing pole in his hand and a grin on his face. Simpson's rendition of the soulful sound of the loon was so bad that even the seagulls abandoned him, taking to the air to put distance between them and the crazed man in the boat. He laughed so hard that tears blotted out his vision. Several more tries to make the loon sound, each one sounding worse than the one before, only brought more laughter and a hoarse voice. It didn't matter because his happy tears became mixed with tears of grief. One last choked call, and surprisingly, the yodel managed to sound decent at the top of the call. Simpson's father must have been smiling in the afterlife.

He wiped away the tears with the back of his hand, saying aloud, "It's okay, Simpson. It's why you came up here," Next he told himself. "Life is never going to be the same. I'm never going to be the same. The one person who defined me and made me a better person is never going to be there for me again."

Isolation

Simpson had begun to accept the irrational act of walking away from the hospital, leaving his grieving children parentless -- yet he didn't feel remorse. He thought that it would be better for them to worry about him than to see him fall apart -- a depth of falling apart that he couldn't have done if he'd stayed. The slight breeze became still and the warmth of the sun caressed his face. Simpson closed his eyes and turned his face sunward. The emotional kickback of seesawing feelings had left him exhausted, taking the fight out of him. The Northern flopped around in the boat, chasing the last of the emotional fog away.

"Alright buddy, I'm with you. Let me get the stringer out of the tackle box." For once, the bright orange stringer was in the right compartment. Simpson ran the stringer's spike through the upper and lower lip of the Northern and clamped it shut. "I'm betting you are closer to fourteen pounds." Making sure to tie the stringer to the seat brace, Simpson lifted the fish over the side. Just as the fish was almost overboard, he noticed the notch missing from the top of the tailfin. It was about the size of a quarter and looked like someone had taken a big hole-punch to the tailfin. "I'll be damned…"

About thirty years earlier, Simpson had caught a similar fish to that one. It hadn't been as big, but it had an identical part of its tailfin missing. A warm sensation swept over Simpson, not a feeling of déjà vu -- more a feeling of knowing when something was all too funky and distinctly not right.

Things were starting to pile up, he was paying attention, and his stomach began to churn. First, it was the unexpected appearance of Sophie and then it was the Northern. It was clearly more than just a set of coincidences -- and if you tossed in the sounds of ghost voices, there was an increasingly persistent feeling that he was being haunted.

The fish plopped into the water with a satisfying floomph. Simpson twisted around on his seat and started the motor -- one pull and it roared back to life, instantly burying the peaceful serenity of the lake. The boat had drifted nearly a quarter of a mile away from gull rock. While the boat was in gear, slowly taking Simpson back toward the fishing spot, he examined the damage to his plastic worm. It might be able to take one or two more hits before needing to be retired to the land of abused and forgotten fish baits.

After finding an old rag tucked away in a compartment inside the middle bench seat, Simpson dipped it into the water and cleaned the wound to his fingers, swearing at himself for also forgetting the first-aid kit. He could easily picture his father standing on the dock with his arms crossed and with a look of consternation on his face. The fishing net and first aid kit would have been sitting on the dock at his father's feet, a quiet testament to his son's lack of thoroughness.

After an hour of circling the rock, Simpson had only caught two mid-sized smallmouth bass to add to the stringer -- but he also had more fish than they could eat in the next couple of days. Lifting the stringer out of the water, he put the fish into a five-gallon plastic bucket. The wording on the old bucket was nearly gone, but Simpson remembered what it once said, "Krieger's Hamburger Pickle Slices." Empty plastic buckets were priced at a premium in Krofton nowadays. Restaurants sold their unwanted buckets for a nice price and it was generally expected amongst neighbors that when you stopped somewhere else to eat on the road, you would ask if they had extra buckets for sale.

Simpson opened up the throttle and let the cool breeze wash over him as he sped back to the cabin. Out of the corner of his eye, he caught a shadow moving along the water's edge on the north shore. Simpson looked more intently at the spot, but couldn't see anything that would have caused the movement. With the bounce of the boat as it skimmed the water, the shadow might have been a tree stump or dark rock that could easily be mistaken for an animal moving. With all that had been just *too coincidental*, it left a feeling of something or someone watching him from the shore.

Simpson's mother had the uncanny ability to tell the moment she walked into a room if a lamp or a vase had been moved a fraction of an inch -- it was that same type of feeling – but the more he scanned the shoreline, the less he saw anything that might resemble an animal.

Adding the unexplained shadow to his growing list of unexplainable coincidences, he turned to enjoy the view of the lake. Down towards the southern portion, you could just make out Kittelson's cabin -- barely a spec at this distance. Squinting against the spray and sun, there were a few relevant details though. Smoke was coming out of the chimney and there was a break in the tree line where the cleared land housed the cabin. Simpson briefly considered heading south to say hello since he had always liked Robert Kittelson, but he had no idea if the Kittlesons still owned the cabin. Bob and Thelma had been in their seventies the last time he'd seen them. Simpson also didn't want to find out that they'd lost a cat. If he visited, he'd be obliged to ask.

Pangs of guilt nibbled at his insides. "*What if the cat belongs to their granddaughter and she's miserable thinking that it is never coming back*." No amount of potential remorse made him alter course though. He couldn't explain it, but he knew that he needed Sophie. Simpson uttered aloud all the reasons for keeping her, but the whine of the motor was his only reply. With precision mastery from years on the lake, Simpson raced the boat towards the dock and then cut the engine in perfect synchronization to enable him to reach out and grab the mooring hook.

Frosted waves whipped against the shore from the motor's wake. Simpson couldn't stop smiling since his father had always grumbled when he came in too fast. "That one was for you, Dad," he stated as he tied off the boat. After unhooking the stringer, Simpson lifted the bucket out and up onto the deck. Grabbing his pole and tackle box, he stepped onto the dock and noticed Sophie sitting on the porch watching him. "

Hey Girl!" Simpson called out, "We're eating high on the fish tonight." Sophie gave a quick *flip* of her tail and yawned with disinterest.

Standing on the dock, looking back out over the lake at the vibrant colors, Simpson felt happy for the first time in a long time -- not a happy without problems sort of happy, but the kind of happy to be away from your problems happy.

Simpson carted the bucket of fish up the dock and set it down by the door to the fish-cleaning hut. He took the tackle box and pole back with him to the cabin and as he sat on the bench next to the door, Simpson rummaged through the tackle box looking for a fillet knife and the ceramic blade sharpener. The cut on his finger was starting to ache and felt warm, so it wouldn't do any good to bandage it before cleaning the fish. The edge of the fillet knife was now sharp enough to do the job.

When he looked up, Sophie had made her way down to the bucket. Standing on her back legs, she leaned in to get a better look. Satisfied that there was indeed something edible in the bucket, she sat down and gave him a, "what are you waiting for" look."

It didn't matter how many Northern Pike you might have cleaned in the past -- they were always a pain to deal with.

Simpson did a respectable job and ended up with two nice filets along with a pile of cat trimmings. Before giving them to Sophie, he made sure there were no bones mixed in. Sophie sensed that there was something for her and her yawls were tempered with fevered anticipation and cat commands. Opening the hut door, Simpson set the scraps down on the ground and had to snatch his hand back quickly before Sophie included it in her feast. Erasing the idea that cats always eat daintily -- Sophie inhaled the fish trimmings in a matter of seconds. When she finished, she sat tall and wrapped her tail around her front legs. Her tongue lapped happily at the fish oil on her lips while Simpson chuckled and told her, "I'm glad I could be of service."

To Simpson, there wasn't anything better than the smell of freshly caught fish frying on the stove. The anticipation caused his stomach to turn somersaults while waiting for the first batch to cook. Then, with what he thought was going to be a great sense of composure, he dipped the next batch in milk and rolled them in cracker meal, lowered them gently into the hot snapping oil of the frying pan, slid them back out with a spatula, slowly placed them on a plate, and then paused for a mere second or two before madly cramming a huge chunk of hot fish into his mouth. He had to inhale a mouthful of air and shift the fish around in his mouth until it was cool enough to swallow. Whatever wasn't eaten immediately would be going into the *now* running fridge. Simpson ate half of the first batch while the next batch cooked and he decided to stop eating before he made himself sick and save the two other fish for another day.

He had brought two plates to the table and placed the platter of fish in the center. Since fish was the only course for that particular evening meal, he initially attacked it like a madman. But his insatiable appetite quickly vanished and he ended up forcing himself to eat the last few bites. Sophie had also lost any interest in another plateful of food and had taken up her usual spot on the couch, lying on top of her head with her stomach turned upwards. Simpson smiled as he said, "I don't blame you – I'm not sure I would be able to lie on my stomach tonight either."

While standing at the sink doing the dishes, Simpson watched the night sky as it settled into a thin, evening light. A shadowy movement outside the window suddenly caught Simpson's eye and just as it had been in the afternoon, the shadow was there and then gone. Something was out there and that something was keeping tabs on him -- a feeling he knew was correct. He dried the dishes, put everything away in the kitchen, and then stoked the fire. Simpson stretched out on his back and a relaxed yawn escaped. It wouldn't be long before he took up his own cat-like position as the warmth of the fire and the comforting sounds of the cabin settling in for the night against the outside chill made it hard to keep his eyes open.

Feeling that he needed to do something more tangible before his mind began to run away with conjecture about who and what was observing him, Simpson collected the mysterious *Our Heart* book from the table and sat down by the fire to read. Nearly halfway through the second chapter, it suddenly dawned on him that it was Vicky's voice in his head reading it aloud. That was quite weird for him since he normally assigned voices to the characters along with pictorial descriptions that matched the author's narrative. The narrator in that story was male, so it should have sounded like a man. Instead, he heard Vicky's voice attempting to impersonate a male voice. She spoke using her husky voice, the one that Simpson always thought of as "vixen" and "sexy."

He put the book down, rubbing the back of his neck. "This is getting stranger by the hour -- shadows that aren't there and

Vicky talking behind closed doors and now in my head," he complained to an uninterested Sophie.

Simpson added some more wood to the fire and paced around inside of the cabin to calm his nerves. Feeling a bit more at ease, he grabbed one of the other books on the table and sat back down. After the first chapter, he noticed that he had quit listening inside his head to hear who might be talking and he was able to actually get into the story.

Everything was as it should be – *no unexplained Vicky voices*. Somewhere along the way, he drifted off into a pleasant sleep. A log popped in the fire, waking him with a start. Sophie raised one eye to glare at him, "Right, girl -- time to call it a night."

After one last stoking of the fire and a session of uncontrollable yawning, Simpson ambled back to the bedroom. The room was quite chilly compared to the sleepy warmth of the main room and he quickly changed into sweatpants and a sweatshirt. The dresser was close to the window and as he pulled out a pair of hunting socks, he could see his breath. It was going to be a crisp night. It wouldn't be long before he'd be sleeping inside a sleeping bag and also under the covers.

Simpson tumbled into bed and as soon as the chill gave way to warmth, his body relaxed and he fell deeply asleep. All thoughts of evil shadows and possessed books were forgotten. In his dreams, Vicky put her head on his chest and tenderly traced circles on the back of his hand with the tip of her finger. He breathed deeply, inhaling the fruity scent of her shampoo. And somewhere in the vast expanse of his dream, a cat was purring.

CHAPTER 7:
A Rainy Day

———•·•⧖•·•———

Over the last week, it had felt as if time was stuck in a repeating loop. The gloomy weather and tedious days were stacked upon themselves with no bright spots to look forward to. If it had been winter and snow was all that could be seen, Simpson might have easily fallen into a blissful state of insanity.

There hadn't been any other shadow sightings and life in the cabin had mostly been predictable and normal. He did get a quick prickle on the back of his neck when he picked up the book from the couch to set it back on the table. That scared the living hell out of him, causing the book to drop to the floor – and it took nearly a day before Simpson had the courage to pick it up off the floor. In a strange, tempting-fate way, he began to purposefully pick it up two or three times a day -- *just because.*

That seemed to have removed any power it had and there hadn't been any other intimidating feelings when Simpson had touched it after that. He had read several more chapters and thankfully, they were in his own voice when he heard the words echoing inside his head. Time was moving forward though because the days were getting shorter. Simpson had been lucky to always have one of those internal clocks and he never needed an alarm clock – well, mostly never needed one. He consistently woke up at six twenty-five, no matter how tired he was or when he went to bed the previous night.

The mornings may have been perceptibly darker, but the weather had been a bit warmer as Simpson cautiously moved through each day in a state of anticipation -- waiting for something and dreading whatever might be coming -- acknowledging that he must face the undefined 'it' without ever knowing the *why* of it all.

He thought about his children and knew that if Trent and Abby had been determined to find him, they would have looked for their father at the cabin. But since no one had been out to see if he was staying there and more than two weeks had now passed, Simpson doubted if anyone would be coming. It hurt to think that his kids were fine with him being completely out of the picture, but then again, it was probably better than what he truly deserved.

With the exception of the much-needed companionship of the cat, the loneliness had sent his thoughts bouncing back and forth from panicked thoughts, to worry about them being on their own without their father, to wondering if they were even slightly worried about where he was, to his recurring waves of guilt about not being there to help them through the pain of losing their mother.

Back and forth he went between his list of fears and the self-loathing that was wrapped tightly around the whole package -- but never did he feel the desire to return -- not yet – the time was not right yet. He still felt that he was undeserving of their love and forgiveness.

There had been a few *bad* moments when Simpson suddenly stopped dead in his tracks and cried uncontrollably. It felt like a rehearsal and he sensed that something even bigger was coming, some sort of episode that would require grieving, so he needed to learn how to process grief in preparation for what hadn't even arrived yet.

Simpson completed every mundane maintenance project on the cabin that he could think of and there was soon enough chopped firewood to last until the following April. The freezer was about one-fourth full of fish, but the yearning for a thick slab of fire-grilled ribeye with a baked potato drenched in butter, chives, and sour cream occasionally crowded into his thoughts. What he wouldn't have given for a big bowl of chocolate ice cream smothered with caramel topping and pecans.

There had been a hilarious moment when Simpson confided in Sophie about his need for beef. As if on cue, the cat bolted for the back bedroom just as he bent over to scratch her ears. "You're a cat, not a cow!" he yelled after her, laughing for several minutes before it all turned to tears again. Every chance to laugh removed one brick of pain from atop the high wall that had been protectively built up against his anguish.

Simpson had not gone there to forget -- but to remember and grieve and prepare for something undefined that was on the way. On the previous day, he dug out a large yellow legal pad and had begun to jot notes down about his life. For every negative thing he had remembered and written down, he had purposely added two positive contributions. He knew that the negativity would drown him if he wasn't careful. It may have seemed like a crazy way to heal himself, but it helped -- taking a hard look at his life and forcing his mind to see the good when he only wanted to dwell in the bad.

Isolation

The good things were actually tougher to remember at first, but once he started doing the healing exercise, or exorcism might be a better term for what Simpson was doing, he had started to feel better -- *slightly better than worthless.*

There was the time when he'd stopped in freezing temperatures and icy rain to change the tire for an elderly couple -- back before everyone had cell phones and you always stopped to help if you could. It wouldn't have been fair to write down the good things about his life where Vicky was concerned though. She had made Simpson better than he really was, made it easy to be loving and thoughtful.

One of their friends was a struggling songwriter who had lost her husband and to help her deal with the loss, she'd written a song about the deep love she had for her husband. The first time Simpson heard that recording, he turned into a blubbering mess. Knowing her as a friend and not just an anonymous musician made it that much more personal. Whenever Simpson felt out of sorts in his life, he would listen to it and remember to be thankful. He had listened to it so often that he could sing it from memory:

"My life has changed, so alone and afraid. Too much quiet, so much empty space. The silence only magnifies my pain. I've cried myself to sleep and drank my share too. Tomorrow still came, the next day the same. Friends would stop by, sometimes they'd try to help me forget, offering their prayers. Give it some time, the hurting will end… Oh, they'll never understand. It wasn't his touch or the way that he kissed me. It wasn't the silly way he smiled, or how my heart broke when he tried not to cry. God knows that he wasn't a saint. No, not even close. He was much more than my one true love…he was my life."

Back then, he had been sympathetic about how she felt -- but later, Simpson could fully relate to all of that pain. Vicky had been his life, his everything, and Simpson could never figure out how some people could bounce back up and smile as if nothing had changed after a devastating event.

By the time he went to bed, the legal pad was nearly half-full. Sophie kept brushing against his legs, trying to get his attention. As he looked down at her, she gave him her "and what about me" look. "Right," he told her. The last entry of the night was *Rescued Sophie from cold and starvation.* Satisfied that she had made her point with her 'psychic cat vibes', Sophie headed off to bed.

Sometime during the night, the wind picked up outside and a cold draft nibbled at his ears. Simpson rolled over onto his side and pulled the covers up to cover his ear. Mumbling something about remembering to check for leaks tomorrow, he drifted back to sleep. When he awoke, Simpson didn't need to hear the pinging of rain outside to tell him it was raining. He could already feel the moisture in his head and joints.

Anytime the barometer changed drastically, he got a sinus headache. Based on the severity of his throbbing head that morning, there had been a major change in pressure. Through half-slit eyes, Simpson fought his way out of bed and managed to wobble toward the dwindling heat of the wood burner. It was cold enough inside the cabin to see his breath and there was only the barest touch of warmth emanating from the stove. Simpson shivered as he loaded it up with wood and fanned the coals with air until they caught and ignited. Every breath rocked the pain in his head and bending over made him dizzy. He reached around behind him and pulled the blanket off the couch, wrapping it tightly around his trembling shoulders as he waited for the heat to thaw out his icy-cold body.

Sophie made her way out of the comfort of the bedroom once the fire was going strong. She plopped down in front of the open door and absorbed the searing heat without a care about singeing her fur. After adding more layers of clothes and swallowing two extra-strength pain tablets, Simpson grabbed the slicker off the back hook, stepped into the fur-lined boots at the back door, and braved the freezing rain in a race to the outhouse. The pounding of his feet as he ran across the slick ground outside sent jolts of pain through his body and he almost passed out from nausea before he could slide his pants down in the outhouse. Only the thought of hanging his head over the toilet seat kept him from throwing up -- that and the fact that there weren't enough pain pills left in the cabin to waste a single one of them if he vomited. He clearly needed another plan for using the outhouse or the foresight to bring the large kerosene lantern out ahead of time.

The moment Simpson opened the back door to come back inside the cabin, he caught wind of it. It was very faint -- and completely out of place in the forest-fragrant wilderness. This time his shivers had nothing to do with the cold or the dampness. Like a locked-in bloodhound, he followed the scent and it grew stronger as he moved closer to his father's bedroom. His nose reacted to it first, then his head and heart worriedly understood -- *Vicky had decided to visit.* It was her perfume that got his attention first, but then it was the slightly ajar bedroom door that captured his full attention -- *headache be damned.*

Simpson's mind was racing with ghostly thoughts and imagined dangers again. It didn't help that what little daylight penetrated into the bedroom was so dim that the difference between darkness and daylight was imperceptible. He felt the cold emanating from within that room, calling for him and reaching for him. Still wearing the slicker and boots, he boldly pushed the door open, determined to face whatever was in the room with courage. His heart was beating thunderously against his chest and

Simpson knew that his hand was trembling without looking at it. As he stepped into the room and turned on the light, Simpson was close to hyperventilating as he prepared for *something* to jump out – but nothing did.

The room was as silent as it was empty. Even the scent of Vicky's perfume had a faded and past-expiration-date smell to it -- like the scent on a shirt days later. It hadn't been his imagination though because lying in the middle of the bed was the book. Simpson felt sick to his stomach and as the blood rushed to his aching head, he nearly fainted.

In every ghost story he had ever read, the ghost or spirit had rarely been one with any sort of redeeming purpose. Mostly, they were malevolent and terrifying. Simpson's heart insisted that it was *his Vicky*, but his head warned him to believe otherwise. He shut off the light and backed out of the room, closing the door. The book could lie where it was and never be touched again as far as he was concerned. The warmth of the fire beckoned him instead, an inviting contrast to the cold from the bedroom. It offered normalcy, or as much 'normal' as could be associated with spirits and doppelganger cats.

He took off the slicker and tossed it on the back of the nearest chair. It slid to the floor and Simpson picked it up, hooking the collar on the back of the chair. He kicked off the boots and pulled the blanket out from under Sophie. Sophie gave him a disgruntled look, but Simpson couldn't have cared less. His mind was numb and a never-ending wave of shivers was crawling up and down his spine.

Simpson's head was pounding out a tune of contrition. What he desired was sleep, the ability to forget about ghosts, and enough of a break to give his headache time to ease. Maybe then, his mind could create a more rational explanation for what his heart

Isolation

believed was happening. If Vicky was actually there to haunt him, she would have to wait until after he awakened.

The warmth of the fire and the comfort of the big quilted blanket had done their job. Simpson had slowly melted into the old couch, moving his body into the best position to avoid the irritating bump by his hip and the worn edge of the armrest. His thoughts waded through a cloudy mixture of wanting to believe and not quite believing. Undoubtedly, he was missing something important, something essential about what was really happening to him, but even as he tried to stay asleep, Simpson recognized that he was in no condition to rationally and logically think about what that could be. His eyes felt as if someone had sewn mini-weights to his eyelids. He could feel himself sliding into the void and he was grateful for that.

With the blanket wrapped around his shoulders and his eyes closed tightly, he half heard Sophie mewing in some distant place, but it sounded dull and without substance. He wasn't sure if she was really in the room or was calling him to sleep in a dream world. Simpson told himself to open his eyes and see what she wanted -- but in the next instant, he was deeply sleeping. He was unable to decipher the cold caress of a spirit hand upon his cheek and when he shivered at its touch, he reflexively pulled the blanket up around his neck. His mind heard the whispers and his heart was aware of the presence in the room as his nostrils breathed in deeply, registering the memory of a familiar perfume.

Time passed in a vacuum and Simpson had no idea how long he had been asleep. His pounding headache had quieted to a dull roar, but he still needed to squint somewhat painfully against the low light inside, looking past the table and out the window where all he could see was an endless expanse of *grey*. The small slits in his eyelids gave way to more open eyes – yet the interior of the cabin still remained gloomy. His neck was stiff and his right hand was numb from being tucked beneath his chin. Inhaling and exhaling carefully in preparation for the pain he was expecting to feel, Simpson pulled himself up. Within seconds, his neck and hand reacted to the increased flow of blood, causing him to grimace and shake his hand vigorously to relieve the pins-and-needles prickling in that extremity.

Simpson could see the lake out the window and it looked angry. The rain was falling so thickly that it was almost as if someone had vandalized a beautiful painting by putting a light coat of grey paint on it. The scene still showed through, but it was obscured by the top coat of paint. He noted that there was one thing to be thankful for -- his head had ceased to pound out bass drumbeats, marching band style. There was no sign of Sophie as Simpson rolled his head around to loosen his neck and bent it from side to side before hearing one satisfying pop that gave him some relief.

The cabin was still warm, so he couldn't have been out-cold for hours, but it felt as though he had slept an entire night. Just like the air outside, his body felt heavy and his mind was weighted down -- *painted grey*. His stomach gurgled noisily since it was hungry, but he was not – yet another one of those weird contradictions. Food didn't sound good at that moment and something on the table caught his eye. It wasn't something out of place, rather, it was something in its place—*the book*.

Our Heart was where he last laid it, not in the bedroom where he had seen it during the earlier haunted episode. One or both must have been imagined. Simpson began to create a set of logical explanations for the entire sequence of events, deciding that the whole episode that morning had been due to his headache -- nothing more than an overactive mind mixed with grief causing the senses to fabricate Vicky's perfume and the book on the bed. The atmosphere inside the cabin felt overwhelmingly *depressing*. Outside it was even worse -- ten degrees colder with rain that was due to change consistency and turn into a foot or more of snow.

Simpson had begun to seriously think about leaving the cabin *sooner* than later. The drabness outdoors and the claustrophobic atmosphere inside the cabin created grave doubts about his present and rather fragile state of mind. If he ended up stuck out there for months, the results were unlikely to be positive.

As if to accentuate that point, the wind outside pummeled the cabin with a howling burst. The front door rattled violently against the stiff wind, sending such a startlingly cold draft across his feet that it was enough to fan the fire. Simpson tossed off the blanket and stuffed the woodstove with more logs, putting the teakettle on the wood stovetop to heat up water. Though not actually feeling hungry, he knew that a couple of packets of chicken soup should quiet his stomach now that it was rumbling boisterously.

He looked for Sophie and couldn't find her anywhere. She wasn't in the bedroom or under the bed, in the main room, or playing hide and seek in any of the cupboards in the kitchen. Simpson even looked up to make sure she wasn't sitting on top of the elk head mounted on the wall. Her absence gave him that itchy-all-over feeling again as he realized that the only place left was behind the closed door -- in his father's bedroom.

Standing in front of the bedroom door, feeling distinctly weak at the knees, Simpson knew that he didn't possess the bravery needed to open it. The hairs were standing up on the back of his neck and arms and he didn't know what scared him more -- finding Sophie in the bedroom or not finding her there.

Simpson could have sworn that as he looked at the door, it was expanding and contracting in sync with his breathing.

Instinctively, he stepped back as his mind continued to process equal amounts of doubt and fear. It was just his own heart beating madly inside of his chest—he understood that, but his mind had begun to convince him that the *thump, thump, thump* sound was actually coming from the behind the door.

In a moment of both sensory overload and awareness, Simpson's vision started to darken in the center as bright halos of white and golden light danced along the periphery. *I'm going to faint*, he realized. The sound level of the thumping increased until its booming volume was painful within his head. Before he collapsed, Simpson fell towards the door with his arms outstretched. The door had felt warm and fleshy -- giving in to his touch instead of remaining solid. Simpson could feel it -- the insistent sense of need from within the room, beckoning him to enter. There was a danger inside the room -- but there was hope inside as well -- hope for answers that he was desperate to learn. It was more than his mind could take and Simpson slumped unconscious to the floor.

A loud and very shrill whistle cut through the blackness and into the place where Simpson was dwelling. In his mindless, darkened state, Simpson rolled his still closed eyes towards the sound of the train. It wasn't a train's whistle -- too shrill and annoying, more of a policeman's whistle.

He forced open his eyes and saw the bedroom door. Everything came rushing back and he sucked in air while pushing himself away from the door in comical fashion. He wasn't laughing though – far from it. The teapot on the stove was exhaling steam in a steady plume and aggressively whistling its impatience. Simpson rose to his hands and knees and began crawling towards the stove. He managed to stand up on unsteady legs, wobble over to the stove, and remove the teakettle as he turned off the burner. Simpson's hands trembled as he carried the teakettle to the table and set it atop the decorative ceramic tile which protected the wood.

"All a hallucination," he told himself – several times -- as he listened to the chattering of his teeth. Returning to the kitchen, he grabbed a large mug and the box of tea bags. There was a bottle of whiskey on the same shelf – and he grabbed that for good measure.

While the tea was steeping, Simpson chugged three large gulps of whiskey. The burning sensation as it slid down his windpipe and into his stomach had the desired effect -- waking him up -- making sure he knew that he was still alive. As another mouthful of whiskey went down too easily, Simpson doubted how long his present state of coherence would last. There was a new plan percolating in the back of his brain -- inebriation into blessed forgetfulness.

The tea was ready to drink by the time the whiskey had calmed his nerves. But with the sly grin of a closet alcoholic, Simpson added a hefty shot of whiskey to the tea. Sitting so he could face the closed bedroom door, Simpson mechanically drank the tea -- raised the cup, took a drink, put it down, paused, and repeated the entire routine. When the cup was empty, it was unceremoniously refilled with straight whiskey. Simpson sipped it slowly, his eyes never leaving the door. The book was sitting on the table -- touched at least a dozen times to prove that it was real.

The whiskey was doing its job as it started to push the "I'm afraid" into the realm of "I don't care." Alcohol did different things to different people. It usually made him smile and knocked the edge off whatever was stressing him out at the time. But at that moment, Simpson regretted that it hadn't turned him into some version of "Mr. Hyde." He could have used the aggressiveness and false courage it gave some people. The first time Simpson shook his head vigorously to knock back the invading cobwebs, he knew that he was ready to face what was behind the door.

Draining his cup, he stood up – but an alcohol rush surging through his body caused him to stumble. Grabbing onto the table for support, he waited until his eyes were able to refocus. The good news was that his headache had disappeared, but the room was now sweltering hot from the wood stove and with the alcohol in his system, the effects of the heat were magnified and caused Simpson to break out in a sweat.

Three bold steps toward the door -- and the rational man he'd tried to bury with the alcohol made a final plea for a redirection of the plan. Simpson ignored him and stepped forward, but the inner-rational-man managed to yell out, "What about a weapon?" That startled him and made him stop and rethink things.

In a bit of Karma, or maybe 'Murphy's Law', the best weapons were under the bed on the other side of the door he intended to enter. Through eyes that persistently jumped around and refused to stay focused, Simpson scanned the interior of the cabin for something to use. He retreated to the table and unsheathed the fillet knife since nothing else within eyesight offered anything more suitable for protection. He couldn't help but chuckle semi-wickedly as he spoke, "What's the best way to skin a ghost?"

The bottle of whiskey looked even more appealing and the rational man inside was saying, "Go on, have another drink." But Simpson shook his still-woozy head and audibly responded, "No, it's time to face my ghost."

He walked with purpose and bit more steadiness as he approached the door and twisted the knob. Gently easing it open, then watching cautiously as that opening grew wider, Simpson clutched the doorknob in a death grip in case he needed to shut the door quickly. The scent of her perfume washed over him in waves of eerie nostalgia. The atmosphere of the room didn't feel hostile this time, just the opposite. It made Simpson feel welcome. Sophie was curled up asleep at the foot of the bed and the book was lying open, page-side down on the pillow. Simpson slowly turned to look back through the doorway at the table in the outer room, but he already knew what he would see -- *the book wasn't there*. When Simpson looked back at the bed, for a brief moment he saw an indentation that was shaped like a body lying on the bed -- but then it smoothed out and disappeared. He couldn't stop the flood of emotions as tears welled up in his eyes. This time, there would be no hiding from whatever was in that room.

By the time Simpson sat down on the bed, all the familiar scents associated with Vicky -- her perfume, the scent of her shampoo, the pheromones that made her unique, had enveloped him to the point that he *felt her*. Grief and need racked Simpson's body with heavy sobs. Falling over on his side, careful to stay outside of where he saw Vicky's silhouette, his back was to the door, his face buried in the pillow. Simpson sensed Vicky all around him, wanting to comfort him but somehow still remaining distant. He gently put his arm around her phantom waist and willingly gave into the emotions surging through his body as Vicky softly told him it would be okay. He never felt Sophie jumping down from the bed or noticed her leaving the room. He also never saw the door gently swinging closed as he fell into a deep sleep.

Dissolve pudding in milk, whip in cool whip. Spoon into 3 oz Dixie cups or ice cube tray and insert Popsicle stick or tooth picks. Freeze. Don't forget you can use other pudding flavors also to change it up!

CHAPTER 8:
Icy Encounter

THE INTERIOR OF THE ROOM WAS DARK AND COLD when Simpson awoke. The color of the darkness was wrong -- suddenly more blue than charcoal as if he was looking through a polarized filter. Lying in the center of the bed on his back, shivering uncontrollably, Simpson's headache had returned with a stabbing ferocity. His body ached from head to toe and the slightest movement made him wince in pain. As he sat up, Simpson cried out, nearly fainting as white halos artificially brightened the room behind his eyes while the real room became painted in darkness. He knew he needed to clutch tightly onto anything real and tangible – and he needed to stay awake.

Simpson nearly fell while getting out of the bed, lurching and stumbling towards the door in the darkness. His left leg and hip did not want to bend and each movement brought him closer to the brink of passing out again, this time from pain instead of fear. As he did a jump step on his right foot to maintain balance, he collided hard with the door when he couldn't lift his left arm to steady himself. Simpson struggled to grip the handle on the door and somehow managed to open it. Chills began to race up and down his spine as soon as the warmth from the outer room wrapped around him like a blanket.

A ghostly reflection of himself in the front window caused Simpson to spin around and seek out the phantom. The thin light from the fireplace had thrown off just the right amount of illumination to give the ominous specter its phantomlike look. Simpson's wobbly mind did the rest to create the ghostly presence. Heart beating wildly and the pain beginning to dim in his leg and hip, Simpson cautiously took baby-steps toward the fire as each step became a little easier than the previous one. He added more wood to the fire and grabbed the blanket, wrapping it around his shoulders. As the fire roared back to life, Simpson stood dangerously close, allowing the intense heat to bore into his legs. The shuddering slowly abated and the warmth lessened the sensation of trauma -- but it did nothing to stop the confusion spinning around inside of his head.

Sophie made her presence known as she stopped and stretched at the door to their bedroom. She gave Simpson a friendly yowl and after weaving between his legs and giving him a flip of her tail, she jumped up on the couch. "What the hell just happened?" Simpson asked as he stroked her fur.

Simpson wearily shook his head, trying to remember what had taken place in the bedroom. There was an intense half-memory of Vicky being in the room, then nothing before he awoke in agony. He wasn't surprised to see the book back in its place on the table. The nearly unbearable heat from the fire had helped to soothe the stiffness and pain in his body, allowing him to slowly flex the stiff knee and lift his left arm. Even the pain in his head had receded to a tolerable level.

Simpson was ready to believe that he had simply succumbed to an alcohol haze -- but then his senses were on high alert and his heart tried to crawl out of his chest by way of his throat. The bottle of whiskey was no longer on the table, nor was the cup of tea. Instead, an empty plate and silverware had taken their place. He recognized the smell of simmering stew wafting in from the kitchen and turned to confirm that there was a pot heating on a low flame. "I have gone utterly insane."

Awash with confusion, Simpson realized that he'd either set the table and heated up the stew in some sort of alcohol-induced vegetative state or Vicky's spirit was capable of doing more than just haunting him. Maybe, it was a combination of the two -- she could possess him and also make him forget what was inconvenient. That might explain the severe pain that he had felt upon waking -- some sort of transference of her pain from the accident and a now-lingering set of effects on him.

Simpson considered all of that as he sat under the blanket, rubbing Sophie's fur into a slick-downed look and avoiding looking at the table. Other than the aroma of stew and unanswered questions, he didn't sense the presence of Vicky's spirit or feel frightened by the implications of what might have happened. Instead, Simpson chalked it up to his grief and use of alcohol. There might have been some weirdly supernatural-love-connection explanation, but for the moment, Simpson was willing to let it simmer without examining any of it. Pushing Sophie off his lap, he retrieved the stew from the stove, carrying the pot to the table. He sat facing the front window toward the lake, keeping the warmth of the fire at his back. The rain had stopped and the clouds were moving out since he could see that the stars were beginning to shine once more.

Simpson forced himself to save some of the stew so he could give Sophie some meat chunks and gravy. She devoured her share of the stew as soon as the bowl was placed on the floor. Outside, it had become increasingly bright as a large bank of clouds gave way to a freshly washed full moon. The moon's reflection on the lake made it appear as if an alien world had materialized outside the cabin's window.

Simpson felt oddly at ease in spite of all that had unfolded over the last few hours. There was still a real danger lurking outside the cabin, but for some reason, he was no longer afraid of the presence within the cabin. He couldn't explain his reasons for feeling that way, but he was convinced that it meant him no harm – whether it was *Vicky* or not. The pain was almost gone, and he was willing to endure it again if it meant that he could connect with Vicky's spirit – even for a brief period of time.

Simpson carried the dirty dishes to the kitchen sink. Then, to prove his belief that the danger was outside, not inside, he opened the cabin door and stepped out onto the porch. The air was brisk and carried with it the strong aroma of pine and wet earth -- a tiny but powerful sense-memory -- a reminder of the fragrance that was carried into a house after cutting a fresh Christmas tree.

Far off in the distance, a loon was calling and then another that was closer answered. Simpson gazed out over the lake, noting the luminance of the moon and the mirror-like calmness of the lake reflecting it. But he paid close attention to his peripheral vision and it didn't take long before a shadow moved and attracted Simpson's attention. Vicky's spirit was clearly not the only one haunting the cabin, haunting him.

Believe in one, you must believe in them both. They were connected to each other, but Simpson was not certain how just yet. Although he now believed that the one in the cabin meant him no harm, he sensed that the other outside would devour him if given a chance. A beautiful, but soulful howl of a wolf echoed musically across the upper end of the lake. Without directly looking, Simpson watched as several shadows raced along the edge of the shore in the direction of the call. One shadow stopped at the water's edge and though he couldn't make out what form it was, he sensed that it was looking back at him. The eyes had a red cast that appeared to brighten and then dim. The moon slipped under a cloud and the form blended back into the mixture of shore and water. As the cloud passed, a large and very real black-and-white-coated wolf had taken the place of the previous shadow. It raised its head and added a verse of its own to a song that was only known to its companions. With one last look back at Simpson, it scampered off into the cover of the trees. The wolf's song felt like a warning meant for Simpson.

He knew they were real wolves, but his gut also said that they were creatures of paranormal origins and substance. They had been bold and braved the closeness of the cabin -- so it was now imperative that he be extremely careful not to be caught off guard or be somewhere unprotected from an attack. He was acutely aware that they meant to do him harm if they could.

Sophie had ventured out and taken her place next to Simpson on the porch -- defiant in the way she sat next to his right leg, her tail wrapped around her front feet. She made it two against the pack -- the odds stacked against them. For some reason though, Simpson worried less about her chances for survival than he did his own.

The cold was settling in again -- both in Simpson's heart and on his skin. Back inside the cabin, he picked up Sophie's bowl and carried it over to the sink. He didn't feel like taking the time to heat up water, so he squirted a little dish soap in the cat's bowl and filled it with cold water, letting it soak. Opening the cupboard, he noted that the whiskey was where it was supposed to be and the bottle was still half-full. A drink was the last thing on his mind though. The true craving, which made him smile, was for a big piece of chocolate cake or a brownie with vanilla ice cream and hot fudge on top. The best he could do at that moment was a chocolate covered peanut-butter granola bar sealed in a plastic bag in a drawer. He didn't even attempt to read the expiration date and simply tore open the wrapper. The granola bar lasted for a two bites length of time as he impatiently stuffed it into his mouth -- just like a kid getting his fix with Halloween candy.

The sweetness of the granola bar only made him want more and Simpson couldn't seem to stop his mind from ticking off a list of all the candy bars and desserts that he would have enjoyed just then. There were too many and it was too sad to dwell on them. In pure *Charlie Brown* cartoon fashion, Simpson yelled out, "Arrgh!" The foil wrapper was tossed into the fire where it glowed with a metallic green before being consumed by the flames.

Looking over at the table again, the book was now sitting in the middle. The bedroom door was closed and unfortunately, a chocolate cake had not manifested itself on the table. Vicky evidently didn't have those types of powers.

Simpson believed that he knew what Vicki wanted and the book was a part of it. It created some version of a conduit for her and connected her to his mind. Without a doubt, Simpson believed that Vicky's presence was real, but his fear of the unknown also created a justifiable state of reluctance. Looking at the bedroom door and then back at the book, he said, more to himself than to Vicky, "I can't."

He didn't tell her that he couldn't because he didn't know how to help her when he was the one who had caused her death. He also believed that he couldn't because once she was in his mind, she would uncover the full weight of his burden of guilt for her death, the remorse he felt for leaving their children alone, and the fear of what was right outside the cabin – what he felt – *what he knew* -- was coming for him.

Simpson grabbed the Sudoku book off the table instead and sat down on the couch. With a pencil in hand, he methodically worked through the first uncompleted puzzle he turned to. Glancing up at the table every so often – he could reassure himself that the book remained in the same place. After he had completed five puzzles, he lost interest in doing another one. *Our Heart* was still in the middle of the table and there was still no bribe of cake or brownies. But Simpson had begun to sense an increased heaviness in the air. Under his breath, he whispered again, "I can't…I'm not ready."

Sophie was restless and she gave him the evil eye as he tossed the Sudoku book aside and pushed himself up off the couch. Looking for a distraction, Simpson remembered seeing a package of sugar-coated self-popping popcorn in the cupboard. As it cooked, the aroma tantalized his nose with the scent of sugary bliss, causing his stomach to growl in eager anticipation of the sweet feast to come.

With the bowl of popcorn in one hand and a glass of ice tea in the other, Simpson plopped down on the couch and within minutes, over half of the popcorn had been inhaled. "Good…so good," he mumbled with his mouth full. Most of the ice tea had been drunk in one large gulp. Sometimes it was the simple things that satisfied the body and mind.

Simpson took a fluffy piece of popcorn, scraped it along the bottom of the bowl to pick up some extra sugar, and then he put it next to Sophie. She sniffed at it and tentatively, licked it, but it stuck to her tongue. Unnerved by this, Sophie shook her head to rid herself of the evil attacker and the popcorn fluttered to the floor where, in a fit of revenge, Sophie pounced on it. Soon the popcorn was being batted all around the room, with Sophie racing after it and swatting it before it could get away. The harder Simpson laughed, the more persistent the cat was at showing the popcorn her best Ninja moves.

Sophie entertained him for quite awhile and he enjoyed the show while he finished off the rest of the popcorn. After she tired of her popcorn chase, Sophie swaggered off towards the bedroom. It was late, but Simpson wasn't the least bit sleepy and it felt as if sleep was all that had been accomplished that day. What he could really use was the mind-numbing effects of watching a classic movie on television or a marathon of some comedy show -- *anything that wasn't about ghosts.* There was nothing scarier than being left alone with one's thoughts, especially when the supernatural was involved.

At precisely that moment a sound came from within his father's bedroom, the sound of someone sitting down on the bed. Vicky's well-timed response to Simpson's train of thoughts prompted him to answer in a slightly strangled voice.

"I can't," Simpson called out, but his voice carried little in the way of conviction behind it. The truth was, Simpson wanted – no -- needed to connect with Vicky. His intuition warned him that if he didn't do it soon, he might never get another chance to tell her how much she meant to him.

Simpson stared at the door with a mixture of fear and disbelief as it slowly swung open. A lump formed in his throat as the acid began to rise in his stomach. There was no ghostly apparition sitting on the bed in wait. Her perfume reached his nose and he gladly inhaled the scent that he had always considered alluring, but it would have been better, certainly much easier if he had already been half drunk. Simpson's heart pounded painfully, trying to burst from within his chest. He tried to swallow again, but couldn't. The book was missing from the table again, silently transported to where it now sat on the bed -- waiting, calling, and demanding his attention. Fear of both going into the room and not going in made him suddenly feel sluggish and stiff again as he gingerly took a step towards the room. The wall lamp over the bed cast a dim light, but with each step toward the room, the brightness began to intensify. Simpson walked unsteadily towards the room, unaware of anything but the light within. Entering the room, Simpson was unexpectedly hit by a set of conflicting sensations. He was chilled and shivering – but also touched by warmth at the same time -- two opposites converging at the center, of which he was the defining point.

There was an odd almost-rotten odor tainting the scent of Vicky's perfume. Simpson wanted to leave since it gave him an intense feeling of unease that crept along his skin, a series of visible goosebumps warning that something was *not right*. He couldn't say what the smell was, but he knew it, recognized it, and it wasn't something that his brain interpreted as being good.

The pull to connect with Vicky fought his desire to flee and won out though. He struggled to bend his unresponsive knees, looking like a drunk as he fell onto the bed once again. The book bounced up and into the air, deflected off his arm, and came to rest against the wall. For a mere second, Simpson panicked -- fearing the arrival of some type of repercussion because of his poor treatment of the spiritual talisman. Carefully, he touched it to make sure it was still just a book and not some object possessed by fire or acid, sent to burn him for his transgression.

Isolation

Simpson exhaled with relief. The book was just a book. He settled more comfortably into the bed, stuffing the extra pillow behind his head and draping the throw blanket across his legs to ward off the chill. This time when he picked up the book, a sensation like an electric current pulsed from the book into his fingertips – surprisingly, a somewhat pleasing and calming feeling.

Before any second thoughts had a chance to stop him, he opened *Our Heart* to the bookmarked page and began to read. Simpson tried to imagine Vicky's voice, but nothing happened. He told himself to relax, breathe, and just let it come without forcing it. Slowly, his breath became less labored and his body began to quiet down. His eyes flew open in surprise as a sharp, stabbing pain attacked his hip, causing him to involuntarily clench his teeth against the pain.

Simpson closed his eyes again, breathed as calmly as possible, and somewhat controlled the pain by shifting his weight off the hip. It helped -- temporarily – before he began to feel other parts of his body aching in unison. Simpson believed that it was a consequence of connecting to Vicky -- feeling her pain.

When he opened his eyes, his focus was oddly crisp and his senses were sharp. The black type nearly jumped off the white pages and he soon lost himself in the story about Jason and Allison. Without even realizing it, Simpson's inner voice had morphed into Vicky's comforting tone. Instead of being afraid, he embraced the sound of her reading the story, letting her take over and enjoying the subtle ways in which she altered her voice to portray each of the characters. Simpson's eyes shut and she continued to read. She paused, and his eyes flew open, afraid she had left -- but then she asked him a direct question.

"Simple, do you remember when Abby had a crush on the new boy up the street?"

"I do," he said aloud. There was a gentle squeeze of his hand. Vicky's fingers were laced together with his. With his eyes closed, he could imagine her lying next to him, feeling her essence all around him. "If I remember it correctly, the boy -- Nick, just as in the story, was a few years older and wouldn't give Abby the time of day."

"He was just like the Nick in the story. Remember how we joked about the two Nicks being so similar?"

He laughed at her thinking the same thoughts as him, and he responded, "Life really does imitate art. She chased after him for a long time, and when she finally did catch him, he wasn't worth keeping."

"Simple, you are so much like Jason in the story. You wear your heart on your sleeve, and I know that you would do anything for me. You don't know how much I love you. I've never been good with words, not the way you are. I'm just plain vanilla to your chocolate, raspberry swirl." Vicky's hand clutched his tighter. Without needing to see her, he could sense the great emotions playing through her. "Simple, it's not fair…"

"Shush now. It's all right Vicky. I'm here and I'm never going to let you go again. I'm ready to join you wherever you are. I don't care anymore about what is right and wrong. My life isn't the same without you."

"Simple, we have so much to look forward to…" Her voice broke and he knew she was crying. He loved her so that the feeling of needing and wanting her overcame him. "This can't be what God intended for us. I need you to be strong, be the hero you've always been to me. I need you to do whatever it takes so we can be together again. Please Simple. I love you and I need you now."

Warm tears rolled down Simpson's cheeks and fell silently onto the pillow, a perfect analogy of the moment -- the separation of warmth from cold, the distance between here and there, and the expectations of his life and her death. A massive and desperate sigh burst from within him and the hand that was holding his own let go. Tender fingertips caressed his cheek and Simpson's lips twitched, then tingled, as unseen lips gently kissed his. He opened his eyes, expecting to look into his angel's face, but there was only the ceiling above him.

"No!" Simpson cried out, "Don't go!" But Vicky's presence was gone and all Simpson could do was roll over onto his side, curl up in a fetal position, and close his eyes tightly against the rising tide of despair. Nothing would hold back the sobs as they took hold.

When he was finally worn out, he slipped into a strangled and broken sleep. Her words replayed again and again and he grappled with the meaning of every word she had spoken. What did she mean by doing whatever it took to be together? In spite of his faith that it was his Vicky, he paused, wondering if the evil entity that he sensed was also around had stepped in and might be attempting to play on his weakened emotional state and encourage him to just end it all.

That vague ripple of an idea went against his nature and his belief system. Even though he was overwhelmed and clouded with guilt, the notion that he might have considered taking his own life to be with her was pushed back and rejected -- sharply. The Vicky Simpson he knew would never ask that of him.

A more important and rather desperate thought abruptly raced through his mind. What if she wasn't dead at all, but was still trapped in a coma -- and he had walked away from the hospital and left her there alone. The part of Simpson's mind where rational explanations lived reminded him of the sound of the monitor as it flat-lined and how his heart broke as he heard Abigail crying at the sound.

Was it even possible that Vicky had somehow survived after he'd walked out? Simpson's heart said that it was Vicky who was communicating with him and that somehow their minds had managed to link together. Stranger things had been reported by others -- and Simpson wanted to believe -- needed to believe in the possibility of the impossible. The tremors had stopped reverberating through his body and his mind had begun to pick at the possibilities that still remained. All he could bring himself to conclude was that he didn't know what to think at that moment.

Unexpectedly, the temperature in the room began to fall, bringing goosebumps once again to the back of Simpson's neck. Like the perfume that told of Vicky's presence, there was also a darker atmosphere, an undefined something or someone that was manifesting within the room again. Like a primitive version of man who operated on instincts to survive, Simpson feared the undefined it -- but was clueless about the nature of the danger that it might hold. Perhaps the connection between them came with a cost that Simpson wasn't sure he could pay. If he had been able to stand up and look out the window, Simpson wouldn't have been a bit surprised to see glowing red wolfish eyes keeping watch on the cabin – on him.

A deathly-cold pocket of poisonous-smelling air began to encircle Simpson's head. His eyes dried up and then burned as if they had been touched by an acidic ice fire. Gasping for air, he rubbed the palm of his hands over his eyes to ward off the cold and try to lessen the sting. The eye pain was nothing compared to the agony in his throat when he inhaled a bit of that cloud of deadly air. It was as if he was trying to suck liquid nitrogen through a straw, causing his lungs to constrict and refuse to inhale the burning and poisoned air.

Simpson rolled off the bed onto the floor, clawing at his throat in a vain attempt to force it to open. With eyes blurred and shut tight, deadly fear washing over him, reaching the warm sanctity of the fireplace was Simpson's only thought. Like an old car trying to start on a frozen morning, Simpson continued to gag and cough, trying to catch a breath. His throat finally relaxed just enough, allowing him to swallow a bit of fresh air as he hugged the floor. Using his left hand to grab the doorjamb for support, Simpson tried to stand up.

The door was almost open when unseen and icy hands firmly reached out, grasped his right ankle, and pulled him back into the room. An ice-cold yet burning fire seared the skin around his ankle and the nighttime quiet exploded with his agonized screams. Simpson's hand slipped off the doorjamb and only a last-second movement of his head to the side saved him from having a broken nose and teeth as he collided with the floor.

"*I'm dead, I'm dead!*" Simpson's inner voice kept repeating those words -- the internal dialogue rising in intensity as he was violently dragged to the rear of the room. Simpson screamed out repeatedly, now completely terrified and consumed by panic. Kicking at the phantom with his left foot was no more effective than kicking the air and it did nothing to free his right leg.

Simpson twisted around, managing to flop over onto his back. The right leg felt immobilized and secured fast to the floor with ice-covered bolts securing it in place. The air above his ankle had a shimmering quality. Simpson had an idea of what it might want -- to crawl inside of him -- and if it did, he would lose a battle he didn't know he was a player in.

A blur of fur raced past Simpson and vaulted unafraid into the heart of the shimmering air. Sophie continued through the air without resistance and her heroics caused the icy hands to release his leg. Simpson was afraid to turn his head and look at Sophie, fearful that she had been turned into a frozen *catsicle*. Instead, she was sitting unharmed near his ankle, staring down something near the foot of the bed. He followed her intense gaze and together they watched the crystal mist-like air, shimmering with deadly beauty, as it slowly rose toward the window and then sliced like a knife through the glass before disappearing into the night. It left behind a spectacular frost pattern on the window. It might have been quite amazing under other circumstances, but instead, it was left as a frosty tattoo of some type of deadly intention.

Simpson scooted backward as fast as he was able until he was safely out of that room. Sophie followed behind, giving him a "Saved your butt" look, and then she leaned into his arm as she walked by. Simpson sat on the floor, halfway between the fire and the open bedroom door, stymied by what had just transpired. The heat on his neck caused a shiver to travel down his arms and along his spine and his ankle throbbed with every beat of his heart. He felt certain that if he looked down, he would see a blistering mess of raw skin where those invisible hands had grabbed him. Every one of his senses was on high alert, so the sound of the crackling fire and the rustle of branches outside the window reverberated like gunshots in a valley.

Simpson was still breathing hard as he studied the dust pattern on the floor where he had just dragged himself from the room. He was instantly aware of the tangy smell of fear that emanated sourly from his body. Whatever it was that attacked had somehow rendered him powerless to protect himself. If not for Sophie, he would surely be dead. He had no doubts that Sophie was a gift from Vicky. Could there be any other reasonable answer for her being there and how she seemed to know what was coming ahead of time? In whatever realm Vicky was dwelling just then, it was filled with monsters that had the ability to navigate their way through borders of time and space and into his world.

Perhaps the cumulative effect of a lifetime of watching supernatural movies and television shows had left a mark on his subconscious, but Simpson fully believed that the presence that nearly killed him was the same entity controlling the wolves, or perhaps masquerading as them. He knew in his heart that it was close to the truth.

The cabin appeared to provide a protective shelter from the wolves, but the icy entity was clearly not bound by the solidity of walls. Sophie was now his only guard against that particular presence until he could figure out if it there was a way to deal with it.

Simpson's gaze shifted to where the book was now resting, once again, in the middle of the table. But unlike the other books stacked on the table, that one particular book was not real -- not really. It was more like a strange form of Ouija board that Vicky had somehow placed there.

Simpson had created another visual image in his head – an hour-by-hour counter that was clicking down as his assigned time was now stacked against him. His chances for answers -- and more importantly, survival – were dwindling and he knew that he was in a race to find out what Vicky needed before the allotted time ran out.

CHAPTER 9:
Too Close Encounter

———•·◄⚭►·•———

He had slept. How in the world had he slept?

Simpson voiced those thoughts aloud as he jerked awake. The fleeting images from his nightmare chased him into the wakening world. Bathed in sweat and reeking of the demons that had tormented him in his dreams, he groaned aloud in pain, "Ahhwwwwlll," The shards-of-glass sensations in his neck were an unpleasant reminder of the broken rest and discomfort of sleeping on the battered old couch.

After the incident with the icy apparition, he had been afraid to sleep and even more afraid to be away from the fire. When exhaustion had finally overtaken him, he had fitfully slipped into the netherworld of nightmares. Simpson's neck gave an unceremonious pop as he moved rather cautiously and attempted to rid himself of the kinks. The pain worsened at first and then eased a bit as his bones resettled. Several more pops and crackles broke the silence of the morning as he first rotated his neck and then twisted his back.

Isolation

The inside of his mouth had a bitter taste and his tongue was beyond feeling hairy, it was wearing a fur coat. Simpson built up as much saliva as possible to moisten the inside of his mouth, probing the inside of his lips and cheeks with his tongue, gingerly feeling the rough spots where he had bitten the inside of his cheeks while asleep. It was a habit that had continued long past his youth -- and it reoccurred most often during periods of stress and anxiety. "Go figure," he said quietly and sarcastically under his breath as he acknowledged the almost-unhuman levels of stress in his life.

It was morning, but the light inside the cabin was dim. Simpson hobbled toward the window to look out at the lake. The sky outside was overcast with large grey clouds obscuring the sun and the lake was relatively calm, unlike his nerves. Sophie brushed against his leg and he nearly sent her flying across the floor, trying to evade the demon that his imagination had immediately conjured up.

Unhappy with his rude response, Sophie warily glared at him from a safer distance. "Sorry girl. I don't think it would be wise to sneak up on me, though I'm sure that in a tussle, I'd end up as the one with the wounds." Sophie ignored the apology and with nothing else to say, Simpson shrugged his shoulders. Turning her back on him as a form of cat-type comment, Sophie jumped up onto the couch and settled into the newly-vacated warm spot.

Simpson studied the clouds with meteorological interest. They had an ominous look about them. Simpson knew that he might be placing more emphasis than necessary on the appearance of those clouds, but the thought of a storm brewing caused a feeling of dread to settle over him. At that time of year, it didn't take much for a heavy rain shower to turn into a massive snow blizzard. "Perfect…just perfect," Simpson swore as he faced the window.

The smart money would be on hitting the road. "Not going to happen," he answered the inner-voice of common sense. There was a reason he'd been led to that place, and he must see it through. From the moment he had seen the picture hanging on the wall in the hospital waiting room, his path to the cabin had been an illogical but predictable outcome.

After stoking the fire, Simpson moved around in the kitchen making breakfast for Sophie and himself. He went all out with powdered eggs and a tin of compressed meat, making enough for four people. Between the two of them, they left nothing in the skillet and didn't even bother with plates. After Simpson stuffed himself with all that he could eat, he set the skillet down on the floor for Sophie. She was also ravenous -- dealing with a supernatural being had apparently brought on a fierce hunger attack. There was also an overriding sense that ingesting something with a bit of substance was vital since their energy was about to be taxed -- again. While she was licking the edges of the skillet, Simpson stepped outside the front door.

What would normally have felt like a simple wintery chill now seemed to be interpreted by Simpson's brain as moist and menacing cold air that intentionally attacked the bare skin of his wrists and face. It only took a few minutes to wind back those thoughts though as he realized that he would have been smarter to grab a coat instead of merely wrapping his arms around himself as he headed down the steps towards the dock. Failing to put on his shoes and wearing only socks hadn't been the smartest thing to do either, but he was drawn by the need to see if the wolves had left any tracks by the water's edge.

The dampness of the sandy soil quickly soaked through his socks and a panic attack grasped at him before he had even reached the dock, suddenly concerned that the wolves were hiding behind the cabin and might have cut him off from its safety. Spinning in his tracks as he looked back, there was nothing to see but the cabin. There were no eyes watching him and there was no movement from the side of the cabin, behind the cabin, or prowling the tree line on either side. Not only did he feel ashamed of the strong and unwarranted fear, he inwardly chastised his stupidity. If Simpson was going to survive long enough to figure out what Vicky wanted, then he was going to need to be prepared for anything -- and *everything*. He also knew that preparation didn't mean panic – he needed to get the panic response under control.

Simpson couldn't keep standing there in the middle of the path, swiveling his head and seeing nothing, since the cold was beginning to win and his body was now shivering violently in reaction to each gust of wind. Taking one deep breath, he moved purposefully toward the dock, then stepped a few paces down the dock to get a look near the water's edge. His first reaction to seeing the wolf prints was a sensation of relief that they were real and not imagined. But the merriment in his brain was short-lived. The wolf's clearly defined path abruptly stopped thirty feet away. The ground wasn't too rocky or grassy to prevent him from seeing the continuation of the tracks -- but they had just ended in thin air.

It was possible that the wolf could have jumped ten feet sideways into the water or it could have been snatched up into the air by a mythical dragon. Where the tracks did stop was in the middle of a small sandy area where over the years many a child's attention had been lost in imagination-filled playtime -- turning sand castles and moats into the visions of their dreams. As if to further drive the point home, a long, musical bray broke through the heavy air further down the shore from the cover of the trees. Simpson's face drained of color. Was that what impending doom felt like?

With no warning, Simpson only had seconds to lean forward as the full contents of his stomach violently erupted from his mouth. He crouched there shaking, waiting for the spasms to pass. Then with hands on his knees for support, Simpson couldn't help but look at the new resting place for his breakfast, expecting to see maggots squirming about. There was nothing scary to see though, making it even more fearful for some reason. If this had been just another script from one of his favorite horror movies, Simpson would at least have had an idea of what to expect next. Instead, he was awash in uncertainty and dread.

He lifted his head back up -- the wobbliness in his legs caused him to take a steadying step backward to catch his balance. Two inches more to the right and he would have stepped on a nasty-sharp jagged splinter protruding from a piece of deck board. In spite of all of the trips back and forth across the dock, it was the first time he had noticed it.

He saw it from the corner of his eye and knew it wasn't his imagination. A shadow had moved behind the outhouse. Simpson raced to the cabin, bursting through the door and then slamming it shut behind him. His heart thumped mercilessly in his chest and if he hadn't already lost his breakfast, it would have been spewing from his mouth at that moment. He had never believed he'd be one of those people that threw up in the face of fear, but he also hadn't ever believed in ghost wolves either.

Simpson's body and mind were already in a heightened state of alertness from the fear that he felt -- and now they were nearing a full meltdown because of the source. Trembling, he turned a chair around and sat so he could look directly out the window.

He couldn't bring himself to look out the other windows and see if anything else was outside and watching. His mind was still strong enough to know that he was being easily led into an imaginative world where werewolves and demons lurked behind each tree. The sound of a squeaking doorknob turning from behind him added to his increasingly irrational state of mind and Simpson was afraid to turn around.

Just as he sensed the cold from the bedroom beckoning to him again, Simpson felt an overwhelming wave of fatigue pressing him down and he knew he didn't have the strength to rise from the chair. Cool micro-drifts of air caressed the back of his neck as a solitary tear escaped his eye. He spent the limited energy that remained by concentrating only on the sound of his breathing, counting to five as he breathed in, five as he exhaled. Airy fingertips touched his face where the tear had tracked down his cheek. He was keenly aware of whose fingertips were touching him -- Vicky's. Simpson did the only thing left to do -- he *prayed*.

But Simpson choked on the words when he got to the part about *delivering me from evil*. The odor of Vicky's perfume was so strong that it made him queasy.

Could that be possible? Was she evil? Was the love of his life trying to torment him or seduce him into suicide -- something Simpson had briefly contemplated as she lay dying in her hospital bed. Now was it being forced upon him? In his grief, the thought of ending his life to be with Vicky seemed somewhat noble, but neither she nor he would ever let the other walk that path. All of these thoughts raced through his head as he continued to struggle with the question -- was she some sort of evil shadow-incarnation of Vicky? Simpson didn't believe so, but how could he explain away the not-really wolves and the cold mist-like specter?

Simpson's eyes may have been tightly shut, but he could clearly imagine her standing right in front of him. Years of memories, years of looking at Vicky throughout the many stages of her life had combined into one substantial image. Her brown hair was long, airy, with soft curls at the ends that fell softly around her delicate, tan, and bare shoulders. She wore the bright yellow sundress that was perfectly flattering to her shape and size and meant to drive him crazy. It had done just that when she wore on their vacation to Cancun and it had created so much love and laughter between the two of them that it had temporarily turned Simpson into a hot-blooded schoolboy. Vicky's lips were a light shade of red and her eyes sparkled, perennially full of the love and happiness of their lives together. When the cold fingertips touched his cheek once more, he saw her slender fingers with the manicured nails painted in her favorite mauve color. Her new wedding ring glistened in the sunlight. But Simpson hugged only air when he reached out to embrace her.

Her presence had briefly chased away his fear of the wolves. Simpson was drawn to the promise of her comfort and felt pulled toward the room where he knew she wanted him to go. If he had opened his eyes to search for the book on the table, it would have been gone, already waiting in that room, waiting for him to open it and read more of the story of Jason and Allison.

Vicky needed him for some reason that was unknown to Simpson at that moment and he felt compelled to ask her – "Why." The sickeningly heavy scent of perfume receded, allowing the air to be touched by warmth. As Simpson opened his eyes, the scene outside the window was a shadowy reflection of the cabin's interior, playing across the window in an eerie type of projection. A shadow without true form, but with just enough substance to be familiar was standing in the bedroom doorway -- waiting. It was undoubtedly Vicky, but when he turned around in excitement to see her, there was nothing there but an open door. Simpson's ankle began to ache where those icy hands had grasped him a few hours earlier. His lungs were struggling to get a breath in the sub-zero temperatures that had suddenly returned to the interior of the cabin. As he felt himself slipping back into a state of fear, another tear slid from the corner of his eye.

A soft humming was coming from the bedroom, clear enough and loud enough so that he could hear it, but at the same time, so quiet that he had to strain to catch the musical whispers. His mind sharpened the song that was so familiar, the song Vicky hummed every morning as she applied her makeup -- *Nights are Forever without You* by England Dan and John Ford Coley. He once asked her why she liked to hum that song and even sing it passionately when she didn't think anyone was around to hear. Her answer was in the sweet smile that lifted one side of her upper lip higher than the other and in the caring softness of her eyes as she answered, "Because it's how I feel about you." Whatever response he could have given would have been inadequate. But that was the moment when Simpson knew he would do everything in his power to protect and love that woman forever.

Simpson's heart was being gripped in a vise of regrets and doubts. With every note that Vicky's spirit hummed, the vise twisted one turn tighter. The tone of her song was sad though, not thankful as it normally was.

As if he was walking in his sleep, Simpson discovered that he had reached the door of the bedroom. He hesitated for only an instant before walking into the frigid room. There was a sense of suffocation as soon as he entered and the muscles in his legs tightened, ready to take flight, but refusing to do so. Surprisingly, the room still smelled as stale and unvisited, almost medicinal, as the day that he had arrived. It made no sense.

The humming had softened and now sounded quite distant and tinny, as if the sound was rising up through the registers from a basement far below. Feeling like the cold was freezing him from the inside out, Simpson found it harder to breathe or even think. The urge to run grew more insistent, but Simpson faced the room and forced himself to take in a deep breath, an intake of air that caused him to gasp in pain and feel as if someone had hit him in the ribs with a hammer.

Hunched over, hands on his knees and his body quivering with an equal mixture of fear and cold, the sad and tender hum of the song continued in the background, offering him an odd mix of peace and *hope?* Holding his left side with his right hand, Simpson staggered to the edge of the bed and sat down. Lying back on the pillow helped to alleviate the pain and his breathing came a bit easier. His throat still felt as if he'd sucked in a mouthful of the ocean, complete with the sand. Whatever Vicky was doing to him was more painful, physically and mentally, than he believed he could bear. Flight was the only option on his mind, but as Simpson attempted to roll over on his side and then drop onto the floor—*he couldn't move.* His mind raced with panicked thoughts, *"I'm going to die…why is she doing this?"*

Simpson yelled at his body to move, pleading aloud to Vicky, "Stop this! I want to live! Please, sweetheart, release me. Tell me what's going on. You don't have to do this!" There was no verbal response to be heard, but the pain in his ribs intensified sharply. The burning sensation on his right ankle was now joined by an agonizing throbbing that attacked his left leg. Simpson's arms were pinned to the bed at his sides. He tried to keep calm by taking shallow cleansing breaths and focusing each of them on the areas of pain. Warm tears streaked from his blurry eyes and rolled down his deathly white cheeks. If he had to endure much more of that, he really would want to die.

A cool touch of air drew a line across Simpson's forehead, pushing the hair back from his eyes. It reminded him of the way Vicky tenderly brushed the hair away from his eyes after they made love. Her touch, always pleasurable in the past, wasn't soothing or comforting just then as the breezy fingertips stroked his cheeks and slowly traced the outline of Simpson's lips. From his peripheral vision, he watched as the book, now sitting on the nightstand, opened and the pages fluttered from front to back until they came to rest nearly halfway through.

Simpson was unable to move and he had no way to grasp the book, let alone hold it to read and make that ethereal connection with Vicky. All he could do was endure the pain and pray for his release. Simpson whispered, "God, help me, please."

He closed his eyes and concentrated on Vicky, adding her to his prayers, hoping it would be enough to reopen the door between their worlds. Cool air lingered on his cheek and then it gently slid away as it grabbed his hand.

"What do you want from me," Simpson blurted out, no longer able to keep the fear at bay. The sensation of his hand being squeezed again was the only reply he received. The volume of the humming rose, then suddenly stopped mid-note. At the same time, the pain in his ankle and leg lessened. She was still present in the room and the scent of her perfume was much stronger, but he was free from the invisible bonds that had physically held him in place. Simpson felt more confused than ever.

As he sat up, the pain in his side was completely gone. *What the hell was happening here?* His eyes darted around the room, anticipating that the icy mist would soon be making a return appearance. But after several tense minutes of feeling that he needed to stay on high alert, Simpson began to relax a bit and breathe more normally.

He needed answers and rather than fleeing when he had the chance, he stubbornly reached for the open book from the nightstand. Simpson scrunched up the pillows behind his head as he laid back down. He started to read but found it hard to concentrate on the story since he was still so edgy and his senses wouldn't fully relax. He had escaped from the battlefront and then turned around to re-enter it. Why? Every few sentences, his eyes leaped from the words on the page to the window at the back of the room. Time passed slowly as he read two more chapters without Vicky ever returning to take over.

Simpson was about to put the book aside when a tingling sensation danced in his fingertips where they touched the book. It gave him renewed hope and he concentrated more diligently on the story. Exactly as it had happened before, Vicky was soon the one who was reading. Simpson closed his eyes and lost himself in her narration.

As she was reading, the sound of her voice fluctuated, getting louder and then very quiet. His first thought was that she was slipping away, but then Simpson remembered what was coming next in the story. It was the part where the grandfather came downstairs to tell Jason that his mother had died in an auto accident. Simpson found it strange that Vicky's spirit was so emotional. Was that normal behavior for a spirit? Hell, what was normal? When he heard her sobbing, Simpson couldn't wait any longer to say something.

"It's going to be ok, sweetheart. I don't know what it is you need from me, but I'm here to help you cross over if that is what this is all about."

She didn't reply and Simpson was about to continue when he felt pressure on his chest. At first, he tensed-up, expecting that the pain would be coming back, but then he sensed spirit-Vicky as she rested her head on his chest. He could actually smell the citrus scent of her shampoo and feel her where their bodies touched. She almost felt real -- *almost*. He could sense her presence, smell her perfume, hear her voice, but he couldn't actually see her and feeling her was open to a subjective debate at best. Opening his eyes to glance around the room, Simpson kept his voice as steady and calm as possible as he asked her again, "Vicky, what is it you want from me?"

There was movement along his arm as the cool air gripped his hand, causing it to tingle with that *knowing* sensation. He was beginning to believe that it was all just a version of muscle-memory of how Vicky had felt before her death. Still, it brought him a bit of hope. "Simple, I don't want to be alone. I need you. It isn't the same without you next to me."

"What are you asking of me?" he cautiously asked.

"I know that I've told you a million times that I love you, but somehow it always seemed pale compared to the way you have of expressing your love for me. I've never been good with words and even though I tried to show you how much you mean to me, I never have quite gotten it quite right when I was telling you. It always came out as silly and humorous, even when I tried so hard to be romantic and sincere."

"That's not true," Simpson replied. "I've never thought of you as silly. Every day of my life, I knew how much you loved me. If anything, I'm the silly one, always trying to prove my devotion to the woman who has always been too good for me."

"You've given me so much, and made my life more than I could ever have hoped for. I just wish…no…I want more. Call me selfish, but I don't want us to end, not yet."

"I don't know what you expect from me, Vicky," he said timidly. Simpson's insides were turning somersaults at the thought of her asking him to take his own life in order to be with her.

The cool air changed into a warm mist as her invisible face drew closer and her voice now whispered in his ear. "Simple, I know you are far away, but I need you to listen to me. There is a way out of this. I know there is. This isn't the end and I believe with all my heart this isn't what God had planned for us. You are too good of a man to accept what has happened. If anyone can find a way to overcome this, it's you!"

Something in her words reached a hidden place within Simpson, a place that was buried deep inside where he had locked the door and then bricked it over to ensure that it was closed forever. There was more to the meaning of her words than he wanted to hear.

"I don't understand. I don't know how to bring you back and I don't want to die. I'm so sorry, but I need to let you go and think of the children instead. Please, sweetheart, don't ask me to die. I already have to live with the pain of causing your death. I won't survive letting you down again."

"Simple, do you remember the day that we met? I'm not talking about in high school at the music contest, but at Luther -- that first night with the Nordic Choir?"

"I remember. I knew you were there before I saw you. Something made me turn around and look over in your direction. The second I saw you, I told myself to do whatever it took to make sure you didn't get away again -- and I've been doing it ever since."

Simpson responded to the cool air kiss on his lips as his heart began to beat strongly with his love for that special woman. He believed that he might be capable of sacrificing everything to be with her -- she was that important to him.

There was a long silence before Vicky spoke again. "I have a confession that I've never been able to share with you. Our meeting and my joining the choir was not coincidental. Pamela Thompson was from my high school and a year older -- your age. She was in the choir and recognized your name from the contests where we first saw each other and because of all the things I had said to her about you. She couldn't wait to tell me that she'd seen you and she even hinted that she might try to get you to notice her, maybe even flirt with you so you would ask her out."

Simpson understood Vicky well enough to not say a word or interrupt her. She wasn't like some women who wore their emotions on their sleeve. She kept her thoughts to herself and only ever shared the occasional things that she needed help with. When she did have something to say, it was better to just let her spill it out in her own way. Simpson drew upon all the memories of her face -- her eyes in thoughtful study, her mouth pursed as she carefully contemplated her every word, to be able to picture her as she spoke.

Vicky continued, "Simple. That moment back in high school, when I looked out across the room and saw you staring at me, I almost lost it. My heart starting beating faster and it wasn't because you noticed me, but because I noticed you. From that moment, those feelings only grew stronger the more I thought about you in the days and weeks afterward. I found out who you were and where you went to school. I even showed up at your spring concert. I was trying to talk myself into accidentally bumping into you. I couldn't do it though because I didn't want to find out that you already had a girlfriend. So I left before the last song ended."

Simpson couldn't believe what she was telling him. It touched him far beyond her words -- and what he wouldn't have given to be able to hold her right then. Simpson could relate to why she had never told him any of this. It would have diminished all the emphasis he had always put on divine intervention and the magical moment of a sweet coincidence that brought them together at Luther. She was wrong though. He would have loved her even more if that were at all possible. "You're always the romantic," she'd said many times about him. Simpson wished now that she had told him. But it also made him wonder why she was telling him all of this now.

"I tried to tell you several times, but I always lost my nerve. You loved me so much and I was always afraid of what you might think -- silly, I know. After a couple of years went by, I was more afraid of what you would think of me for not telling. Simple, you are one of the sweetest and most caring people that I have ever been around -- more than two of your Aunt Carol and Grandma Beth put together."

Simpson had to fight to keep his escalating emotions under check. He knew the real point of her telling was yet to come. His stomach was tied in knots. Just knowing that he wouldn't be able to follow through and kill himself for the woman that was his everything was likely going to be enough to kill him anyway.

"Simple, I love you with all my heart. I knew there would be a day when one of us would pass on, but I always believed it would be far in the future when we were both in our nineties -- and when one of us went, the other wouldn't be far behind. That's the way it was supposed to be."

Simpson's throat constricted just then, forcing him to hold his breath. Vicky squeezed his hand and her airy fingers caressed his cheek.

"This isn't the way we were supposed to end. We were destined to meet and live to a ripe old age. I know this with all my heart. Life without both of us is no life for either of us. I don't know what to do, but I know that I can't go on without you. I need you Simple. I can't do this alone."

Simpson heard himself responding -- "You aren't alone. I know that all of the people that have meant so much to us are waiting for us where you are going. Time will pass in the blink of an eye. It might be twenty years here, but a second for you -- I believe that. God wouldn't allow us to feel the anguish of being separated from the ones we love without giving us the means to cope. I'll be there with you before you know it. Just don't ask me to come now. I can't. *I can't.*"

The cool air caressed his hand and Simpson could have sworn that the air turned warmer with her ghostly touch. She was so real, but yet, she was only as real as his imagination could recreate her. An instant later, she was completely gone.

"Don't leave!" he screamed into the emptiness of the room. Remembering what had happened after the last time he was in that room, Simpson bolted upright and practically jumped off the bed. Scanning the room, especially near the window, he didn't see any signs of a return visit from the dangerous icy intruder. But as he entered the main part of the cabin, the first thing he noticed was how dark it was. Not middle of the night dark, but definitely dusk. He couldn't have been in the bedroom for more than an hour by his estimation, two at the most. But judging by the lack of remaining light outside, the entire day had slipped away.

Simpson sensed the presence behind him and spun quickly to face the icy mist that had returned and was hovering in the doorway of the bedroom. It slithered up and down, forming beautiful geometric patterns, but it wouldn't cross beyond the door's threshold. For whatever reason, the bedroom seemed to be some type of waiting room between the states of here and there -- a way station where both worlds could briefly coexist.

He gathered his courage and took two steps closer to the apparition. As he approached it, the movements became more agitated. Even the blue hue of the mist sparkled with a fiery blood-red tint. It was angry -- and it was deadly. Simpson scooped up a chunk of firewood from the bin. Holding it outstretched like a sword, he moved in closer to the mist.

It responded by darting back from the doorway and hovering over the bed, vibrating and shooting off sparks. It became an ever-changing, amazing spectacle, like looking into a kaleidoscope within the dimness of the room. Simpson dared not cross into the room. He faked an attempt to step into the room, but at the last instant, he pulled back short of doing so. Instantly, the apparition shot forward to the edge of the doorway and Simpson clearly felt its dead coldness from where he stood. More importantly, though, he could feel its need -- its desire.

Anger was welling up inside him and he rather foolishly wanted to take a swing at the mist with the chunk of firewood, but caution held him back. Instead, Simpson took deliberate aim and tossed the log directly into the heart of the mist. It was barely perceptible, but for a millisecond, the wood caught, then slowed inside the mist before continuing into the room. The mist looked thinner where the wood had penetrated it. The colors within the mist intensified and sharp flashes of lights shot back and forth. In one last spectacular flash of color, the mist expanded until it filled the doorway.

Then it began to reshape itself into a form -- *a mirror image of Simpson*. It might have been just his own reflection shining back from the surface of the mist, but seeing his face materialize was terrifying. He fell back a step and the *Simpson-mist* stepped forward. As soon as the mist-foot crossed the doorway though, it vanished. The rest of the mist dropped slowly to the floor and slithered away along the edge of the bed toward the window, all except for the mist-face, which hung suspended and bodiless.

Simpson nearly screamed when the face began to grin at him. The grin widened farther than a natural face and the teeth stretched downward and elongated to form sharp points. The pupils of the eyes turned neon red and a wolf-like snout stretched outwards. With an unholy howl, it darted toward him before it exploded into nothingness once it breached the doorway.

From outside the cabin, a chorus of howls answered. The sound came from everywhere and completely surrounded the cabin. Instead of stopping, their call grew in volume and need, demanding their due. Simpson couldn't move. He had never been so scared in his life. *"God help me,"* was his only thought.

He immediately wondered if he should burn the book. Simpson felt sure that it was the conduit that allowed Vicky, and now the creatures, to cross the threshold into the world of the living. But if he acted hastily and burned the book, it would also end his connection to her -- and that alone stopped him from doing it. When he looked down again, Sophie was sitting at his feet, her tail flicking in the air behind her as her eyes watched the front door. He followed her gaze and then his heart dropped to the pit of his stomach as the door began to shake behind whatever unknown force was attempting to gain entry.

This time, howls of frustration penetrated the interior of the cabin. Simpson was cemented to the floor, unable to move and with nowhere in which to flee. The sweet scent of Vicky's perfume wafted by on a cool breeze, kissing the nape of his neck as it moved past him towards the door. Instantly, the baying on the other side changed from indignation to howls of pain. Then they retreated, moving away from the cabin until he could only hear them by straining for the sound. Simpson was living in the worst nightmare that he could have imagined.

To be perfectly honest, death had begun to look as if it was the only possible outcome, whether by his own hand, courtesy of the ghost wolves, or by some other yet unknown factor. His death now appeared to be inevitable.

How long had he stood rooted to that spot? An hour, minutes, even *a lifetime could have passed.* Time wove its pattern differently here -- more proof that the supernatural had bent reality. Simpson's only refuge was to escape into his own mind because simply walking out the door and leaving the cabin was now out of the equation.

He searched for moments of happiness to focus on, then he panicked and began hyperventilating when his imagined version of Vicky's serene face morphed into a wolf. With persistence and concentration, remembering her loving eyes, her sensual smile, and her delicate nose, those moments gradually became more fixed in his brain and he was able to climb down from that point of isolation and away from the fears that had wrapped tightly around him.

Simpson replayed their lives, one happy memory at a time until he felt secure enough to let himself to return to the then and there. It may have been dark outside, but it was warm inside the cabin with the freshly stoked fire. He didn't care if a spirit or the cat had done it. As for Sophie, she had disappeared again and Simpson wondered if she wasn't part ghost-cat as well -- always there when he needed her and missing when he wasn't actively thinking about her.

Simpson asked himself, "Am I insane?"

The answer wasn't forthcoming, but he knew that he was close to that state -- not quite ready to jump off the pier yet, but definitely thinking about it. What was happening to him was not something he believed could be possible—movie possible, book possible – yes -- but come face-to-face with it -- no.

He thought about how many of society's beliefs are overlaid with plausible doubts. Science and religion had been fighting each other for centuries. Good versus evil, angels versus demons, not to mention Christianity duking it out with Scientology. They had become a world that believed in everything and in nothing. You could ask yourself all the "What ifs" you wanted to, but until faced with the unbelievable reality removed of preconceived certainties -- no one would ever know how they would react.

There was definitely a grey world where the unexplainable occurred and those greatest-possible-fears lived. Somehow, Simpson had been dropped into the middle of that world, and it was slowly closing in on him.

CHAPTER 10:
The Wolf At The Door

The previous days had passed in slow motion, but Simpson had neither the courage nor the desire to venture outside the cabin or reconnect with Vicky inside. Wrapped in a blanket and huddled in front of the fire, he fluctuated from nightmarish naps to trance-like periods, doing his best to convince himself that he was surely just sick, delirious, and suffering from a hallucinogenic fever – *certainly a viable opinion.*

Unfortunately, he still retained enough conscious thought to realize that no amount of heat or extra-strength aspirin was going to chase away those particular chills. The other part of Simpson, the one who was dwelling in the supernatural realm at least part of the time, believed the chills were an understandable side-effect, a human-world symptom of his ghostly encounters. Either way, he was nearing a point where he was standing on the precipice looking down and didn't know if he'd be able to retreat before taking an airy step that never ended.

Isolation

Sophie was very much aware of his shattered state and she hadn't left Simpson's side for the better part of two days. Simpson ate sporadically, drank coffee -- albeit laced with whiskey now that the bourbon had run out -- and managed to keep the fire well stoked. He had enough wood to make it through that night -- but the next day was going to be another story and he knew he would need to open the back door and venture outside to collect more firewood from the pile stacked against the back of the cabin.

He should have been making a serious attempt to save himself before it was too late, but Simpson couldn't seem to pull himself out of his semi-catatonic state. Even worse, when he awakened from his latest nap on the couch, there was blinding whiteness out the front window -- *snow*. Early winter snowstorms were common in Northern Minnesota, but warm weather following them wasn't. One way or another, his days were numbered in that cabin.

The *almost* wolves had not made an appearance since *that night* -- so everything other than Simpson was pretty much back to normal. The movie image of a hero standing calmly in the eye of the hurricane was where the climactic ending in every movie suddenly ramped up the music and prepared you for what was to come. It was also the point when all hell broke loose. That was where Simpson found himself – waiting for hell to arrive. Under other circumstances, the big falling flakes of a first snow would have been beautiful, stirring warm thoughts of hot chocolate, snow angels, and classic old-fashioned movies. But on that day, it served as a sign that his time had probably run out.

Simpson didn't remember doing it, but at some time during the fitful existence of his last couple of days, he had retrieved the shotgun from under the bed. It was resting in the corner of the dining room and there was a box of shotgun shells sitting on the corner of the table. The question of what good it would do against the spirit wolves proved to have only an elusive answer.

A dark thought ran through Simpson -- did Vicky place it there as a reminder of what he should do to *be with her?* A big part of him wanted to open the front door, walk blindly into the heart of the forest, and take his chances. Surely, the wolves would not expect him to leave the comfort of the cabin. Surviving them had become the least of his worries -- surviving, period, was no longer a concern. After two days stuck inside his own mind, Simpson no longer believed that there was any chance that he would survive. What he wanted to know was the *why* and only one person had that answer -- *Vicky.*

In a case of blind stupidity, he'd been overwhelmed by the feelings of impending doom and had concluded that he had no way to fight the supernatural forces. But what Simpson had failed to factor in was having a boat and being able to use it to save himself by motoring down the lake to Kittelson's cabin. Either the Kittelsons or someone else had been there when he went fishing as Simpson had noticed the smoke coming from their property. Every time he'd seen the wolves, they had been land-bound. It didn't mean they couldn't morph into fresh-water sharks as they had in one of Simpson's hallucinations, but it was at least something to temporarily rally around and give him some much-needed hope.

Still feeling feverish and frantic, Simpson sprang off the couch and headed into the bedroom to get dressed. He stopped as he put on the top layer of long underwear, beginning to let it fully sink in that it was snowing quite heavily outside. He knew his way around the lake quite well, but if the wind picked up even the slightest bit, then navigation would become perilous in a blind-out snowstorm. Too many rocky shelves permeated the lower part of the lake and boating under a bright burst of moonlight was much safer than attempting it in inclement weather.

"Damn it all to hell," Simpson cursed, though it didn't have much of a punch to it.

"Ok -- think!" he said aloud in the bedroom while pacing back and forth and hoping that he might hear some much-needed suggestions. He asked the room, "Wait out the snow or try anyway?" The room gave its reply in the form of creaking boards outside the cabin. Turning to the window, Simpson absorbed the direction and movement of the snow, frowning as he watched it blowing more horizontally. "Wait out the snow."

Simpson bounced out of the bedroom and into the kitchen. Feeling better than he had in the last few days, he opened the cupboard and took down the bottle of whiskey. Twisting the cap off, he took a long pull, holding it in his throat and then swallowing it all to feel the burn all the way to his stomach. Gasping for air, Simpson spat it out, "Here's to you, you evil SOB's!" Now that he had a plan, he had renewed hope. Once the lid was screwed back on the bottle, he put it on the shelf. He wasn't the least bit surprised when he noticed the book *Our Heart* lying on the kitchen counter. "Sorry Vicky, not today -- got to keep my wits about me."

Simpson realized that there was a strange connection that bound them all and that included Sophie, the wolves, and the icy apparition. In his brief bursts of slumber and in his alcoholic stupors, he'd spent the better part of the last few days lost in contemplation of those plausible and implausible connections. Every time Vicky visited, the wolves, or whatever they really were, were nearby. When Sophie showed up, so did Vicky. The painting of the cabin back at the hospital had led him there -- and so on.

Until that morning, Simpson had believed Vicky was the center of the connections -- but now he wondered if it wasn't him instead -- or possibly it was the cabin at the center of the supernatural funk. The funny thing was that both the wolves and Vicky seemed to want Simpson dead -- but when Sophie and Vicky combined, they seemed to be protecting him from the wolves.

Clearly, he didn't have the right answers yet. The weather in northern Minnesota could turn on a dime, the next day might be sunny, and rarely did blizzards last more than a couple of days without some kind of a break between passing fronts. The smart money said he should wait for a better chance to boat down the lake.

Simpson could have easily fallen back into an alcoholic pattern while he waited out the storm, but his insides told him the wolves would be showing up soon. First Vicky came and then the pain stalkers. It was Simpson's new nickname for the underlying form of the ice mist and the sometimes-wolves. But he still wasn't completely sure if they were one in the same.

The icy mist had morphed into a semblance of the wolves, but it might only have been that -- the entity's ability to read his mind and know exactly what scared him. The wind was starting to pick up, a cold whistling and scratching *"I want to get in"* sound came from outside the kitchen window.

Simpson's picture-perfect snowy postcard was quickly turning into an immobilizing blizzard. He needed to get a load of wood safely inside and dry -- he just didn't want to do it. He pumped up his mental courage and threw on a rain slicker to keep the snow at bay and protect his clothes, then undid his belt and added a sheathed knife to it. This particular knife had the widest blade and was the sturdiest fillet knife he had -- and it would be next to *no-good* against a charging spirit wolf. It was like a stiff shot of courage and Simpson liked his whiskey any way he could get it lately.

Before heading outside, Simpson went to every window in the cabin and studied the tree line through the blowing snow. There was easily over four inches of snow already out there. With a steady wind, it wouldn't take much to create major drifting, especially if it continued to snow at the same rate – but he didn't detect anything unusual outside.

Sophie entwined herself between his legs in either an indication of "it's been nice to have known you," or "best of luck to you." Simpson reached down and scratched her behind the ears. "Don't worry girl. You're not getting rid of me quite yet."

Looking out the window, he opened the back door a crack, paying close attention to any potential movement outside and ready to shut the door quickly if something charged at him. Seeing nothing, Simpson swung open the door and stepped out on the small landing. Thankfully, the wind was beating against the cabin on the opposite side of the firewood stack. He raced up and down the steps, grabbing handfuls of wood and tossing them back inside the door on the floor. When the pile in the hallway looked insurmountable, Simpson stopped. As cold as it was outside, he was thoroughly soaked in perspiration – partly from the sudden burst of activity, but mostly out of fear. Only once did he stop, thinking he heard the wolves rushing at him from the front of the cabin. Simpson dropped the wood and crouched into a fighting position, knife in hand, while slowly backing up toward the door. When nothing but the wind moved past the back of the cabin, he returned to the task.

It took him awhile to cart the wood from the hallway and stack it in the main cabin. He'd gone a bit overboard and the woodpile was more than double the size of what could normally fit in the bin -- so he started piling the excess underneath the window and along the rest of the sidewall. Even Sophie mocked him from her observation perch on the couch.

Every time Simpson happened to glance over at the table, the book had shifted to a different spot, as if it was trying to seize his attention. He finished stacking the wood and stoked the fire. Washing his hands at the sink, he noticed that the wind outside was blowing the snow past the window at a good clip, but it appeared as if the visibility had improved a bit. Simpson could see the dock, now white, and the boat tied to it. A smarter man would have made sure to pull the boat up on shore and cover it with a tarp. Unfortunately, there wasn't a smart man around.

A loud explosion of shattering glass shattered the silence of the cabin from the hallway through to the back door. Simpson could only assume that the door had burst open and violently smacked against the wall. The explosion-like sound it made and even more troubling, what had caused it, had forced the muscles in his body to tighten and his heart to almost stop. He sucked in his breath and turned around, his body's instincts firing on all cylinders as survival triumphed over fear. Instead of running down the hallway, Simpson ran to the shotgun in the corner, sliding the last several feet but still managing to keep his footing where the floor had wet spots from where the wood's snow coating had melted.

Grunting loudly as his left shoulder took the brunt of the impact with the wall, he scooped up the shotgun and raised it to his shoulder, pointing the barrel down the hallway. Snow was whipping through the open door and stretching its way down the hallway. There weren't any wolves – but Simpson's finger stayed on the safety as he cautiously moved down the hallway. Sticking his head out the door, Simpson didn't see any signs of tracks or wolves waiting in the snow or by the trees.

Exhaling hard, Simpson realized that he must not have latched the deadbolt securely and the wind must have caught the door at just the right angle, slamming it open against the wall. Still feeling cautious, he used the barrel of the shotgun to push the door away from the wall as he looked for any movement outside. Then he slipped his body in behind the door and pushed it closed.

The window in the door was actually four panes split by a cross and only the two on the left-hand side were broken. During the winter closing of the cabin, the window was protected by two pre-cut sheets of plywood secured to both the inside and outside of the door. Unfortunately, they were both sitting in the shed out back.

What snow was still blowing had a fine icy quality to it, no longer the big fluffy stuff. That was Minnesota for you -- weather changes on a whim. Simpson shut the door and slammed home the deadbolt, making sure that it latched firmly this time.

Simpson was aware that she was behind him. The familiar scent of her perfume wrapped around him, moving against the wind current coming through the broken window, and blowing in the other direction. He shook his head *no* -- and the perfume kissed his lips. Simpson tasted her essence in the same way he'd tasted her sweet kisses so often before. It broke his heart.

"I can't, not until I get the window covered up and the hallway clean." She ignored him, his cheeks tingling with her kisses and his eyes became moist where her invisible lips had touched him. He felt something wet just below his eye and reached a finger to his cheek, wiping away the spectral tear that was all too real.

Simpson fought against the urge to give in and go to her instead of snagging the slicker off the back of the chair and pulling it on. Concerned more at that moment about avoiding contact with Vicky and her desires, Simpson set his body in motion and walked out the back door without thoroughly checking for the wolves. He had inadvertently left the shotgun behind, resting on the table where it could do him no good.

The sensation of the snow pelting against his face felt more like cold sand. He jumped down the steps and slogged as fast as could toward the shed. The snow was already creating a good-sized drift between the back of the cabin and the outhouse. Simpson heard an excited howl as he climbed the last step into the shed. He pushed the door open and quickly shut it behind him, cursing a blue streak under his breath. After finding the flashlight and turning it on, he swore at the back of the door, "Just what in the royal hell were you thinking?"

The panels for the back window were stacked with the others along the south wall. Simpson grabbed the pair and hustled back towards the door. If he thought about it, then time would slip away and render him more slow and stupid than he'd already been. The best opportunity was right that minute, so he opened the door slowly, looking cautiously outside. A moving shadow was coming down the lane, another one not far behind. They had three hundred yards to cover and he only had thirty, yet Simpson was willing to bet that it would still be close. He stopped only briefly to pull the door closed and set the latch.

Carrying the boards in front of him, Simpson leaped off the top stair and into the snowdrift. In the first five yards, he gave up fifty to the advancing wolves. Several more shapes formed along the trees behind their leader. Simpson made it to the steps up to the back door just as the wolves burst their way into the yard.

If Vicky hadn't opened the cabin door and then closed it behind him, Simpson wouldn't have made it without having to fight his way in. The lead wolf hit the back door amidst a swirl of fur and snarls, mere seconds behind him. He could smell the raw stench of anger reeking from the animal, its frustration and desire creating a truly sickening smell. The wolf had its snout pushed through the broken windowpane, teeth bared and saliva spewing from its yellowed teeth. Simpson raised the board and brought it down with his own angry force, connecting quite effectively with the wolf's snout. Simpson was defending his domain and didn't have time to wonder how whether or not a board could hurt an ominous spirit, nor did it stop him from displaying a satisfying grin when the wolf yelped in pain and fell back into the snow. It would be much later before he would have the time to rethink what had happened and how he'd been able to hurt the spirit wolf. Simpson put the bottom of the board in the metal holders and quickly twisted the securing clamp latches into place. He didn't know how many wolves waited outside the door, but the chorus of their unified baying was loud as it penetrated the cabin. For once, Simpson wasn't afraid, he was angry.

The wolves circled the cabin, baying as they moved, conveying to Simpson that they could wait longer than he could hold out. The biggest fear to be wary of was if one of them burst through the front window. As if reading his mind, a wolf stopped in the center of the window and peered in. His hot breath and black nose were inches from the glass, causing it to become cloudy. When the wolf stepped back, Simpson was afraid it would attack the glass. The shotgun was back in the corner by the window and not on the table where he'd left it. *Why?* What was this game that he was being forced to play?

His knife was still clipped to his belt. Instead of losing sight of them by going into the bedroom to retrieve the rifle under the bed, Simpson thought it would be better to wait and see what the wolves did and then escape into the bedroom if it became necessary. He held his breath watching and waiting for the wolf to move. Instead of assaulting the window, the wolf jumped off the deck and headed around the side of the cabin.

For the next two hours, the wolves circled the cabin. Simpson nervously paced inside, going from window to window, making sure to stay a safe distance from the glass and completely away from his father's bedroom. It was strange, but the whole situation felt different this time -- *more real*. He had also smelt Vicky's perfume and felt her ghostly touch, but there weren't any answers forthcoming about why the wolf felt pain when it was hit with the board. The only thing Simpson could come up with was that these were real wolves that were under some form of possession.

Perhaps the shadow entity had taken control of an actual wolf. In every supernatural movie, you kill the host and then you still have to deal with the entity. It didn't bode well if this was the case and he didn't have any other more normal ideas that sounded better.

Sophie was uninterested in his rambling thoughts, his wanderings around the cabin, or the wolves outside the door. Every so often, Simpson would catch a glimpse of her sitting by his father's bedroom door, looking at him or looking at the door. She was not a cat -- of that, Simpson was now sure. If anything, she might have been a spirit guide or a totem. The cat might even have been the reason he had the ability to connect with Vicky. Somehow, it all made sense if he could allow himself to believe. Believe – he had no choice now but to believe. Simpson's furry little protector wanted the door to the bedroom open and it wasn't so she could go in.

The book had vanished from the table more than an hour before, coincidentally, coinciding with Sophie's interest in the closed bedroom door. He had barely beaten the ice demon out of the room last time – so could he be equally lucky this time?

Simpson didn't think so. The room was the way station and the book the conduit. Simpson presumed that it wouldn't work the same way if he weren't in the room.

He told himself that he was not afraid -- not of death and not of the entity, but the time left to choose the lesser of two evils was quickly approaching. Based on everything that had happened thus far, Simpson had an unfounded hypothesis that the spirit wolves and the entity in the room could only hurt him – but not kill him. Dying was going to be his choice alone, even if the nudges in that direction were strongly urging him to do so and the pain caused by contact with the entities continued to be excruciating. It felt right. However, the wolf that attacked the door could most assuredly have killed him – it wanted to. This was what confused Simpson the most. Could both of those possibilities be true? Perhaps, but only if you believed that reality wasn't confined to human-defined rules.

Was there some unspoken rule that bound the spirit entities to a certain code of conduct? Who set those rules? Simpson wondered what the great theologians would have believed if they had been there to express an opinion.

Sophie tilted her head slightly towards him as she fixed her gaze on him. *"Well, what are you waiting for?"* emitted from those intelligent and not very cat-like eyes. *"Don't you know that Vicky is stuck somewhere between here and there."*

Maybe that's what she was saying, or maybe she simply heard a mouse in the bedroom. In the scary movies that he loved, a troubled spirit could never pass on if they had unsettled business that was left unfinished. This time, Simpson was the one who was feeling unsettled though!

It was time to toss away the imagined movie script and follow his heart. Sophie yawned, her pink tongue elongated and then rolled back up inside her mouth. "Glad you find things so boring," Simpson pointed out to her.

Outside the snow had settled down, fluttering by the window now -- more due to the wind and less caused by new snowfall. Still, there was more than enough outside to make roads difficult to travel on without being plowed or having the right vehicle to drive through deep drifts. Simpson tilted his head up and prayed for a little luck, that this was the end of the snow and not just a break with more bad weather to come.

Simpson wanted a drink. His nerves were shot and his body was worn out from being on edge for hours at a time. The wolves had gone silent – but both he and they knew that they were simply biding their time. They could afford to wait for as long as it took. Sophie gave him a reproachful look when he headed to the kitchen and not to the bedroom door. He didn't need the drink, didn't really want it, but he was lacking the courage to enter the bedroom at that moment. Besides, a drink was a good excuse to stall for a little while longer. In some strange way, Simpson wasn't worried about the wolves outside. He knew he was going to be dealing with them soon enough -- so this moment was about one last conversation with Vicky. Whatever the outcome, he would be leaving the cabin the next chance he got. *I've made my decision and I want to live*, he thought to himself.

Simpson poured a stiff shot of blackberry brandy into a glass, swirling the deep red liquid around, noticing its thickness and smelling the rich aroma. Downing it in one swallow, he held it in his throat for a few seconds, then let it tingle on his tongue before swallowing all of it. It still made him cough as the brandy burned on the way down.

The blurry line between rational and irrational speculation was mentally exhausting. Was this what happened to you before you ended up being dragged to an institution in a straight jacket with foaming spittle dripping from your mouth? Human brains were not wired to deal with things outside of the normal realm in which they dwell.

How many soldiers had lived for the rest of their lives with the atrocities they had to witness or even endure? That was a modest taste, much like thriving on watching horror on television and getting ramped up by that short adrenaline fix. But when faced with the reality of the horrors, Simpson knew that most people would simply fold up their tents and willingly eat their food from a proffered spoon for the rest of their lives.

Simpson added another, smaller shot of brandy to the glass. Why that was important, he didn't care -- but knowing it still meant something -- a meager acknowledgment that facing his fears was nobler with a clearer head. No swirling, no study of the brandy, just a tilt of the glass and he slammed it home. Holding the glass in his hand, he considered turning it upside down and banging it on the counter or even throwing it against the wall. Simpson's attitude had crossed into the "I don't give a damn, bring it on" stage. The brandy, along with a certain amount of increased determination, warmed up his insides. The endorphins were firing now and ready for a fight.

Simpson put the glass in the sink and the bottle back in the cupboard. He gave the cabin a serious look, running a hand along the counter to feel the wood, touching several of the carvings and pictures hanging on the wall as he made his way from the kitchen to the table. In a way, he knew that he was saying goodbye to the cabin and his father.

Sophie understood his emotional state, rubbing up against his legs. Simpson bent over and ran a hand across her back. She arched into his hand, pulling her body along his palm. He was saddened by her touch because he didn't know what would happen to her if he was no longer there. There was a strange certainty he felt -- that when the time came to leave, she would already be gone and it wouldn't do any good to try and find her.

Sophie purred loudly, something she rarely did. The sound of it struck him hard, nearly making him cry. This was goodbye. She made another couple of passes around his legs and under his hand -- then she hesitated, sniffing at it. Her tongue darted out of her mouth and licked his fingers as Simpson smiled at her. She might have been Vicky's spirit guide, but she had also helped to guide him. Sophie stretched her front paws out as far as she could reach while her back end was raised high in the air in a perfect cat bow. One last knowing look and then she darted off into their bedroom. There was no need for him to go and see if she was there—*she wouldn't be.*

Standing tall, Simpson faced the door to the other bedroom. His heart was beating faster with the anticipation, both good and bad. Three feet from the door, it slowly swung open. There was no icy entity waiting in the doorframe and from inside the room, Vicky was singing softly. With one last glance around the cabin, he surrendered to the sound of her voice and stepped into the bedroom.

CHAPTER 11:
Time Had Run Out

SIMPSON WAS IMMEDIATELY ENGULFED BY THE SMELL of her perfume and something else. It was there, but barely perceptible -- a tangy medicinal odor being masked by the sweet aroma of perfume. He knew that smell for what it truly represented -- *death*. Throughout his life, he had walked through it, smelt it, and even gagged on it. Every trip to the nursing home to see his great aunt Gladys when he was younger or the last moments spent in the hospital room waiting with a loved one who didn't have much time left in this world were but a few times that Simpson had been coated with this smell of doom. It stayed with him and he couldn't wash it off fast enough. He never forgot the scent for what it was -- *the end*.

Simpson had a girlfriend for a short time in high school who worked at a nursing home facility. She helped on D-wing, the place where they sent you to die. They might have easily used other letters, like "M" for mortuary, because that was what came next. One night, when he picked her up from work to go out on a date, she'd freshened up before coming out -- but as he hugged and kissed her, that odor was there, just like in this room, clinging to her. It ended up being an awkwardly uncomfortable date and was the start of the end between them. He could never get past that smell and Simpson was too embarrassed about his behavior to ever tell her why he'd been less than affectionate and unwilling to hold her close.

Simpson knew that everyone faced personal weaknesses. They may have wished that they could be better people, but sometimes they simply weren't. It wasn't always about how to face a set of fears, but there were some things that created more of an internalized reaction -- an *"ick"* response – that made people walk away rather than stay.

That episode in his past was Simpson's skin-crawling ick and he still hated himself for it. All these years later, he continued to berate himself, feeling that he had let those people down who needed his support the most. That was the same skin-crawling, stomach-churning feeling he had just then -- that desire-for-flight feeling -- to leave and brush the invisible scent-bugs off his clothes. But Simpson wasn't going to be granted an opportunity to flee this time. The choice had been confirmed the moment he heard the door gently close – and it wouldn't be opening again for him -- even if he had tried.

Simpson scrunched-up his nose, trying to avoid the medicinal reek and concentrate on the sound of Vicky singing. As he took the last few steps to the bed, each one became more leaden and painful. His ribs began to ache and he nearly lost his balance since his left leg wouldn't bend at the knee. Simpson had to drag the leg the last step. There was a sharp stabbing pain behind his right eye, forcing it closed as it began to water. Spittle dribbled down his chin from the corner of his mouth. He couldn't close his lips together and when he tried to raise his right hand to wipe it away, it wouldn't move. Whatever had happened to Vicky in the accident was now manifesting itself in him. Simpson's throat was constricted and raw, making his breathing nearly impossible.

He attempted to scream out from the horrific pain he felt -- but he found that he could barely utter a sound. He was left with no choice but to flop backward onto the bed since his body would not cooperate, nor bend. Simpson's left leg stuck straight out, unnaturally extended past the side of the bed without bending. The pain intensified as he struggled to inch fully onto the bed. Tears ran freely from his eyes and his nose bubbled with snot as the pain reduced him to the state of a wounded animal. His mind saw the hot-white halos of excruciating pain as his body hurt more than it had ever hurt before.

With sad humor, Simpson's one thought through those crashing waves of pain was that he hadn't drunk enough to make it through this encounter. He wasn't a science fiction superhero who could mentally extinguish all pain, so he had no choice but to suffer. Between tears and gasps of pain-encumbered breaths, his strangled-sounding voice begged and pleaded first with Vicky and then to God to end his suffering.

Apparently, neither of them was listening. If anything, his pleas gave them a reason to turn the dial up on the pain meter. The last thing out of his mouth was an agonizing scream so piercing that if he hadn't been sure it was him, he would have sworn it came from an injured animal. Simpson's mind shut down, but not before the deafening sound of nothingness quieted the blood-drums beating in his head. He had succumbed to the nothingness, retreating from a pain so absolute that his mind had no recourse but to shut down all of his senses in some measure of self-preservation. He had been beaten physically, his bones ground together until only white-hot lights danced in his field of vision.

In Simpson's state of senseless transcendence, he was, unexpectedly, oblivious to any physical feeling. His body just was. He couldn't make it respond to any commands from his brain and his vision was fixated on an unusual spot on the ceiling. There was, rather oddly, a strange crispness in his vision, almost as if it was magnified. He easily saw the little details of every brush stroke in the dried paint and in the blotches where the brush had been lifted. Outside of his peripheral vision, the details were blurred and darkened. From the other side of the door, he recognized the sound of Vicky's voice, first soft and jumbled and then becoming clearer as it swelled and filled with rich, vivid tones and volume. The stronger Vicky's voice became, the calmer he became. Simpson couldn't move, but his mind began to relax as the pain continued to subside.

Simpson had never experimented with drugs -- not even when they had been readily available and offered during his college years. To explain to someone what his current sense of being felt like, he'd tell them it was as if it was drug-induced. The mind was sharp and focused while the body seemed to be of no consequence. He couldn't tell if he was breathing. It was as if someone had plucked his mind from the body and placed it in a jar. Simpson tried to move his eyes to the side, only to find that they were locked onto the perfectly round paint bubble on the ceiling. It had such depth and smooth contours -- fascinating in its simplicity. It made him happy just looking at it. He listened to Vicky's soft and tender voice and it brought comfort and contentment. The last vestiges of Simpson's fear drained away and he was ready to do whatever Vicky needed.

"Simpson, do you remember the day that we took Trent to the emergency room after his appendix nearly burst? He'd been having abdominal pains for several days but didn't want to complain -- that age when twelve-year-old boys try to prove they are more man than just a kid. I completely lost it when I realized what might be going on, but you were rock-solid. You told me that if you hadn't been there that I would have handled it just fine -- *but you were wrong*. I knew then -- guess I've always known -- you are my compass. I might get off the path, but you point the way back. Well, I'm so far off the path right now that I'm not sure there is a way back."

"Sweetheart, you have always been stronger than you believe you are. When somebody needed to take charge, you never hesitated. When anyone challenged one of the kids, you stood toe-to-toe with them. I had nothing to do with that -- it was all you. I stand by what I said. You can handle whatever is thrown at you."

"I know you believe I'm this tough woman who can command a room full of volunteers to get the job done -- but again, you'd be wrong. Not a day goes by that I don't thankfully pray about how glad I am that you are by my side. Some people are born strong and others, like me, need that special person to keep them centered, just in case they fall off to the side. I know you are going to tell me that I could do it without you. That's just it -- I don't want to and many times, I can't. I'm a better person because of you."

Simpson was a loss for words. He wanted to wrap her in his arms and hold on to her for dear life. He couldn't and he wouldn't ever be able to again, not in this world. Simpson could hear the pain and anguish in her voice and in her words. The thought of letting her down, mixed with his devotion to her, made him a willing listener and almost eager to hear what she expected him to do. How could he not contemplate the thought of being with her forever or trying to live the rest of his life without her? It pulled at the deepest core of his emotions. Simpson remained silent and listened with an open heart.

"You are the kindest and strongest person I have ever met. You always felt like you sat in the corner of the room and let the world move past while you happily watched it go by. That isn't true. You are one of those rare individuals who are so humble that they don't have a clue about how much they are loved and respected by others. Not just by your family, but also by all those you have touched with your compassion and understanding. The world needs everyone who can make such a positive difference -- it needs you. But I'm selfish and I need you more. Time is running out and I'm…scared. I don't know what to do. I don't want to be without you. You have to come back to me. Your life is in danger and I can't hold them off much longer. Please, Simple! Come back to me…"

Simpson rolled off the bed just as the icy mist began to descend upon him from above. It might have been his inner-senses warning him of its approach or Vicky calling him into action. Either way, he barely escaped as it viciously settled into the spot he'd just vacated. Vicky's words pounded repeatedly in his skull, "come back to me…come back."

She didn't die – surely that's what her words meant – but unless he could get back to the hospital in time, she would. There was clarity within her message -- she needed him to survive. The bedspread began to turn frosty where the mist rested upon it. Dark shades of red pulsated throughout the mist. Simpson back-crawled through the doorway into the main room of the cabin just as the mist raced towards him. Again, it stopped at the door's threshold. But this time, rather than morphing into a wolf's head, it became an icy silhouette of Vicky.

Simpson watched in fascinated horror as the misty lips silently whispered his name. Her hair blew in a wind that could not be felt and the scene before him was both beautiful and terrifying. When he didn't move forward, it vibrated in apparent anger and frustration, multicolored lights blinking in a vast universe of cold. The mouth yawned open farther than any human mouth would have been capable of doing. Pink twinkling tears raced down sunken cheeks from sightless eyes, dropping onto the floor and quickly evaporating back upward into the unearthly form. The features turned dark and menacing as jagged teeth elongated and filled the oversized mouth. It made no sound but Simpson could hear it screaming in his mind. He pushed further away from the danger. His hand brushed across something on the floor. Keeping his eyes on the apparition, he picked up what he recognized as the book.

Simpson wasn't surprised to see that it was *Our Heart*. He couldn't hold back his grin as he raised the talisman and threw it into the center of the screaming apparition. It didn't shoot through it. Instead, it stuck in the center like a fly in a spider web. The icy mist spun in circles as it tried to shed itself of the book. The book appeared to grow inside of the mist, but then Simpson understood that it wasn't getting bigger -- the mist was shrinking as the book absorbed it. The book hung suspended in the doorway as the evil face was pulled inside, the eyes the last to go. They were sightless, but Simpson felt their unholy stare nonetheless.

The book held its place in the air for a second longer before falling flat onto the floor. Simpson looked away to find Sophie watching him from near the stack of firewood along the wall. When his gaze returned to the bedroom, the book was gone. He was sure that he would never see the book again. Simpson also had the sinking feeling that his time with Sophie had ended as well. In the blink of his eye, she now sat majestically on the other side of the doorway where she hadn't been a second ago. There was a melancholy in her eyes. He was right -- their time was nearly over. Sophie walked over to where he sat on the floor and nestled her head into his side. Simpson petted her soft hair and whispered, "Thank you for everything." She looked up, holding his gaze. There was great understanding in those eyes. She rose up on her back legs and placed the paws of her front legs on his chest. Her eyes locked on his as she began licking his face, first one side and then the other. As she did, Simpson had to fight back the sorrow.

"I promise," he heard himself say aloud. What he was promising, he didn't know. He just knew that it was imperative to tell her. Satisfied, she returned to a sitting position, the tail wrapped around her feet and its end gently flicking up and down on the floor. Simpson tenderly stroked her hair and she closed her eyes, smiling as only a cat can do. "Be safe," he said to her, and then for added measure, "Be careful." She opened her eyes and Simpson saw his reflection in them. Sophie yawned and headed for their bedroom. He knew that if he were to follow her into the bedroom, she would not be there. Each bedroom seemed to be a doorway of sorts -- his father's room let in the icy mist and allowed him to connect with Vicky. His and Sophie's bedroom gave her passage to the place she came from.

Outside, the wind feverishly attacked the side of the cabin. Standing up, Simpson went to the kitchen window. The snow had made everything look clean and fresh outside. Branches in the pine trees hung low with the weight of the damp snow and the dock looked several inches taller. He could only imagine how much snow had accumulated inside the boat. A shadow twitched at the corner of the cabin. It could have been a snow-plumped tree blowing past the overhang of the roof, but it moved in a way that a tree couldn't, snow-covered or not. With his face plastered to the window, Simpson tried to gain a better angle to see what was making the shadow. It had to be directly behind the cabin, just out of sight. He hustled into his bedroom to get a better look out its window.

Simpson had a similar look on his face to the one that countless explorers must have had when they came upon the Grand Canyon blocking their way -- *his chance of escaping was going to be nearly impossible.* There was always a way and a chance, but the odds were becoming stacked against his success. Outside there were at least a dozen wolves -- all of them keeping a close watch on the cabin. The nearest one to the window took a step forward and instinctively, Simpson backed up. It stood on its hind legs, which allowed it to place its nose at the bottom of the windowpane. The wolf's paws were slightly higher on the glass, and as one paw slid down, its sharp nail etched a ragged line into the glass. The *chalk on a blackboard* sound pierced at his ears and nerves. Simpson backed slowly out of the bedroom while keeping his eyes on the window.

He opened the door on the wood stove and loaded it full of logs. The fire began to burn hot and smoke rolled out into the cabin. He adjusted the flu and the flames inside the stove rose in height as they lapped at the oxygen in the stovepipe. The heat did little to stave off the chills. Even if he made it to the boat ahead of the charging wolves, Simpson still needed to start the motor and get away from the dock before they attacked. There wasn't any snow falling now, but the skies looked dark enough, which indicated it could start again at any time. A blizzard might be both a blessing and a curse, giving him the chance to slip out undetected, but also making navigation tricky. He could try to reach the boat in the cover of darkness, but again, navigating the lake would be iffy at best.

Simpson was willing to bet that the wolves outside the door were of the *real* variety this time. They may be possessed or controlled by the demons, hell-bent on slaughtering him, but being real meant they could be injured or killed. Simpson purposely took a glance over at the shotgun -- it would suffice if the wolves were charging and at close range. The rifle under the bed in his father's room would be of better use to pick off the wolves from long range. The book had only temporarily taken care of the icy mist -- it would still be there guarding the room. Getting to the rifle might be easy -- *escaping from the room could be the difficult part.*

This was a time when he could have used his spirit guide, but Sophie had gone back to where she came from and was unavailable. He also didn't feel positive that Vicky would be helping either. Simpson made tight circles around the interior of the cabin, thinking and unthinking plans to retrieve the rifle. The light bulb went off as he passed by the stove in the kitchen for the tenth time. Tucked in the corner by the refrigerator was one of several fire extinguishers kept on hand. It was one of those idiotic thoughts -- using a fire extinguisher on an icy mist -- but it felt right. He collected another extinguisher from his bedroom and set it down by the door to his father's bedroom. This one would be the backup.

Simpson stood in front of the closed bedroom door and ran through his intended plan several times. He needed to be mentally prepared and able to change direction in an instant. Not only did he need the rifle, but he must also collect the bullets from the top drawer in the dresser, which was the farthest away from the safety of the doorway. There would only be one opportunity to get both -- no second chance -- as the icy entity would certainly prevent any future attempts.

Dancing back and forth from foot to foot, Simpson tried to build up the courage to enter the bedroom. Visions of mist wolves and alien monsters clawed at his thoughts. For whatever reason, he suddenly thought of the giant marshmallow man from the film *Ghostbusters*. He didn't know what he was up against, but his mind needed to be clear and focused. In every science fiction movie, the evil spirit always manifested itself as some form of the greatest fear of its victim.

Simpson began breathing in and out, calming his nerves and stoking his adrenaline. As ready as he was ever going to be, Simpson ripped the plug out of the fire extinguisher. He pulled the trigger and shot a spray toward the center of the bedroom door, smiling as it *swooshed* out and splattered on the door with a wet plop. There was a rustling sound coming from behind the door and then the sound of glass shattering as a picture must have crashed to the floor. The entity knew that it was time.

In the movies, the scenario of what happened to the hero when he raced headfirst into a closed room full of demons crossed through Simpson's thoughts. He quickly pulled his hand away from the doorknob, suspecting that it might be booby-trapped.

Leaning in toward the door without placing his ear on it, Simpson listened for tell-tale sounds. It was quiet -- *not good*. With no idea where the mist entity might be, Simpson held the fire extinguisher in the ready position, took a deep breath, and then angrily kicked in the door. It burst open, splinters flying as it slammed back against the wall. The entity was hovering over the bed and pulsating in an array of dark colors -- burnt red, then dark green, and intense black-blue. Simpson pulled the trigger before he even had a chance to think about doing it. The jet stream caught the bottom of the mist, causing it to skirt sideways. Adjusting his aim to lead the entity, he hit it full-force before it could dart free and escape out the window. It managed to stay upright for a second and then collapsed to the floor, making a sound like a snowball hitting a half-frozen water puddle. It vibrated on the floor, particles of ice being thrown off, burning acid-like where they hit the floor. Simpson raced forward and coated it with the remaining contents of the fire extinguisher until all he could see was a pile of white foam.

Simpson's mind told him that the mist was far from dead and he'd better hurry, so he jumped over the foaming blob and yanked open the top drawer of the dresser. The box of bullets for the rifle was almost at the back on the left side. He grabbed them and the box of shotgun shells resting next to it. When he spun towards the bed, the foam was vibrating and casting off droplets as if it were a dog shaking off water. He dropped the fire extinguisher and bolted to the side of the bed, sliding the last couple of feet on his knees. Simpson reached blindly under the bed and caught hold of the gun's protective case, pulling it out. He tossed the gun case out of the bedroom, just past the doorway where it landed with a soft thud and then skidded across the floor -- *too near the fire*.

Simpson was back upright and on his feet when the icy mist, still shimmering with the coated foam, grabbed hold of the arm holding the two boxes of bullets. Screaming out in pain at the mist's touch, he desperately clutched the bullets to his chest. Hot yet icy pain raced up his arm making it numb and useless. Simpson's eyes watered as he fought against the blinding pain behind his eyes. The mist held him in place, beginning to attack him in his mind as well as his arm.

Simpson's eyes started to glaze over as the voices in his head cooed, "Stay, Simple, there's no hurry. You'll come to like what we have to offer you. It's a magical, happy place. Soon, you won't even mind the pain -- you'll look forward to it, enjoy it."

Simpson shouted back, "I love her and I will never abandon her!"

"But you already have," it spoke into his mind, complete with the bone-chilling sound of maniacal laughter.

Simpson's hand was losing its grip on the boxes of bullets. It was so hard to think straight and stay focused.

He'd been caught out in a freezing rainstorm without proper protection one time in the past. Walking up the road to the nearest gas station, had it not been for the kind elderly couple that stopped to pick him up, he might have succumbed to hypothermia. That was exactly how he felt now. His mind felt muddy. If Simpson didn't make it out of the room in the next few seconds – he knew he never would.

Using his right hand, he reached across his body and took the boxes of bullets from his dead arm, tossing them in what seemed like slow motion past the open doorway. He marveled at the way the boxes exploded on impact with the floor, sending bullets flying towards the fireplace.

Simpson managed to take a step toward the open door and then paid for it as sharp stabs of pain knifed his legs. Yelling at the top of his lungs, he took another step and then crumbled to the ground as his knees gave out. Falling forward, he stretched as far as he could, giving up his body as it slammed hard onto the floor. Simpson twisted at the last second to land more on his right side, arm out-stretched, where he could just grab the doorjamb with his right hand. He pulled with everything he had.

"Where are you going Simple? Vicky isn't out there. She's in here with us -- waiting!"

Simpson pulled his body forward a couple more inches closer to freedom and then ungodly pain shot through his ribs and squeezed the breath from his chest. He didn't care --his mind now resting in the place where determination triumphs over impossibility.

He pulled again and his head broke through the opening of the doorway. Instantly, his mind became clearer and the voices were completely silent. But in his mind, Simpson replayed the last sounds he had heard – the levels of frustration and outright anger in their final screams. With every inch that he gained into the main room of the cabin, the pain and immobility in which the icy mist held him slowly fell away. At last, Simpson was able to drag his useless legs completely past the threshold. He lay on his back, his torso twisted around so he could look into the bedroom. The icy mist continued to expand, filling the entire interior of the room in a grey cloud of blurred lines. It looked as if he was trying to see the room through a scratched glass bottle that was held up to his eye.

Simpson swept the floor with his hand until he snagged a stray bullet for the shotgun. It took painful effort, the confrontation with the icy mist still affecting him, but he managed to sit upright. He tossed the bullet at the open doorway and wasn't surprised when it rebounded back. The room seemed to be solidly filled by the entity. Simpson should have been amazed or even worried by this new wrinkle, but what he felt was a state of disinterested neutrality. The bedroom no longer mattered -- nothing mattered other than saving his skin and getting back to the hospital where Vicky was still alive and waiting.

Simpson fought the urge to simply lie on the floor and sleep. He was tired and stressed and his muscles screamed as he tried to stand up. Swaying from side to side, he took several steps toward the center of the cabin, stopping when he reached the table, using it for support. A loud and angry howl erupted from just outside the front window. Jerking his head up, Simpson's fear meter hit a new high as he studied the two wolves sitting on the porch. The larger one had its snout in the air as it sang to the rest of the pack. The smaller wolf took a step toward the window. Its eyes were yellow and not demon red. But those eyes were confrontational as they looked in through the fragile safety of the window's thin glass, *"Your time is up!"*

Simpson spun around wildly and sought out the rifle and shotgun. For a brief moment, his panic rose, worried they had both been moved back into the ice-blocked bedroom by spirits. The rifle case lay just behind and partially under the table. He bent and picked it up, putting it within easy reach on top of the table. The shotgun was on the couch and he didn't remember putting it there. The bullets were scattered all across the floor, forcing Simpson to get down on his hands and knees to gather them up. He put shotgun shells in his shirt pocket and back jeans pocket and rifle bullets in both of his front pockets when he was jolted by the sound of the glass exploding in the front window.

The largest of the wolves stood on its hind legs, spittle dripping from a deathly snarl, as it looked in. Simpson didn't feel panic this time -- he felt ready. Reactions and instincts were all that mattered now.

Reaching behind, he grabbed the shotgun from the couch. The wolf's paw shone red with droplets of blood. Sharply ragged splinters of glass hung dangerously in the window casing and the hot breath of the wolf steamed the outside glass.

Simpson checked to see if the shotgun was loaded as he stood up. He cocked one of the shells home as he moved sideways to put the table between him and the wolf and made sure the safety was off, trusting that three other shotgun shells were still in the chamber. The wolf looked as if he anticipated an attack, stepping down from the window and backing up to the edge of the porch as Simpson cautiously made his way toward the broken window. With every step he took closer to the window, the wolf backed away by an equal distance. Simpson couldn't sense or see the other, smaller wolf in his peripheral vision, but he believed that it was close by. These wolves were real, and they weren't -- so Simpson would play it the only way he knew how -- *take nothing for granted.*

Leaning against the wall, he stuck the barrel of the shotgun out the broken window, resting it on the sill. The wolf had jumped back off the porch, purposely keeping one of the porch's columns between them. Those actions reconfirmed Simpson's belief that it was more than a normal sort of wolf. He heard the follow-up sound before being able to see what had caused it. The smaller wolf had been hiding out of sight on the porch, but as it raced toward the barrel of the gun, Simpson heard the sound of its toenails scraping on the deck planks. He pulled the shotgun back through the window as the wolf grabbed at it and fired directly into the wolf's open jaws.

The blast reverberated inside the cabin, causing Simpson's ears to ring and the recoil of the shotgun smarted against his shoulder since he hadn't had the time to correctly brace it. The smaller wolf crumpled onto the deck just below the window. Then, as Simpson quickly re-targeted the large wolf, it snarled menacingly and bolted around the side of the cabin before he could lock another shell in the chamber and pull the trigger.

Simpson didn't venture out on the porch to look at the wolf. His rational mind said it was dead and there was no way it could have survived the shot. But the irrational side, which had been living through the parade of supernatural events during the last few weeks said, "*Don't be stupid.*" There was a fine line between reality and perception -- to live, he had to pay attention to both.

Fine flakes of snow drifted lazily on a gentle breeze outside the front window. Far down the lake, in the direction Simpson needed to go, he could see a patch of sunshine warming the dark bluish-grey waters of the lake. It was a sign -- *time to go!*

CHAPTER 12:
Where There's Heat…

It was just as Simpson feared -- each stop to look out one of the windows diminished his hopes of making it *anywhere* alive. The cabin felt squeezed by the growing number of wolves surrounding it, but he only counted five that he was certain were real. Most of them shimmered slightly, causing him to believe they were shadow wolves instead.

If there were such a thing as good news in the context of his predicament, then it would be that the shadow wolves seemed to be bound by some sort of rules that were unknown to him. So far, they hadn't made it into the cabin, when obviously they should have been able to. Simpson's plan was simple -- kill the real wolves and take his chances with the shadow wolves. If nothing else, removing the bigger threat might buy him a little extra time.

It would have been nice if the .22 caliber rifle had been an automatic, or at the least, had the ability to hold a clip full of bullets. His luck -- it was an older gun that needed a bullet loaded in the chamber each time before it could shoot. The alpha male of the wolf pack, as determined by Simpson, kept a safe distance away. He was the general in charge of the forces preparing to attack. They might have been mostly wolves, but they had definitely been enhanced with added intelligence and an element of something *dark,* which was controlling them. This made them even more formidable. Soon, they would charge the cabin, knowing he couldn't kill them all. In a pure counter-flank attack, the shadow wolves attempted to draw his attention while the others gained entrance into the cabin.

A mangy looking grey wolf stood back by the outhouse. The wolf was looking toward the front of the cabin and was mostly concealed by the building. Only its front quarter was visible. Squatting down below the window sill in the bedroom, Simpson reached up and unlocked the windowpane, then cautiously removed the screen. He didn't need to crank out the window very far to have a clear shot. Simpson cursed under his breath as the first couple of cranks squeaked loudly before the frame popped free from the sill and opened several inches. He was afraid that the noise would scare the mangy wolf, but it was still staring directly at the front of the cabin. That stare bothered him enough that he felt compelled to see what was holding its attention. He left the rifle below the window and grabbed the shotgun off the floor, staying low as he moved into the kitchen.

Leaning over the sink to look out the window in the general direction of the mangy wolf's gaze, Simpson was flabbergasted to see a pair of wolves gnawing at the rope tying the boat to the dock. He fought back his first instinct to charge out the front door, blasting away with the shotgun, hoping to either hit one or scare them off. Of course, making it back to the safety of the cabin would be a challenge. The wolves would maul him instantly for blindly opening the front door and giving himself up – but if

Simpson did nothing, the boat would soon be history -- floating uselessly in the current of the lake and out of reach.

Simpson ran back into the bedroom and stuck the barrel of the rifle out the window. He took a deep breath as he released the safety. There was a cold breeze pushing through the open window, strong enough to rustle an old calendar hanging on the wall. It was also cold enough to make his eyes smart. The mangy wolf stood transfixed. It had moved out a little more into the open and Simpson sighted his aim a little lower on the brain portion of the skull. Animals often duck when they hear a loud noise, just like humans. As he eased the trigger back, the sound of the gun's report broke the pristine silence.

As anticipated, the wolf ducked into the bullet. It took two steps forward, shaking its head as if it were trying to toss off an invisible pest. As quickly as he could, Simpson ejected the spent cartridge and slid home another round. The wolf was staggering, but still alive. He sighted the crosshairs on the heart and pulled the trigger. The wolf jumped up, crying a pitiful howl. In mid bawl, it abruptly stopped and the wolf toppled over sideways. Simpson pulled the barrel of the gun inside and quickly cranked the window closed as an angry chorus of howls rose all around the cabin.

Running into the kitchen, Simpson vaulted up on the counter by the window over the sink. He used the end of the rifle barrel to break out one of the upper panes of glass. He got up on his knees and stuck the rifle out the window. The boat was still tied to the dock, and the two wolves had stopped chewing the rope to look around and wonder about the commotion. One stayed back while the other moved halfway between the boat and the cabin. Simpson aimed and pulled the trigger – but this time nothing happened. "Holy Mother of all…," he cursed.

Pissed at himself, he slammed back the bolt and ejected the bullet. He dug several replacements out of his pocket and tossed them on the counter, grabbing one to put in the chamber. The closest wolf tried to run for cover behind the cleaning shack, but the next shot hit it in the rear leg, causing it to roll over on the ground. The following shot put it down for good. The remaining wolf on the dock stood frozen, staring at the cabin where the rifle barrel protruded. Its shoulders were hunkered down and it bore its teeth.

Simpson had it in his sights when the glass next to him exploded inward. For a brief moment, Simpson was dumbstruck, not reacting to the window, but still trying to take out the wolf on the dock. The general had launched himself up at the window. Simpson was covered in shards of glass but luckily, none had hit him in the face. The wolf let out an ungodly howl as it jumped up again and managed to loop a paw through a broken spot, nearly catching him across the thigh with its razor-sharp claws. For a mere instant, their eyes locked. The wolf's eyes shone with a pure hatred and fury, but Simpson glared back with his own wrath.

"You bastard! You're next!" he yelled at it. Its reply was a deep guttural growl, and then it brought its head forward quite violently, jaws clamping down on the crossbar in the window frame. The wolf tore it from the frame as it fell backward from the window. Simpson jumped down from the counter and kept the rifle pointed at the gaping space where a large part of the kitchen window had been. "*Shit!*" he thought, this was more a means of distraction. He turned to the front kitchen window and saw three shadow wolves just outside, and the wolf on the dock was frantically tearing at the rope with its teeth.

Simpson grabbed a can of peas off the counter and hurled it through the top right windowpane. He had the gun shouldered and remembered the bullet this time. Adrenalin could just as easily give you composure as it did nervous energy. Staying away from the window, he looked down the barrel of the gun and laid the mark on the wolf on the dock.

The penetrating crack of gunshot brought the general racing to the window. Simpson reloaded and shot through the lower glass windowpane in an attempt that was purely chance. It missed, but the wolf retreated off to the side of the cabin -- but the wolf on the dock was still working on the rope. He sighted in again and pulled the trigger. The wolf jumped as the bullet struck home, hitting it in the front shoulder. From this distance, Simpson doubted that he could kill it without hitting a prime spot. It was, however, enough to scare the wolf as it hobbled away from the boat and moved up the dock in search of better cover. Simpson took aim, and the next bullet hit it just below its left eye. It swayed, took two steps, and then fell into the water.

The sound of wolf cries rose all around the cabin and chilled him to the bone. Their harmonized tone was a mixture of anger and sorrow that penetrated deeply into his head. Once frozen memories from childhood nightmares filled his thoughts. As a small boy, Simpson's parents had taken him to the zoo in Des Moines. He'd been fascinated by the wolves, especially a large grey and white male. As unaware children sometimes do, he stepped under the bar and before his parents could pull him back, he'd put both hands to either side of his face as he pressed against the glass enclosure. The wolf charged at the glass in a ferocious fit of snarls and teeth. For years thereafter, Simpson's nights were filled with nightmares of that moment. Now, he understood why the supernatural entities haunting him took the form of wolves. They were his childhood trauma made real.

Simpson shook his head to dispel the nightmarish memories. Falling prey to latent fears of his innocent past would only exacerbate the current problem and he didn't have much time before the wolves would begin to regroup. By his count, three were out of commission, leaving only two that he considered to be of the living variety to threaten the interior of the cabin. It wouldn't be long before the shadow wolves called in their living reinforcements to command and possess.

Trying to come down from his edgy state of hyper-awareness, Simpson had a brief moment where he felt as if he was losing his grasp on reality again. What would follow afterward? They could bring in bears, beavers, maybe an attack of birds -- definitely the non-human cast of a movie that scared him when he saw it as a youngster.

Simpson began to think that he understood what was really happening. Vicky's body was hovering between the realm of the living and the next one, stuck in an in-between place that she had somehow managed to drag him into. He had become an unwelcome pawn in the in-between world, something that needed to be dealt with. Throwing away all the rational explanations, (not that Simpson had come up with any), it was the only theory that made sense.

The world often accepted, somewhat believed, and mostly hoped that the stories from near-death survivors were true. Having someone else share the same visions and stories as the person experiencing them would be revolutionary – it would change the world. He couldn't have been the first to make this sort of connection with the in-between state, and if there were other survivors, they must have all taken a vow of silence or never survived long enough to tell anyone. Death was most assuredly after him.

Simpson shivered and his brain was pulsing with feverous ideas about what was unfolding – but he knew that he must rely on his firm will to live and desire to make it back to Vicky if he was to survive. That felt true and more important than killing the wolves. The shadow wolves could only hurt him if he welcomed death. However, the real wolves could kill, but they were being commanded by the shadow wolves -- so maybe they too, could only kill if Simpson allowed them to. It was not a theory he was eager to test.

There was a thunderous sound as something hard hit the back door -- then the sound of groaning wood caused Simpson to jerk his head around toward the sound. The wolves were trying to break in through the back door. How many were there? Only two were left – or did he miscount? A last-ditch plan came to him. He tossed the rifle on the counter and ran back into his bedroom.

Simpson grabbed a wool sweater and the hooded rain jacket off the hook on the back of the bedroom door. It had a pair of insulated gloves in the pockets. The forceful attacks on the back-door continued as he hurried into the dining area of the cabin to grab the shotgun. He added a shell to the holding chamber -- four shots and then time to reload -- not much hope against a pack of wolves, but maybe just enough to make it to the boat. The wolf hit the backdoor again and it held, but for how much longer. He patted his hip to make sure the hunting knife was strapped in place and thought, *"What I wouldn't give to have a machete."*

Racing between the two front windows and looking out, Simpson didn't see any signs of a real wolf, only the six shimmering shadow wolves standing between the boat and the cabin. Four shots -- his theory was soon going to be tested. The wolf hit the back door and this time a chunk of doorframe splintered off and skidded down the hallway. The next hit was likely to take the door out.

Under the kitchen sink was a tin can of kerosene used to fill the lanterns inside the cabin. Simpson flung open the cupboard door and yanked the tin out from the back of the shelf. It was only half-full. Twisting off the protective cap, he sloshed the kerosene on the floor of the cabin and grabbed the fireplace matches off the table. He stood with his back to the wall by the front door. It might have been smart to open it first, but doing so might have alerted the shadow wolves and thwarted his plan.

Simpson both looked and felt like a vagabond hero just then, the one willing to do whatever it took to win. He held at least a dozen matches in his right hand with the shotgun tucked under his arm. His left hand supported the shotgun and the box of matches with the strike plate facing his right hand. One chance -- it was going to be all that he got. He would need to light the matches, toss them on the kerosene, open the front door, and then shoot whatever was in his way. Oh -- and kill the wolf that was advancing from inside the cabin after it broke through the back door.

His eyes felt burning-hot from the intense concentration on the back door and the effects of inhaling the kerosene. Looking around the cabin, knowing it would be the last time he ever saw it, Simpson somberly said aloud, "Sorry, Dad."

Simpson could have sworn that Sophie was rubbing against his legs, but when he looked down, she wasn't there. He struck the matches and watched as the flames rose higher on the group of matches that he held tightly. The back door burst open, slamming against the back wall as a large grey wolf with blood seeping from several spots on its head cautiously advanced into the hallway. Its right eye was shut and bulging out, twice the size of the other.

Its nose was *Rudolf* red and it wobbled as it walked -- feeling the effects of using its head as a battering ram.

Another wolf crossed the threshold and stood beside the other. It was smaller and rather beautiful, in a deadly sort of way. It bared its dazzling white teeth, teeth that stood out against the yawning darkness of its dangerous mouth. Simpson watched the younger wolf as it hunched down and prepared to attack. He didn't hesitate as he tossed the matches toward the center of the kerosene when the wolf bolted towards him.

The room exploded with a *kawoomph* sound as the kerosene ignited. Blue and yellow flames raced across the floor and surrounded the wolf. Instead of continuing towards Simpson, the wolf froze in panic and as it stopped in place, it gave the flames an opportunity to latch on. It jumped and danced a violent jig, yelping in pain and horror. Terrified eyes sought him out. A brain that was clearly operating with more than mere animal instincts suddenly ignored the flames, burning hair, and melting flesh, and propelled itself forward. Having already raised the shotgun to his shoulder, Simpson pulled the trigger. The wolf took the close-range blast in the face and crumpled dead to the floor.

The kerosene burned hotter with each second as the cabin's well-seasoned timber welcomed the embrace of the flames. The damaged wolf stayed put on the other side of the growing fire. Ejecting the spent shell and loading the next one, Simpson opened the front door to face what he had already expected to be there. The instant the door opened, cold air raced in and drew the fire closer. It was like standing in the doorway of a sauna and then stepping out into winter's fury -- one whispered promises of warmth, the other death. In this case, both promised death.

The general, the wolf in charge of the rest, stood directly opposite the screen door. Instinctively, Simpson fired the shotgun from the hip through the door. At such close range, it shouldn't have mattered, but his shot only grazed the large wolf, causing it to skitter sideways out of view. He ejected the round and loaded the next, using precious seconds to dig in his pocket and then chamber two more shells. The screen door, or what was left of it, was between him and the wolf. Simpson kicked it open and walked purposely out onto the porch. From the corner of his right eye, a grey shape jumped at him. In true action hero mode, he twisted around and blasted a shot into the chest of the wolf, all the while dancing sideways to avoid the dead animal's body from colliding with him.

Believing the general would attack from the other side, he pivoted and fired -- *at nothing*. Pumping the shotgun, Simpson swung it from side to side in an arc as he backed down the steps. The heat from the fire in the cabin had caused the snow on the porch roof to melt rapidly and he got drenched as he crossed past the roofline. The shadow wolves didn't move from their position in front of the dock or attempt to advance. Simpson wasn't concerned about them -- the general represented the immediate danger to him.

Simpson was stuck in the middle of an imaginary hurricane with no genuinely positive outcomes -- move toward the dock and take on the shadow wolves, stand by the cabin to be consumed by the fire, or take his pick and move to either side of the cabin to face the general, who had to be hiding nearby, waiting for his opportunity to strike. The snow was nearly a foot deep and Simpson's poorly constructed hiking boots were already letting the moisture penetrate and chill his body further. He continued to make circles in the snow as he decided where to go next. His feet moved him toward the shadow wolves since the boat was his only real option and they were between it and him.

The heat from the fire raging throughout the cabin made the outside air feel like an Arizona summer. Simpson raised the shotgun and drew a bead on the shadow wolf in the center. He didn't really believe he could kill it -- or even hurt it. He was also reluctant to waste another shot or be forced to reload if any of them attacked.

The shadow wolves looked a bit like real wolves, but their coats were duller and lacked detail and color. It was as if you were looking at them without wearing your glasses. But the closer he moved toward them, the denser they became, taking on more definition and becoming fuller. Simpson felt an instant spiritual chill when he locked eyes with them. He felt compelled to look away or else run the risk of being hypnotized by their gaze.

The shadow wolves might not be able to physically kill, but like Medusa, they might be able to turn his mind to stone and transform his wish to survive into the image of an ancient stone anchor sinking endlessly into a black ocean. From the increasingly fevered corners of his mind, an idea for revenge erupted -- *the propane tank*. It would surely blow up and cause shrapnel to be shot outward.

Simpson had no option at that moment but to move toward the shadow wolves, screaming forcefully at them, "I want to live, damn it! Leave me alone!" Instead of backing away though, they closed in and stood shoulder to shoulder. Simpson's mind was a jumbled mess of fluctuating good sense and wild indecision. Should he run through them, shoot them, or take his chances by running for the road? Each choice that he fleetingly pondered seemed doomed to fail.

The windows of the cabin blew outward, pelting Simpson with shards of glass as the searing burst of heat pushed him forward. The shadow wolves made no movement and seemed completely disinterested in the cabin's destruction. He held the shotgun out in front as he took a cautious step toward the wolves. He kept his sight over the top of their heads, but kept the leader in the gun's sights and made sure not to make direct eye contact with them. Simpson began to pray the "Lord's Prayer" as he inched closer.

The shadow wolves left no tracks in the snow and cast no shadows of their own for him to focus on. Simpson's mind buzzed with a loud static, distracting his thoughts and breaking his concentration, making it hard to stay alert. He shouted aloud, "Stop it!" But yelling didn't curb the insects inside his head.

Simpson pulled the trigger before losing the ability to do so. The recoil snapped the shotgun hard into his shoulder. He'd been holding it loosely and now his arm smarted from the backward impact. The shadow wolves stood where they were – still, unmoving, and no worse for the spray of shotgun pellets.

The swarming insects inside his head grew louder in volume so that he could no longer hear anything else but that annoying buzzing sound. Simpson felt an unexpected urge to close his eyes and he struggled to keep them open. Just as the levels of fatigue began to wrap around him like a cloak, the shadow wolves slowly spread out around him. They didn't walk as wolves would have done, but they shimmered sideways instead. Simpson took a step forward and then collapsed onto his side. The world seemed to be uneven, tilting first one way, then the other.

Simpson struggled to make it back up onto his knees. The shotgun was lying just off to the side but appeared to be shifting positions due to his distorted vision. He felt along the snow until his hand brushed the stock of the shotgun. Simpson pulled at it with such a weak grip that he wasn't sure he'd be able to pick it up, let alone fire it. He was nearing the dangerous point of passing out.

His stomach couldn't stand the ride any longer and it let loose of what little contents remained. Simpson's mind was quickly turning to mush as warm streams of tears slid from his eyes, chilled on his cheeks by the cold air. Without thought, he used the back of his hand to wipe away the snot dripping from his nose. His eyes registered the blood on the back of his hand, yet his mind only took in the inky redness, not the full meaning of what it really was.

The world around him started to spin. The shotgun was forgotten as Simpson could only envision peaceful quiet -- the type of quiet one could only relish by just letting go and giving in. "No!" he shouted at the wolves, "I won't!" Simpson crawled forward on wobbly arms and knees, swaying like a sickly dog. He was less than four feet away from the nearest shadow wolf when he noticed a movement off to his right. It came from the far side of the cabin and was artistically backlit by the roaring blaze. *Here comes the general*, he thought to himself.

Although Simpson's vision had little in the way of clarity, the general seemed to be brighter and fuller in size. There was a sudden and noticeable change in tone as the buzzing became louder, rougher, and less harmonized. Simpson's eyes regained a little stability and he could see the general approaching. His brain processed the information that the wolf who was charging towards him wasn't the general – it was not even a wolf. The animal was a Siberian husky with the bluest of eyes and a full black and white coat of stunningly bright fur. Simpson knew her name, much as he had known Sophie's name. The dog's name was Talini, and she had been his dog and best friend as a youngster. It was fitting that she was here precisely at this moment since her name meant *"snow angel"* in Inuit. Talini was going to be his next guide. He only hoped she would be taking him to safety and not to the place where Vicky waited -- *though they might be one and the same.*

The nearest shadow wolf began to quiver more rapidly and the others moved quickly to place themselves between the husky and Simpson. Talini bore down on them, her lips pulled back in a fierce snarl. It was her protective nature and one that Simpson had seen her use in his defense as a boy when he'd been threatened by another dog. She was met head-on by the shadow wolf to his far right. Both were up on their hind legs, front paws grasping for a hold, as teeth ripped at each other.

Simpson understood that it was a unique situation -- that neither of those creatures were of this realm. He bet that if he touched Talini, she'd be real to him. Maybe the shadow wolves would be real too, but he didn't think so. Talini got her mouth around the underside of the shadow wolf's neck and he heard the howls of pain in his head. She swung the wolf violently to the side, tossing it like a stuffed toy. The cries of pain in his head were abruptly silenced and the shadow wolf lay motionless on the ground. It both melted into the snow and evaporated into the air simultaneously.

Talini then turned to face the next wolf, but she was brutally knocked sideways by the general's unsuspected attack. Talini and the general circled each other and then came together in a singular mesh of ripping teeth and flailing claws. Simpson spied the shotgun half-buried in the snow and grabbed it. The buzzing in his head had been softened enough that he could see without everything spinning around and stand without throwing up. He cocked the shotgun and stepped toward the two animals locked in combat, hoping to save the one who came to save him. It didn't seem at all strange to hear the words "*no*" and "*go*" compassionately spoken inside his thoughts. It was Talini's canine voice, humanized and speaking to him.

Perception is what we are willing to believe. As a kid, Simpson had wished to have ESP because he knew Talini would have spoken to him. For whatever reason and far beyond his current level of comprehension, she was there to protect him and, if necessary, give up her life without any hesitation.

Every fiber inside of Simpson wanted to march into the fray and fight with and for his best friend, but he understood that she would be fine, just as Sophie was fine. It was time for him to use her intervention as an opportunity to escape. He walked right past the two shadow wolves still standing between him and the dock -- but he had to twist sideways to slip by without touching either of them. They never moved or tried to impede his progress. Looking down at them, he wondered what would happen if he touched one? Would his hand continue into them unobstructed by fur, bone, and internal organs? They weren't exactly evil, but exactly what they were, he couldn't say. The way they hummed inside his head gave them robotic attributes – as if they were doing the task that was expected of them without the benefit of any feelings or objectivity. They needed hosts, like the general, to command.

Walking down the dock to where the boat was tied, Simpson unsheathed his knife. The rope securing the boat had nearly been chewed through and it only took one swipe of the knife's blade to cut the remaining rope fibers. Sheathing the knife again, Simpson pulled the boat along the dock, picking up speed as he maneuvered it backward. At the end of the dock, he jumped into the boat, landing in half-melted slush and frozen water. At first, his graceful pirouette kept him upright, but with the backward motion and side swaying of the boat, he lost his balance and fell roughly onto the bench seat. The bruise on his upper arm would heal but losing the shotgun over the side of the boat wouldn't. It was a stupid mishap, careless, and would most assuredly cost him and make his death more probable. Simpson had no delusions that he was safe simply because he was in the boat.

The drawn-out angry cry from the general caused Simpson to scramble up from the bottom of the boat and find a perch on the seat. Looking back toward the dock, the general was standing at its end, head raised to the sky. His fur was spotted with dark red blood. Their eyes locked. "I'll kill you, you son-of-a-bitch," Simpson swore at him. The general snarled in return. *"If I only had a gun,"* Simpson silently cursed.

Simpson turned on the gas flow and squeezed the bulb to prime the tank of gas. Setting the choke to full, he pulled on the starter cord. She fired up on the fourth pull. After running it until the sound of the motor evened out, he reduced the choke and twisted the accelerator higher. The motor spat a couple of times and then settled in.

The general watched with visible hatred, his shoulders scrunched in a killer's pouncing pose, his mouth opened in anticipation of his victim's throat. Simpson had no doubt he'd be seeing him again before his escape was secure and he was safely on the way home. In one of those moments of clarity, his intuition hinted that safety wouldn't be found at home either. He had opened the bottle and let the genie out -- so putting it back wasn't an option. The shadow wolves needed him to be isolated -- something that he'd been aware of since the moment he'd seen the painting in the hospital waiting room.

Simpson cranked the engine fully open and steered the nose of the boat in the direction of Kittelson's cabin. The wolf hadn't moved from the end of the dock, but as he made the turn south around the point at the far end of the bay, Simpson glimpsed him racing along the shoreline. It was three miles to Kittelson's cabin by water, nearly five by road, and nearly the same if you tried to follow the shoreline. He ran the probabilities through an over-exerted brain. Simpson would get to the cabin first -- maybe have five to ten minutes before the general arrived -- *not much time to convince Robert and Thelma about the danger.* Who was he kidding? With his current run of luck, he could only hope that they wouldn't shoot him on sight.

He'd covered half the distance before noticing there wasn't any smoke coming from the chimney. You couldn't see the other cabins on the lake without jogging around Pine Ridge and following the lake past the cluster of islands all the way to the east end. Kittelson's was the closest to the main road, but even so, it was still a treacherous six-mile hike back up the lake road, not counting the danger from the wolf on his tail. If the Kittelsons weren't home, then the odds weren't much better that the others would be either. Simpson looked around the boat, hoping something had magically appeared that would help him break into Kittelson's cabin or at least give him something to use as a weapon -- a hefty pry bar or even an ax would have been nice.

The only other pet Simpson had during childhood was a turtle named Spike. He just couldn't see him playing a part as a spirit guide though. Each of Simpson's guides had done their best and it was up to him now. What he needed was a ride. Robert might keep a snowmobile in a shed. Even a scooter or skis would be a blessing. The one thing he couldn't do was to stay for too long at the cabin and allow the shadow wolves to recruit new hosts. They might choose to upgrade to black bears. He had to keep moving regardless.

Simpson had almost talked himself into trying for one of the other two cabins -- the farther away from the general, the better

Isolation

-- when the motor gave off a loud *ping*, followed by a *whump*, and then nothing at all. The silence was a worse feeling than when he lost the shotgun over the side of the boat. He knew that sound, and it wasn't good. The motor was useless to him now.

There were no such things as coincidences -- *Simpson saw it all now*. Everything was being played out like a chess match but on a grand scale. Simpson moved his piece and then whoever it was that sat across the board moved their piece. Any hope of outthinking them wasn't just unlikely, but nearly impossible. His father's cabin had been symbolic of the queen -- *protecting him*. He'd sacrificed her to wipe out some pawns and maybe a bishop. His opponent's queen was now maneuvering into place to set a trap that he wouldn't be able to escape.

Simpson lifted the motor prop out of the water and locked it in place. It took a little effort, but he freed the old rowing oars from underneath the middle bench seat. Having to reach into the semi-frozen water in the bottom of the boat didn't help, but smartly, he'd taken off his gloves before submerging his hands. He placed the oar pins into the slots on either side of the boat and let the oars hang out over the water. Simpson took a hard look at the shoreline and didn't see any movement. Taking a cleansing breath, he dipped the oars into the water and began the first of many pulls. "God, if you're listening, I could use a little help…"

CHAPTER 13:
Kittelson's Cabin

Within a matter of minutes, Simpson was sweating profusely. The sweater that had previously kept him warm in the cold air as the boat churned down the lake now felt cumbersome and heavy. With every stretch of his arms, he could feel muscles flexing and sweat dripping, not to mention the aches and pains of an old body trying to do too much, too quickly. Simpson didn't dare stop though -- *time was no longer his, the queen was in position, and it was his move.*

The choice had been made -- it was Kittelson's cabin or bust. Simpson wasn't capable of rowing the extra four miles to any of the other cabins with a possible hope that someone would be there. There wasn't any doubt in his mind that the shadow wolves had something to do with the motor's problem. Coincidences were no longer per-chance happenings -- they were merely a part of the larger and deadlier game he had found himself playing.

Kittelson's boat dock came into view from behind the tip of land that stretched out into the water and provided a natural cove.

The cabin itself wasn't anything spectacular -- modest and efficient, as most of the cabins on the lakes up here were. Simpson stopped paddling and let the gentle swell of the current drift the boat into the dock. It took him awhile to catch his breath as he scanned up and down the shoreline for signs of the General. He was out there -- *and he was waiting for his opportunity.*

Simpson stretched his neck from side to side to rid it of the stiffness that was already settling in. Now that he'd stopped rowing, the cold air had attacked the inside of his open jacket, sending chills that rippled through his body. The air smelled as clean as the snow looked on the ground when he took a few seconds to inhale deeply. He didn't know what the temperature was just then -- or what it would be that night or the next day. If it stayed below freezing and the sky maintained its overcast appearance, then he was in for an icy cold escape. Simpson needed to catch a break. Krofton would be a rough twenty-mile hike without one.

Kittelson's had two other structures near their cabin. One was the outhouse and the other a good-sized storage shed. His hopes rested with what was stored inside the shed. It was possible he might find transportation and a weapon. If there was a gun on the property, it would be inside the cabin -- but Simpson doubted he would have enough time to find out before the General arrived – and that was if he found nothing of use inside the shed.

Thirty feet from the boat dock, Simpson saw the first shadow wolf. It was standing behind the outhouse -- eyes blazing red. Those eyes meant it was sending an invitation to the others, letting them know he was there. Even if he headed to the other cabins, the shadow wolves would find him -- *there would be no escaping them.* The front of the boat became grounded a couple feet short of the dock. Simpson had unintentionally picked the shallow side for his approach. He grabbed what was left of the tethering rope and made the leap easily enough onto the dock and pulling the boat only far enough up to tie it up; he secured it to the nearest eyehook.

A movement behind Simpson made him turn around. A second shadow wolf had made its way to the dock, stopping at the dock's first wooden plank. Simpson wasn't afraid at that point -- *just annoyed*. He didn't like the idea of the shadow wolves creating an army of fierce attacking rabbits, chipmunks, or even busy beavers. The thought of beavers actually made him cringe. Those teeth, sharp enough to tear trees apart, would cause massive damage if they managed to lay into him. Simpson gave the shadow wolf his best, "Come and get me grin," along with a cocky, one finger salute. It just stood there, its red eyes the only color contrasting with the inky blackness. He took out the hunting knife and held it in his left hand as he walked briskly up the dock and past the shadow wolf. It made no movement, just like the others, but Simpson heard it in his mind -- like radio static buzzing and an android sounding voice trying to convince him to stop whatever he had planned. It conveyed how his life would be better if he quit running. "Kiss my…" Simpson didn't finish the mental thought reply.

Coming out of the trees, off to his right was a real wolf. It wasn't the General and was barely half as large. This one looked unsure of itself, taking cautious steps forward and then swinging its head side to side as if trying to shake off a swirl of annoying flies. It had a mostly grey coat that was mottled with black patches. The left eye was a deep golden color and the right eye was missing, a nasty scar encasing the empty black socket. Heightened instincts told Simpson to stay off to the side of the missing eye. He would need to make it past the wolf in order to get to the shed. His only other choice was to go for the front door of the cabin on

Isolation

his left, away from the wolf. He'd already made a mental note of the shuttered windows of the cabin, an appearance that clearly meant *closed for the season*. It was unlikely that the door would be open and even less of a chance that Kittelson had graciously left a key under the welcome mat. Where there was one wolf, more would soon follow.

At that moment, it was a stalemate. The wolf kept doing the funky head-swinging thing while pawing at the ground -- a bull preparing to charge the waiting matador came to mind. It could be stalling, waiting for backup -- probably the General. He backed away from the wolf, moving across the front of the cabin. If it became a situation where he needed to run, he wanted the cabin between them -- giving him a little extra time to make it to the shed. At the corner of the cabin, he saw an old ax sticking out of the stump by a stack of firewood lining the cabin's side. There were only two reasons for the ax to be lodged in the stump. Either it had been forgotten or it was all for show and stuck there. The cabin was closed, so it might have simply been forgotten. The odds weren't in his favor, but his luck had to change sometime.

As Simpson inched closer to the side of the cabin, 'one-eye' trotted closer, keeping a consistent distance between them. He would only have seconds to race along the side of the cabin and grab the ax before the wolf bolted after him and caught him. If the ax was stuck solid, he would somehow need to grab it and also be prepared to use his knife, all in the blink of an eye. Even if it came free, he still needed to be in a position where he could wield it. Seeing no other options readily available, Simpson angled toward the cabin's corner. The wolf hunched down, in preparation for a chase, as if knowing that Simpson's plan was to run. Simpson put the knife back in the sheath as he stepped backward. He kept his eyes locked on the wolf's lone eye. At the corner of the building, it took a step forward just as Simpson leaned forward and opened his arms as if welcoming its charge.

    The wolf didn't know what to make of Simpson and started doing the head-swinging thing again. Simpson rationalized that the shadow wolves must only be controlled telepathically and not by possession. It was the same way when he heard the buzzing in his head while getting close to them. They could communicate with him but not control him, only the other animals served that purpose. Simpson took an aggressive step toward the wolf and it reacted in kind by taking two steps backward. Simpson grinned, showing his teeth in an equally wolf-like manner. He felt that he was right -- it was waiting for reinforcements and if provoked, it would attack. He turned his back on the wolf and walked casually around the side of the cabin. The second he was out of sight, Simpson dashed for the stump with the ax.

    The snow was deeper on that side of the building and it slowed him down. The instant his hands wrapped around the handle of the ax, he heard the growl of the wolf. Putting his right foot on the stump, he pulled up on the handle for all he was worth. It didn't budge and although a big part of him knew it was useless to keep trying, the survivor inside kept trying anyway. Simpson glanced sideways at the wolf that was now less than ten yards away and crouched low, gums splayed back from its teeth and its one eye murderously taking him in.

    He was still pulling up on the ax, hoping for the last second miracle, when Simpson felt it -- that small give in the wood as it began to let go of its hold on the ax. He put all his faith and effort behind trying to free the ax, screaming "Aaahhhh," out of desperation and anger. The wolf sprang forward, bounding through the deep snow as Simpson kept screaming. Seconds seemed to stretch out like a dramatic slow-motion movie footage. Just as the wolf

Isolation

leaped forward, the ax pulled free from the stump, frozen splinters of wood clinging to the glistening blade. Simpson swung the ax in a sweeping arc and connected brutally with the inside of the wolf's mouth.

The wolf's growl instantly turned to an agonized yelp of pain. Simpson's left shoulder was jolted hard by the off-balance swing and the ax's impact with the wolf. Instead of lodging in the wolf's mouth, the ax carved through and the continued motion sent both of them sprawling in different directions. Simpson couldn't hold on to the ax as it flew out of his hands and into the snow. Scrambling to his feet, the wolf groggily pawed through the snow as it sought the safety of the trees. The tortured sound emanating from its ruined mouth caused Simpson's insides to momentarily churn with regret. The wolf was nothing more than a pawn in a deadly game and even though it had meant Simpson great harm, he still felt empathy for the wolf. He found the ax buried in the snow a few feet away. The wolf continued its pitiful crying, lying in the snow where it had fallen, its paws walking in the air. Simpson made his way to it and before he could talk himself out of what needed to be done, he swung the ax and silenced the wolf's pain.

Simpson made his way around to the back of the cabin through the thick snow. Once he bridged the back of the cabin, the snow depth eased, allowing him to walk more normally. With every step, he scanned the trees for signs of additional predators. Simpson studied the storage shed as he made his way towards it. The heavy double wood doors were closed tight, chained, and secured with a large padlock. Two shadow wolves stood on either side of the shed. Their blazing red eyes let him know that he needed to hurry.

Standing in front of the shed doors, Simpson sized up the lock and the best trajectory for swinging the ax. Based on the way it was hanging, he took one step to the right. *"No, you don't want in there. Come with us and know peace,"* the shadow wolves projected into his head. "Sorry, but I have other plans—like living," Simpson shouted back at them and then swung the ax, blunt end squarely connecting with the padlock. The recoil from the pull of the chain and the downward force of hitting the metal caused him to cry out. His left shoulder throbbed with excruciating waves of pain. He'd either pulled a muscle or slipped the socket. Simpson cautiously rotated the shoulder without causing the pain scale to increase too much -- but when he lifted the arm up, he felt it -- that unholy pain that makes you want to scream and hop on one foot as you swear to the heavens above.

Simpson sucked in breath through gritted teeth until the pain subsided. His breath came in ragged *poofs* of smoky air. He brushed the blurriness from his eyes and bent down to look at the padlock. It was severely dented, but it still held and was unopened. Using only his right arm, he clumsily pounded at the stubborn lock. He knew what needed to be done, but he just didn't know if he could.

"One more," and then, "Common on, give me a break," Simpson pleaded with the lock as he continued to pound on it with the weakened effort of using one hand. With hope failing that it would give, he backed up and grabbed the ax with both hands again. He didn't need motivation -- knowing that the General was coming was enough. What stopped him was the knowledge that he needed his arm to survive. If it became useless with what was ahead, he wouldn't stand a chance.

He shifted to the left side and prepared to swing the ax in a flat arc using the injured left arm more as a guide. On the downswing, he released the ax with the left hand before it hit the lock and let his right arm take the jolt of the impact. The ax head hit and bounced back hard off the door, spinning sideways as the handle caught him on the forearm. His sweater was so thickly padded that his arm weathered the blow.

The lock hung loosely on the chain and as Simpson pulled it free, the chain slipped from the door pulls, making a clanking racket as it fell on the stoop. He managed to open the right-hand door a mere foot before it lodged against the packed snow caused by his own stomping around. He kicked ferociously with the toe of his hiking boot at the mound, then with his heel, and succeeded in making the gap just large enough to wedge his body through. Simpson used his body's weight to exert enough pressure to push the door open another foot.

The side window of the shed was boarded over, much like his father's shed. But the gap between the roof and walls let in some light and took a bit of the edge off the dark interior. With the door open, he could make out most of what was inside. His spirits sank when he didn't see a snowmobile or a scooter -- not even an old bicycle.

It was mostly full of fishing items and yard-care tools. What looked like a pair of minnow dip nets hanging on the wall near the back, turned out to be a pair of old snowshoes when he got close enough to see them. Unpleasantly surprised and disappointed that the shed didn't have more in it, he rummaged around the shelves and added a container, sealed with matches, into his now empty pocket of shotgun shells. Bullets wouldn't do any good without a gun. Hanging from a hook, he found a hatchet in a sheath and quickly unhooked his belt to slip it on. Simpson stuffed several chemical hand warmers into another pocket. He smiled when he lifted down an old lifejacket to find a daypack hanging on behind it. He stuffed a smaller plastic tarp inside it along with half a can of camping fuel and a ratty, mouse-chewed blanket.

It took looking in the third tackle box before he found a compass. Simpson added a spool of heavyweight fishing line to the pack and a half-used roll of duct tape. His internal clock was ticking loudly and the alarm was seconds from going off. He had spent too much time in the shed and Simpson was one foot out the door when something tugged at his thoughts, pulling him back inside. He looked around, not recognizing what it was that had stabbed at his curiosity. Damned if he knew what it was he wasn't seeing.

Simpson noted the fishing equipment, life jackets, paddles, an old rake, shovel, and some chains hanging on a peg in the back corner. He didn't have time to check out the boxes on the lower shelves. What was it about the chains -- something about them wasn't quite right. They weren't hanging straight -- there were kinks at the lower end, mostly concealed behind a folding chair. When he moved the folding chair aside, he could finally see that the chains held four bear claw traps. Simpson grabbed all four and added them to the pack. Then he hustled out of the shed and was about to start his trek when he thought about the open shed door. He pushed it closed and then quickly wrapped the chain between the doors and ran the hook of the damaged padlock through the chain. It would have to do.

Simpson slipped both feet into the harnesses of the snowshoes and ran the straps around his boots and into the buckle. In his normal life and with all of the hills around their place back home, he had become proficient at using snowshoes on beautiful winter treks through the snow-encrusted woodlands. Today wouldn't be a peaceful ramble though and instead of walking up the lane and down the road, he headed in the opposite direction. The road would take him in the direction of the General, and by now, his new band of followers.

Isolation

As a kid, Simpson had spent plenty of time walking that road and hiking through the woods. The main highway was six miles away by road and maybe three miles away as the crow flies. It had one large ravine and multiple hills to climb to get there, but it also had more opportunity to stay ahead of his hunters. Three miles to go at a mile per hour, if he was lucky. That goal was not nearly enough time to keep the wolves safely at the rear, but perhaps it would be long enough for him to find safety in the ravine and lay a trap for them. Three hours would also be pushing the end of the daylight.

If the sky opened up and dumped a blizzard down on him, then the compass would be his only tool for navigation. Simpson said a silent prayer to keep both the snow and the wolves away as he stepped from the clearing into the trees.

CHAPTER 14:
A Trek to Remember

Simpson had barely trudged a quarter of a mile before he was physically wasted. The added weight of the hatchet and knapsack, along with the heavy sweater, made him feel as if it were eighty degrees outside instead of thirty-something. Perspiration continually dripped into his eyes and needed to be wiped away every few seconds. He had taken his raincoat off so it wouldn't keep so much heat contained within it. That wasn't destined to be the smartest idea if it got cold later, but Simpson didn't believe that there would be a later if he didn't make it to the road.

The snowshoes were both helpful and cumbersome. Any stray branch hidden under the snow grabbed at the snowshoes' webbing and he'd already fallen twice. The last time, thrusting out his left arm to break his fall reminded him it wasn't capable of supporting his weight and he had to give in to the bolt of pain in his shoulder. Simpson ended up lying face down in the snow for several minutes until the pain passed. The cold snow on the side of his face helped to ease the fire radiating outward from his shoulder.

The snow wasn't as deep in the denser parts of the forest, but Simpson still kept the snowshoes on. It was too time-consuming to stop and take them on and off and he wanted to make it to the ravine as soon as possible. The other side was steep, but there was a special path up that he'd discovered as a kid on one of his hiking adventures. Near the top of the ravine was a cave he'd found that had a chimney chute at the rear of the cave. The moss grew over the top of the exit, making the hole nearly invisible. As a kid, Simpson had climbed out of the chimney many times. The present worry was whether it was still open or if he could still fit through it and be able to climb out using his injured left shoulder. He prayed for enough time to check it out before the wolves cornered him. If he crossed the ravine far enough ahead of the wolves, he would then take a gamble and keep going. If they had caught up by then, he would try to trap them in the cave. Simpson hadn't completely thought through the how of that idea, but he still had more than a mile ahead of him to come up with a viable strategy.

Simpson made the effort to stride along at a pace that kept him moving forward without over-taxing his remaining stamina. As his breathing became more regulated, he concentrated more on the sounds of approaching danger or for any sign of threatening movements within the trees. He crossed over numerous sets of animal tracks -- deer, rabbit, and one that he was sure belonged to a black bear. Those caused his heart to race. He didn't like the idea of the shadow wolves using a bear to come after him – but thankfully, the track was headed in the opposite direction from Simpson's trek -- *not that it couldn't turn back his way.* For the most part, the winds were calm and the temperature was holding steady. It might only drop a little during the night or even rise if a warm front moved in. Simpson's plan did include being stuck out here because his father had made sure to teach him the benefits of always being prepared for the unexpected.

Working his way along a side hill, one snowshoe caught under the other and caused him to lose his balance and slide backward down the incline on his rear-end. After skidding for several feet, he reached out and grabbed onto the trunk of a small pine tree. It stopped him from going any further down the hill, but when he stood up and let go of the tree, it snapped back. Simpson was doused with cold snow that had been shaken loose from a larger pine tree by the whipping motion of the smaller pine. He did the only thing one could do in that type of situation -- cursed and then laughed at his own clumsiness.

Two hours had passed since Simpson left Kittelson's cabin behind. He was worried that he might be headed in the wrong direction, but then he broke through the tree line and came up on the east side of the ravine. It was more than six hundred yards across at the widest part and fifty feet at the narrowest point.

There were plenty of peaks and valleys, but none as distinct as this one. His father had shared an Indian legend that spoke of an angry god pulling the hill apart to let the great lake run free. In the process, surging waters had swept down from above and washed away a large tribe of wayward Indians. Their settlement had once thrived in the lower portion of what was now Switchback Lake valley. To see it best, Simpson's father had taken him to the highest spot on the old logging road that snaked its way around the vast acres of forest. It had been one autumn after the leaves had fallen so that he would be able to see the angry god's handprints on either side of the ravine. It didn't take much imagination and his mind easily pictured the great Indian god digging fingers into

Isolation

the hill and ripping it apart. To a young boy, it was a truth never doubted and Simpson had been in awe of the great god that split the mountain. The middle finger on the east side of the ravine was where he'd find the path leading up to the cave.

Whenever he had hiked the ravine in the past, his biggest concern had been loose rocks breaking free and sending him toppling down the ragged hillside. Simpson had never wanted to admit that his father had been right in his stern warnings because that would be meant he had to admit that the older man was right.

Simpson had been lucky on more than one occasion when the ground became unstable beneath his feet, but it was also the reason he had stumbled upon the cave. He'd been testing his skills as he imitated being an Indian hunter who was following the tracks of a great buck. Simpson tracked the deer up the path from the bottom of the ravine. He also had a slingshot in his back pocket in case he found a willing squirrel to shoot a pocket full of rocks at. Halfway up the trail, Simpson saw a rock with a long silver streak running across it. His twelve-year-old brain believed that it was going to be the next great silver strike and he'd be rich. But as he started climbing the boulders to reach the rock with the streak, he realized it wasn't silver after all, just as the rocks gave way below his feet.

He'd held on to an exposed root with his right hand, clinging to it as his heart tried beating its way out of his chest. One larger rock hit another and then others cascaded together until it sounded like a thundering herd of buffalo charging down the side of the hill. As quick as it had begun, it ended. The path that he'd been walking on minutes earlier was now covered by rocks and debris. It wasn't a California level of rockslide carnage, but it was terrifying enough to a boy of twelve.

When Simpson regained his nerve, he slid back down the hill on his rear. Looking back up the hill, he spied the new hole in the ground back where a larger boulder had broken loose and uncovered it. Three days passed before he could return and explore what was within that eerie darkness. Between fishing with his father and a steady string of rain showers, time passed slowly and Simpson could only fantasize about his next adventure -- the Indian treasures waiting for him inside the cave and the spirit gods he would have to outsmart to claim them.

Simpson headed up the ravine in the opposite direction of the way out, his mind caught between thoughts of the past and his current predicament. The direction he was taking also led him closer to the advancing wolves. Simpson believed it would be wolves and not just the General -- the shadow wolves had rounded up reinforcements. Unfortunately, the safest way down from that side meant heading in that direction. He'd walked about four-hundred yards when he came across a large buck standing just off the edge of the ravine, under the protection of the trees. It watched him advance -- *studied him*.

The shadow wolves had eyes everywhere. There were a few times on the trek when he had caught one of the shadow wolves out of the corner of an eye, but when he turned to look for them, they were gone. Simpson hoped to God that he never had to learn what their intentions for him were.

The deer continued to follow his movements without any trepidation. Simpson picked up a bent elbow of a branch and threw it like a boomerang at the buck. It hit the tree five feet to its left -- *the buck didn't jump, didn't run, it just stared at him*. Simpson walked past it, treading cautiously, still mindful that it could charge and try to butt him into the ravine. Where the buck stood above the ravine, it was mostly straight down and deadly, but it only turned its head to watch his progress and after another couple hundred yards, it was gone when he looked back.

Simpson came to the side runoff channel that intersected the ravine and carried high waters from Boynton Lake or spring runoff down into Switchback Lake. He took the snowshoes off to climb down the side of the runoff to its bottom. Surprisingly, the snow wasn't as deep in the runoff as he'd anticipated and he was able to stuff the snowshoes into the pack and hike along the side and bottom of the runoff channel.

Simpson came out into the ravine and stood transfixed by the beauty of the landscape. The high ridges dotted with pine trees and the snow covering the floor and atop the rocks like winter hats made the ravine look both breathtaking and isolated. Behind him, he heard the wolves calling to each other. As their soulful baying filled the ravine, the tone became richer as the rock walls collected the sounds and funneled them forward.

Simpson didn't need an alarm clock chiming in his ear to know that he was out of time. He started running, cognizant that one slip could be the end for him. A broken ankle, or worse, and he wouldn't be able to defend himself against their attack. If he even did survive the wolves -- *the shadow wolves would send new enemies.*

The cry of the wolves grew, filling the ravine, making it sound as if they were closer than they actually were. Still, it spurred Simpson on as he ran without regard to his heart and lungs that begged for compassion. He'd caught a small break -- the snow had been blown across much of the ravine's floor until it had compacted into one large drift. It stretched most of the way across and not too far from where the ancient God's index finger had creased the opposite side of the ravine.

As he ran, Simpson could see the ground and most of the larger rocks strewn across the ravine floor. He jumped over a fallen log and landed badly, fighting to keep his balance as he toppled forward. At the last second, he thought about his damaged left shoulder and did his best to protect it as he hit the ground. That was a mistake. In saving the shoulder, he cracked his head on a rounded rock that looked like a snow mound. Simpson's head collided with the rock hard enough to cause vibrant white light and stars to waltz across his vision. Rolling over onto his back, he closed both eyes and breathed deeply, trying to fill his head with needed oxygen and clear his vision.

Sweat from his burst of exertion poured into his eyes and he took off his glove to brush it away with his fingers. As soon as Simpson felt the stickiness of the liquid, he realized that it wasn't sweat after all -- it was blood. *"Shit!"* As soon as he sat up, the flow intensified. Simpson crawled to the nearest pile of snow and grabbed a handful of it, holding it to his head. The cold felt soothing, but the heat from his head and the warmth of the blood turned the snow into a red slush that dripped through his chilled fingers onto the ground. Eyes stinging from the mixture of blood and salty sweat, Simpson clutched some of the snow in his other hand and used it to wipe his eyes. "*I have to get moving,*" he thought. Holding fresh snow to the wound on his forehead, he attempted to stand. He made it -- but only for a second as the world spun around and he fell to the ground, sliding into darkness.

Simpson didn't know how long he was unconscious, but it was long enough for him to feel the effects of the cold on his body when he tried to sit up. He shuddered as chills raced down his spine.

In his blackout dream, he'd been dancing with Vicky at their anniversary party. He was going to dance with her all night long

-- forever. She told him how much she loved him and then kissed him with more passion than he deserved. She pulled away, her arms still draped around his neck and smiling her half-sweet, half-sexy smile at him. Simpson was ready to carry her off to the cloakroom when she looked him deep in the eyes and said, "Simple. You have to wake up. Please wake up now, your life is in danger!"

Simpson opened his mouth to reply, but she was gone. Her beautiful face replaced by the blurred sight of rock walls and snow-crusted pine trees. After a few seconds, the *thrumming* wound on his head let him know that he was truly awake. It beat savagely against his inner-skull, just behind the eyes. Simpson raised his nearly frozen, ungloved hand to touch the gash gingerly, remembering the amount of blood that had been gushing from it earlier. The blood may have ceased flowing, but now there was a large knot on his forehead. Instead of leaning over at the waist, he went down on his knees to pick up the pack and the snowshoes. Simpson took a tentative step toward the center of the ravine. He wobbled and then pin-wheeled his arms as he managed to stay upright. The next step was a little better and by the time he had taken a dozen, he had regained most of his control over his body and didn't feel as if he'd fall.

He was nearly across the floor of the ravine and about two hundred yards from the path up the other side when the wolves howled in unison behind him. It was a haunting sound -- both beautiful and sinister. The echo of their song made it sound as if there were more of them stationed all around the inside of the ravine. Simpson had no idea how long he'd been unconscious -- an hour, more, or mere minutes. Whatever amount of time it had been, it had been too long. What little edge he once had was fading fast.

Simpson ran the rest of the way to the large, distinctly-shaped boulder that marked the path up the side of the steep wall. The deepening snow sucked at his boots and the last few yards felt like he was running in the mud. As his head pounded wickedly with every step and in unison with his panicked heartbeat, Simpson could only pray for a break, a miracle that another rockslide had not covered the cave's entrance. The old familiar handholds once used as a child were still there as he stepped up and reached for each of them, maneuvering his way carefully up the side of the hill. The snow made the climb difficult -- his boots slipping and his fingers numb as he pulled upward by grasping onto cold rocks etched with snow. Simpson didn't stop until he stood by the imposing rock that he once believed was the head of a dragon that had been turned to stone by a wizard's spell.

The rock didn't look much like a dragon's head anymore, more like a sorry looking gopher. Maybe it had always been a gopher – *children had more imagination and freedom to see the world as they wanted to*. The entrance to the cave was several more yards above the rock, but that particular part of the climb was going to be the most difficult, even without the addition of slippery snow. From where he stood now, he couldn't see the cave's opening since it was further up the hill. The marker he had always used to guide him was a pine tree high up on the hill and slightly bent at the top.

It was still there, guarding and pointing the way to the entrance of the sacred Indian god's tomb. Simpson had spent many blissful years searching the cave and nearby hills in hopes of discovering untold riches. As a teenager, Simpson came up to the lake to go fishing less often -- girls, sports, and *girls* did that to you -- so he exchanged his youthful fantasies about bountiful and undiscovered treasure for dreams of hopeful kisses and home runs.

He'd never forgotten the memories of that cave though, even as it became more of a symbol for him over the years -- changing the meaning to suit him as his life changed. Simpson believed every child had one special place that they held deep in their hearts, a place of perfect solitude where fantasy and reality coexisted. You would never convince him that the whispers inside of the cave were the wind and not the spirits of Indian gods or heroic fallen warriors. Much like invisible friends, who was to say what was real.

The wolves bayed again, rapidly snapping him out of his daydream. They were in the ravine and coming hard. Simpson climbed another thirty feet up the path to where it narrowed as it cut between two steep sidewalls. Doing as he'd done as a kid, Simpson stretched his legs apart and using his arms to keep steady, he climbed upwards between the walls. First the left foot on the outside wall on the rock ledge, then the right toe in the crack, back to the left, and lastly the step on the rock sticking out like a tongue with the right foot as he reached for the exposed root of a pine with his right hand. Swinging his left leg around to find a stable place on the only flat-topped rock, Simpson hefted his weight a couple of sidesteps to the left until he was able to scramble over the top of the wall. The hill was still steep and with the snow covering on top, if he took one wrong step and slipped, he would slide violently back down that rocky surface and shatter his bones -- or worse.

Simpson took off the pack and tossed it the last fifteen feet up the hill to where he knew the level spot was waiting. Carefully, he crawled upward, grasping at anything within reach to help him. Simpson retrieved the pack and slipped his arms through the straps. His left shoulder was shrieking in protest after that workout, but he had to ignore the pain as he gingerly made his way sideways to the opening of the cave.

There was a welcoming dark spot in the middle of the snow and Simpson couldn't help but smile when he saw it. The entrance was still open and hadn't been covered by debris and rocks. The chimney was fifty yards away, over the crest of the hill. He should have gone over to see if it was open, but leaving tracks that lead towards it would give away his plans. Possessed wolves or not, for his plan to work, they must believe he was in the cave, trapped, and without a way out. He had to take a chance and do it on faith alone.

The opening to the cave was more than wide enough for a normal sized child, but now that Simpson was an adult and twice the size of his boyhood self, he shucked off the pack and dropped it down into the hole. It landed with a dull thud as it hit the cave's floor. He scrambled out of the raincoat and sweater, tossing them down into the darkness. Sitting on his butt in the snow, Simpson hung his legs into the yawning mouth and began scooting slowly forward, trying to feel for the rock step below his feet. With his left foot securely on the step, he dug his fingers into the snow at the lip of the entrance and wiggled through the opening while his right foot searched for the next place to step. He had just planted his foot on the familiar flattened rock and lifted his left foot free to step down to the cave floor when suddenly, his right foot slipped off the rock and Simpson tumbled the rest of the way down into the cave. In the end, he was mostly unscathed since only his right wrist caught a glancing blow from a protruding rock on the way down. The worst part of the fall was holding on to the ledge and having to endure a new shot of pain in his left shoulder.

The fall was not far, only a few feet, much shorter than it felt like when he was younger. The entrance allowed enough light in to see most of the main cave. It looked familiar, but different -- another example of the perspective of a child versus that of an adult. On a good day, if he jumped straight up he might be able to catch the lip of the opening. With the light coming in from above, Simpson could see why he slipped. The rock he had spent hours beating away at to make a step was completely coated with ice. He rotated his left shoulder a bit, wincing at the movement. The main cavern was nearly thirty feet long by eight feet wide and the ceiling was mostly taller than Simpson was. What he had hoped to see was still right where he'd stacked it all those years ago.

The plan he'd had to spend a night in the cave had backfired after asking for his father's permission. Simpson had thought his father would identify with the adventurer inside of him, but instead, he gave Simpson a set of lectures about why it wasn't going to happen. And just in case he had any sort of crazy ideas about sneaking out, Simpson was told that he would find himself ineligible to play football come fall.

It had been lucky for Simpson that it rained all night and the next day. He was close to choosing the cave over football because he felt sure that if he spent the night in that cave, he would somehow absorb the energy of the great Indian gods in his own vision-quest and learn something remarkable. It was one of those lessons about growing up -- when the need to test the imagination sometimes won out over simple logic or the sternest of parental warnings.

After the rain, his mother had arrived with his aunt and uncle and their two kids, Ben and Sarah. The cave adventure had to be pushed to the back of his mind – and he also didn't want to share the idea with Ben -- the stereotypical older cousin who enjoyed making younger people's lives more complicated.

Back in the present time, Simpson knew that if the wolves trapped him inside the cave, then no one would ever find his body. His plan was to do the opposite and trap the wolves instead. He knew the shadow wolves would send their minions in after him. Simpson desperately needed *all* of them to come after him -- if not, then he wasn't going to make it home. Simpson began collecting the unused firewood from long ago. Many of the pieces were little more than rotted chunks of wood mush. Fortunately, there were also plenty of good ones, enough to make a pyromaniac happy. He lugged all of it to the front of the cave, just below the entrance. Simpson took out the old blanket from inside the pack and then built a teepee fire stack around the blanket. The air from the entrance would draw the flames upward and with luck, stop the wolves from getting out while also smothering them with the smoke.

Simpson emptied the gas from the can onto the wood and the blanket. He almost added the old wooden snowshoes, but something inside nagged at him to take them with him. He headed to the back of the cave and the narrow passageway leading into the next chamber. He couldn't see much of anything and had to feel his way along the wall. The ceiling that he was once able to walk upright in was now low enough to force Simpson to walk slightly bent forward. He had forgotten about the pointed rock on the sidewall and he banged his right knee into it. After a loud, quick burst of swearing, he rubbed it until the funny sensation left -- *he wasn't laughing though.*

After fifteen feet, the passageway opened up and he could see a sliver of light coming from the chimney at the far end of the chamber to the left. Unzipping the pack, Simpson took out the four traps. With the aid of that light, he set the traps and retraced his steps into the darkened passageway. Simpson spaced the traps along the floor in the darkest stretch. He stuffed the raincoat and sweater into the pack along with the snowshoes, zipped it up as far as the snowshoes allowed, and shouldered the pack.

The chimney chute was smaller than the entrance and a completely vertical climb. It would be a challenge with a bad shoulder -- however, the option of failing and dying in the cave gave Simpson all the reassurance needed to make it. It was *the moment*.

He waited for the wolves, pacing in and out of the darkness. So many things could go wrong, and everything had to go right if he were to have any chance. Simpson took deep breaths as he stood at the corner where the passage emptied into the second cave, and where he could see the hope in the light of the chimney and hear the sounds of death from the main cave.

A long, lone bawling came from close to the entrance to the cave. Simpson heard it from both entrances but could tell that it originated at the main one. It was time -- they were coming. He grabbed the pack and snowshoes and ran to the chimney. The cave narrowed into a V where the chimney chute was located. Climbing the chute was going to be like climbing a doorframe as a kid – he would need to put his back against the wall and use his legs to give support as he inched up the wall. Now that he was an adult though, as he moved up, he knew that the gap would be significantly narrower. Simpson had once been able to make it far enough up so he could grab onto the nylon rope that was loosely draped inside the chute and tied to the tree outside – then use it to pull himself up. There wasn't a rope any longer and this time he would need to use whatever strength and agility he had left to make it back to the top.

Using the carabiner clip, he hooked the pack to a belt loop. Simpson pressed his back against the wall and extended his left leg to the other wall. With his hands by his hips, he pushed up and locked his right leg into place. Without his sweater, the roughness of the rocks began to cut into his back as he inched his way up. In less than a minute, Simpson was more than halfway and the gap had begun to narrow. That meant his legs needed to be more constricted, which also made it harder to gain ground. He was still too far from the top to get a hold of the opening and Simpson used valuable seconds looking for possible hand and foot pegs to grip or step on. A rock overhang was just above him and he knew that if he was able to reach it, he could pull himself up and escape through the opening. Using his right leg and foot to hold him steady, he twisted his body sideways, stretched upward, and barely grasped the rock.

More howls from the wolves echoed across the opening above and from the interior of the cave below. Simpson pushed himself to climb faster while his shoulder burned with pain, causing him to clamp his teeth together firmly to silence any scream that might escape from his lips. One yell and the plan would be lost. Simpson reached his left arm up and through the opening, digging his fingers into the snow until he found enough firmness to pull his weight up. A couple more shifts from side to side with his feet and Simpson's head and shoulders were through the opening. He kept his foot on the rock ledge below the opening. Now he waited for the next sign to go.

The wolves were silent. They were in the cave or still trying to figure out how to get in. The cold air made the perspiration on his neck and face feel like ice cubes were melting and dripping down his spine on a hot summer's day -- both refreshing and chilling. A loud metal clank was followed by a wolf's pain-filled howl, a sound that echoed through the cavern below. The wolf retreated rather than coming forward -- *that was good*. It left the other traps still sitting in readiness for the others. Simpson thought he could hear the scraping of toenails on the rocks as more wolves bounded into the cave. They were still relatively silent, but it was about to turn into a mêlée for survival.

That was the cue to go. Simpson scampered out of the hole just as the shrieking howls of another wolf caught by a trap reached his ears. He ran across the hilltop, the pack banging against his leg as he ran. Reaching into his pocket, he pulled out the glass jar with the matches in it. There weren't any wolves in sight when he reached the top of the hill. Simpson sprinted toward the entrance to the cave, sliding to a stop on his knees at the entrance. Twisting the lid off the container, he poured all the matches into his hand and noticed that they were the kind with the striking bulb on top. As he dangled the end of the pack-strap over the ledge and into the opening, Simpson noticed that he couldn't see any of the wolves. That meant that they had to be back in the passageway. The fire teepee was below him, but some of the logs had been knocked off and were lying several feet away on the cave's floor.

Taking a deep breath, Simpson struck the matches along the corrugated roughness of the pack-strap. He watched as the matches burst into flames and as he held them lower, the flames grew and lit up more of the darkness below.

The General was standing at the edge of the light -- looking directly up at him. His eyes glowed red and his teeth were bared in ferocious displeasure. Simpson smiled and dropped the matches precisely onto the waiting firewood and blanket. For the briefest moment, he didn't think the fire would start, but then a loud *whoosh* was followed by a beautiful blue flame that rippled through the wood and blanket as they exploded in perfect symmetry. Simpson instantly felt the heat rising upward. He kept his eyes locked on the General, able to see him clearly in the light from the fire. The General exposed more of his teeth and Simpson heard the unbridled rage in his growl.

Simpson sat back and pulled the tarp from the pack, opening it fully and covering the cave's entrance while packing snow onto it to hold it in place. The fire would search out the chimney for oxygen and hopefully cause the wolves to suffocate in the smoke. Layering more snow on the tarp, Simpson noticed that the heat had begun to cause the snow on top of the tarp to melt and puddle. As the smoke caused the tarp to billow upward, he cursed at his stupidity. If the tarp gave way with the weight of the water, it might extinguish the fire below. Simpson raced around the tarp piling more and more snow on it, hoping it wouldn't slip into the cave. More howls rose from below – sounds that were both panicked and pain-ridden. Simpson grabbed the snowshoes to flip water away from the center of the tarp where it had begun to puddle over the cave's entrance.

As the chances for the smoke to escape were diminished, the howls from below sounded even eerier as they reverberated throughout the caverns before being channeled out the chimney.

Simpson saw the smoke rising into the sky from over the hill and at about the same time, the howls of the wolves grew silent. There were no feelings of satisfaction about killing the wolves -- or any remorse. What Simpson did feel was suspicion -- *it was too quiet*, too soon, *too everything*.

He backed a few feet away from the tarp, pulled the hatchet from his belt, and held one of the snowshoes in the other hand as his eyes darted back and forth from the tarp to the crest of the hill. The tarp bubbled in the center and Simpson raced forward with the hatchet raised high, crying out as the fearless warrior wanting to live swung the hatchet hammer-like on the center of the rising bubble. Repeatedly, Simpson pounded at the form beneath the tarp and still, it crawled forward. Finally, he heard the sickening crunch as the hatchet crushed the General's skull.

The tarp quit moving and then, almost magically, it began to stretch apart as multiple holes started to appear and expand. Simpson smelt the stomach-turning odor of burning fur and flesh along with the toxic smell of burnt plastic. The fire below ignited and flared upward as fresh air fanned the flames. The General's body began to sizzle and the smell churned Simpson's stomach. Simpson was disgusted by the damage he'd inflicted on the animal's face and head and couldn't take another minute of it. Using his foot, he pushed the body into the opening of the cave and the wolf landed on the smoldering fire, causing ash to billow upwards.

Simpson turned away from the opening, gathering up the pack and snowshoes. He walked nearly a quarter of a mile before feeling that he was ready to stop and put his sweater back on. It reeked of death and the cold air had done little to clear his nose or eradicate the smell from his clothes. The warmth of the sweater temporarily calmed the clammy numbness of his upper torso, but not the conflicted feelings.

One thing nagged at Simpson. Where were the shadow wolves? Ever since leaving the cabin on foot, he'd only seen possessed animals. Why weren't they trying to get close to him and *bug* his thoughts? He didn't believe that was a good sign.

The trees were thinning slightly as Simpson pushed ahead towards the road that would take him back into Krofton. He kept checking the compass to make sure he headed west where he would eventually hit the blacktop. If his episodes of terror were truly over, then he might be lucky enough to secure a ride before the shadow wolves could regroup and stage another attack. Simpson seriously wondered if he would ever be out of their realm of reach. Would they someday find him alone and unsuspecting and then take him? Simpson understood that his unnatural adventures would forever alter the way he viewed his life. As the snow began to deepen, Simpson stopped and strapped on the snowshoes. His inner voice had guided him well thus far -- and it was saying that hope wasn't far away.

CHAPTER 15:
To the Road

SIMPSON SLIPPED INTO A FUGUE-LIKE STATE. He walked, breathed, but wasn't really aware of where he was going. A couple of times, he had to overcome the dullness in his head and swim to the surface of awareness long enough to check the compass heading. He had no recognition of time or any sense that he'd been trudging north, in the wrong direction, for quite a while. Simpson kept the compass outstretched in his hand and started back westward.

The voices reappeared in his head and kept after him, scolding him for killing the wolves, saying he must have enjoyed it. They offered sanctuary if he would just come to them. Simpson did his best to fight back with a voice of reason telling the condemners that he hadn't had a choice. Other voices joined in, reprimanding him for not staying at the cabin because now he would die, lost in the wilderness.

In a brief moment of clarity, Simpson noted that some of the voices were different in tone and message and he knew they were his own inner voices trying to get through to him. But at that moment, the distinction between sanity and insanity was in the details. The shadow wolves had certainly been in his head -- maybe they were still in there, subtly chipping away at his resolve. When one of the voices said it would be beneficial to sit down and rest, Simpson snapped back angrily, "Leave me alone!"

Maybe this was the way it was meant to go -- if you survived the physical attack, next came the mental assault. A never-ending raid on your mind until the only thing left was the bliss of eternal craziness. No matter how Simpson tried to shut the voices out, they wouldn't be silenced. He sang every song imaginable, even making up lyrics when he wasn't sure of the words. It helped to keep the voices down and allow enough distraction in his head that he could focus on the direction that he needed to walk in.

Simpson heard the snap of a breaking twig and spun around expecting to see a charging wolf. Instead, it was a doe running away. She must have been lying behind a fallen tree trunk when he'd walked by and spooked her.

The deer was the first animal he'd seen other than a scattering of birds flittering in the branches of the trees. Simpson was confused and dismayed when he looked down at the compass. When he first read it, it pointed east -- but a second later, it pointed west. He blinked several times, closed his eyes for a second, and tried to clear his mind. When he opened them quickly, the compass pointed west again. With the overcast sky and the height of the trees, Simpson couldn't really be certain what direction he was actually traveling in.

He had stopped singing and the voices were once again talking, telling him to trust the compass, he was going in the right direction -- *don't worry*. But Simpson was definitely worried now. He had an hour, maybe two, left of daylight -- plus the darkening skies of dusk in which to find the road. The matches were gone, he had no blanket, and there was no tarp to use for protection against the elements. His clothing was less than *insufficient* to protect against the rapidly falling temperatures. That wasn't the most terrifying part though. If he didn't make it to the road before dark, the shadow wolves would have a new army ready to attack him.

Simpson was exhausted and his spirit-well was damn near empty. Dropping to his knees, he bowed his head and prayed, "Lord, if you're listening, I'm asking. I'm asking for another chance to see my children, to tell them how sorry I am for running away and to beg their forgiveness for my weakness. I want to hold them in my arms and tell them how much they mean to me, how much I need them and love them. Lord, most of all, I want to see my wife. I want to feel the touch of her hand, kiss her sweet lips, and hold her in my loving embrace. She needs me, they all do. I've no one to blame for this predicament but myself, but I'm asking. Please -- let me live."

Simpson kept his head bowed in prayer and his eyes closed. He pictured Vicky's face, those eyes that shone brightly in her love for him. The quirky little smile that always melted his heart -- he held on tightly to that image in his mind. It helped and his mind became more settled and less frantic. Calmness surrounded him and the voices in his head were silenced at last. When he opened his eyes, the compass pointed east. Simpson headed back the way he'd just come from.

As he walked, instead of singing songs, Simpson talked to God. He thanked God for all the wonderful things in his life and made a list of promises about all the good deeds he would do when he arrived safely home. Simpson asked for forgiveness and repented for all the wrongs he'd done with his life. At the same time, he also acknowledged that if it wasn't in God's plans for him to survive, that was okay. He knew God would take care of Trent and Abby. Simpson asked God to save Vicky because there wasn't a better person to save -- and to let her know he'd be waiting for her.

Simpson walked past the spot where his tracks had made a U-turn. He kept the conversation going -- the deeper the conversation, the more at peace he felt. It also kept the voices at bay. Simpson thought he caught a glimpse of Sophie sitting on a log, but as he looked closer, it was only a squirrel -- *not even close to what Sophie looked like*. He ran out of things to say and could sense the voices circling at the fringes of his mind, preparing to attack again.

Simpson noticed a large broken-off tree trunk sticking out of the ground several yards away and headed towards it. When he read the compass, west was again behind him. This time, the voices were trying to be a bit more subtle as they whispered, "*trust me.*" He took a bearing from his previous footsteps and using their direction as a guide, marked a boulder a good distance away. When he read the compass, the boulder was on a northerly heading. It was enough to cause doubt.

Simpson wasn't sure what to trust. He was out of ideas and it felt as if the forest was more than just trees. It surrounded him as it closed in tighter and prepared to suffocate him with insanity once he gave up his fragile hold on reality. From up ahead, in the direction of the boulder, Simpson heard a dog barking -- but he couldn't see the dog. It was Talini and he needed to put his trust in her -- *he knew this*, more than he just believed and wanted it to be true. Simpson walked on and followed the direction of her barking, the compass now put away. The remaining value of his life was now going to be a reflection of faith.

The voices in his head were not amused. They screamed for him to turn around, telling him he was being led into a trap. But Simpson followed those barks without wavering and when dusk started to dim the daylight, the barks sounded closer and came more frequently. Simpson heard her bark for the last time when it was closely followed by the sound of a truck's engine getting closer and then fading away in the distance. He broke out of the trees and clambered up the side of the ditch and onto the road. Remarkably, Simpson was standing by the sign for the T-intersection of County Road 56 and Le Pierre Road. A sign pointed straight ahead to Krofton -- fifteen miles ahead -- or right on Le Pierre Road and six miles to Blanchet.

Simpson took off the snowshoes and put them back in the pack, not sure why he was still holding on to that pack. It would be of little use now, but still, he carried it with him as he began the long trek toward Krofton. As he passed the T-intersection, he gave considerable thought to Blanchet since, after all, it was only six miles away.

The wind was able to reach him now that he was out of the shelter of the trees. Simpsons boots were wet, as were his socks, but his feet still felt warm as long as he was on the move. The brisk wind was at his back as he headed south down the road. The baseball cap on his head did little to keep his ears from feeling the bite of the wind. Raising the pack up by pulling forward on the straps, Simpson was able to block off a little of the wind. Hopefully, a vehicle would pass by soon and he would be able to snag a lift into town.

The old highway was mostly clear of snow in the middle, but the outside of the lanes and shoulders were snow-packed. Simpson walked down the center, marking the fastest pace he could maintain. Three miles per hour would take five hours or more to walk into town -- *all of it in the dark*. The sky had cleared some and the moon was just beginning to appear, giving enough light to navigate the road. Simpson kept a steady gaze on the ditches and along the edge of the trees for signs of retaliation by the shadow wolves. Ever since he had set foot on the blacktop, the voices in his head felt *gone*. It didn't mean that he was home free though since he still expected them to come after him. Five hours would be plenty of time for them to mount another go at him. He'd used up his bag of tricks and the only things left were fishing line, duct tape, and snowshoes. He only had a knife and hatchet to use as weapons. That might be enough to fend off one attacker, but not a pack.

Simpson had walked close to three miles without seeing another vehicle and he kicked himself for not running toward the sound of the truck's engine that he had heard earlier. The road ahead was curving sharply downward. This part of the road was a treacherous three-mile section that wound through hills and thick timberland. It was also where many a driver had hit a wandering deer because of the tight curves in the road. If the shadow wolves planned to take him, it would surely be here. Simpson let the natural decline in the road pick up his pace as he stretched out his stride. His heart raced, not with the increased exertion, but with self-inflicted thoughts of wolves tearing him apart.

Simpson climbed to the top of the second hill, out of breath and glad to be free from the enclosed feeling of darkness in the valley when headlights shone toward him from the direction of Krofton. He stood alongside the road and waited for the car or truck to see him -- not willing to stand in the middle of the road in case the shadow wolves had the ability to control another human. If he could get them to stop, then maybe he would be able to convince them to turn around and take him to Krofton.

He thought about putting the knife and hatchet into the pack before anyone caught sight of them. It wouldn't help his cause if he looked like a hollow-eyed, weapon-yielding maniac -- *even if that was exactly what he looked like just then*. Not wanting to give up the ready protection that they provided, he slid the hatchet as far as the belt loop would allow toward the rear of his leg. It would have to do.

The headlights of the vehicle were riding high, so he figured it was a truck or SUV. Simpson started waving his arms the instant that the headlights cast their beam of light at his feet. All the screaming and arm waving did absolutely no good though as the truck drove right past him as if he weren't even there or worth any consideration -- *not even a slowdown or tap on the brakes, even as it was safely past.*

Simpson shouted after it and even ran a few paces behind, wildly waving his arms, hoping the driver would reconsider. A string of slurs, a passing moment of despondency, and then he was walking the next rise down and back up the hill. He tried coming up with valid excuses for the driver not being willing to at least stop and see if he was hurt or in the midst of an emergency. The reasons not to stop up boiled down to something as simple as self-preservation. Maybe it had been driven by a young girl under strict orders by her father not to ever let anyone in his truck. Simpson had no choice but to release all of his fanciful conclusions and just concede to the benefit of the doubt.

By the time he'd crested the next hill, the driver had been given a free pass. Who was Simpson to deserve compassionate consideration anyway? As the night bore down on him, the wind eased and the temperatures dropped. Surprisingly, he didn't feel tired or cold. Instead, there was more of an invigorated spirit with each passing mile. The closer to Krofton he got, the more hope he began to allow himself to feel. It didn't erase the fear of the wolves though. He would be looking over his shoulder for them for the rest of his life.

CHAPTER 16:
Looking For A Ride

Simpson spent the next three hours walking the road without another vehicle passing by. The exuberance he'd briefly felt while walking down the center of the highway had thoroughly dissipated. The cold had found its way in around the edges of his rain jacket, prickling his bare ears and numbing his hands. Since they were only wearing the thinnest of gloves, he kept his hands tucked under his armpits to keep as warm as possible and tried pulling down the sleeves of his sweater as an extra layer of makeshift gloves. He was dead tired now and getting more so by the minute. He hadn't come across any recent mileage signs for Krofton, but by his recollection, it was still nearly five miles to the center of town and the Gas & Go filling station. They would have a phone that he could use to call Abby to let her know he was okay and on his way home. The more he thought about calling, the more his tired mind fought him, coming up with irrational reasons why she wouldn't even take his call.

Simpson hoped the gas station would at least offer him an opportunity to catch a ride out of town headed south. He already knew that before seeking help, it would be best to use the washroom and clean up as well as he could. If he didn't make himself look somewhat presentable, his chances of catching a ride would be slim.

"Oh, crap!" burst loudly from his mouth as he frantically slapped at his back right-hand jeans pocket -- no wallet. To make sure, he patted the left one as well -- *no wallet*. Outside of the compassion of others, a bus ticket was now out of the equation, as was paying anyone for a ride or even grabbing something hot to eat and drink. He pictured his wallet sitting on the dresser back at the cabin. The picture that had meant so much to him of Abby, Trent, and Vicky at Abby's wedding had been incinerated to nothing but ash. Bad decisions and their effects were piling up again. It had been so easy to run away and now that he was trying to get home, everything was stacked against him.

Simpson stumbled and nearly fell when his toe caught an ice chunk on the roadway. "Damn it all to HELL!" He yelled aloud, more as a means of breaking the silence of the night rather than because of the pain in his toe. He limped for nearly a hundred yards before his anger receded and long after the toe felt good enough to put his weight back on it. He was mumbling to himself and oblivious to the fact that the darkness in front of him had begun to lighten. It was hearing the sound of a heavy motor churning from behind that caused him to snap out of his foggy mental state and take note. He stepped to the side of the roadway and waited for the vehicle to approach.

He had no idea what time it was, but it was late enough that this might be his last chance for a ride. Simpson decided to play chicken with the vehicle in hopes that he could get it to stop.

Moving to the center of the road, he was soon bathed in a haunting yellowish glow. The vehicle, a car by the positioning of the headlights, wasn't traveling at the posted speed. If anything, it was creeping along at a snail's pace. By the rumbling coming from the engine, it sounded like an older car. Simpson began to shout and wave his arms as he crossed them back and forth in front of himself. The car, already going quite slowly, decreased its speed and then rolled to a stop several yards away. The driver hit the high beams and Simpson had to put his hands in front of his eyes to cut out the intensity of the beam as it shone on his face.

He didn't know whether to approach the car or wait for the driver to make the first move. For all he knew, the driver could be loading his shotgun. Simpson actually wondered why everything he did seemed to fit within the plot of a horror movie. He suddenly had visions of chainsaws, machetes, and hockey masks and he worried about the intentions of his potential savior.

Taking a deep breath, Simpson yelled, "Hey! I don't mean any harm. I'm looking to get a ride into Krofton." He'd been thinking of a plausible excuse to use and decided upon staying closest to the truth. "I was up at my cabin for a late fishing weekend and got caught in the snow storm. The battery died in my car and I had no way to call for help -- so I've been walking."

Simpson stood where he was and waited for the driver to acknowledge him. He was about to repeat himself when the driver dimmed the lights and crept the car forward. It was hard to tell the model of the car or how many people were inside, but Simpson noted that it was indeed an older car and in the background silhouette of the light in his eyes, he presumed there was only one person in the car. He stepped away from the front of the car and moved toward the driver's side and now that the headlights weren't blinding him, he recognized the car's general shape.

For a second, it made his heart catch in his throat. His head shook in amazement -- *there are no coincidences.*

The driver's window began to crank down, all the while emitting the familiar creak of window glass that has settled off-kilter and must be forced up or down with persistence. There was a faint bluish glow coming from inside the car and it surrounded the driver like a halo, obscuring the features and the sex of the person sitting behind the wheel. Simpson found it hard to swallow and after everything he'd been through, seeing a car on this stretch of the highway, exactly like his grandfather's car, was another stab at his rather wobbly mental state.

From the bluish glow, a deep baritone voice called out, "Mister, you look like you've been fighting in one hell of a war. The way I see it, anyone that is walking this road past midnight is either drunk or in need of help. Since I didn't see you swaying, I'm guessing you need some help."

Simpson thought *you have no idea* -- but instead, he replied, "Help would be most appreciated. I'm hoping you could give me a lift to the Gas & Go in town."

"Shouldn't be a problem since that's the only place this road will take us unless you're wanting to do some wolf hunting Lots of them around these parts you know -- then we could head back in the other direction. Either way, you best hop in."

Simpson didn't know what to think about the hunting comment. It felt out of place, but it also had a double meaning to it. *There are no coincidences*, and *I'm not in Kansas anymore* were the thoughts that were racing through Simpson's head as he walked around the back of the car, hoping to see if anyone else was in the car. He also wanted to get a look at the license plate and rear bumper. His grandfather's old car had a bumper sticker with a peace symbol on it -- much faded from the years and tattered around the edges. The only part of it still readable was the symbol itself, though barely. The bumper sticker had been put on in the mid-1970's by some kids in the neighborhood as a prank. Grandpa had left it on without ever trying to remove it. His license plate was one that the veterans would purchase to show their patriotic spirit and to be recognized for their past service to their country. Grandpa's response to anyone who ever asked him about the conflict between his sticker and the license plate had been, "The goal is always peace, in which there would be none without the sacrifice of those willing to uphold it."

The back of car didn't have a bumper sticker, but in the reddish glow of the taillight, Simpson was certain that it once had -- and in the same spot. The license plate was a plain and normal one for Minnesota. He prepared himself for his first sight of the driver. Moving around to the passenger side of the car, he opened the door. Simpson didn't know what to expect as he lowered himself into the seat.

The car smelled fresh, not what he thought an old car should smell like. The crisp aroma of freshly polished vinyl mixed with a familiar scent of after-shave, one that Simpson couldn't quite place, were the strongest fragrances. For a moment, he really did expect to see his grandfather sitting behind the wheel of the car -- *possibly a younger version of the man he remembered.* But the man behind the wheel bore no resemblance to anyone he'd ever seen.

Simpson was aware of the hatchet handle sticking out noticeably from his left leg. Now that he was sitting down in the light of the overhead dome, the blood from his battles with the wolves showed dark red against the faded blue of his jeans and there were bright stains on his hands. He knew he should quickly say something before the driver asked him to explain or insist that he leave.

"Funny you mentioned wolf hunting because I had a little problem with one before I came out on the highway. I made a trek through the woods, thinking I could cut some time off my walk, but it almost cost me my life. I think the wolf might have been rabid -- couldn't really tell. It was weakened, a good thing that it was, but still it chose to attack me. I had no choice but to kill it with my hatchet. Guess the blood splattered me pretty good."

Simpson kept his eyes focused on the driver while he'd imparted his partial truth about the wolves. It was hard to determine any emotions from the driver, one way or the other. The meager glow from the interior dome light slowly faded out as he studied the face of the man who said nothing. The driver's eyes were brown and the whites were bright. Those eyes drew him in, making it difficult to look away. He felt remorse for not telling the whole truth, as if looking into those eyes broke through the layers of half-truths and caused him to acknowledge his personal feelings and regrettable self-judgment. For some reason, Simpson felt ashamed and humbled -- a feeling he couldn't explain having.

The man's hair was dark brown and shaggy -- nearly shoulder length. He had a full beard that looked as if it had been trimmed recently. There was a small vertical scar, about an inch long, running from of the corner of his right eye down. Simpson thought to himself, *lucky he didn't lose that eye*. The driver looked as if he couldn't be over forty. The man's left ear was pierced and had a silver Celtic cross dangling from it. Simpson couldn't be sure, but as the dome light dimmed and then went out, he thought maybe the man might also have a tattoo on his neck.

"It seems you had luck on your side by only encountering a lone wolf. Most times, they patrol the woods up here in a devilish pack. I can tell you that fending off one of them is tough enough, but a pack will eventually take down even the most prepared man," the driver stated matter-of-factly as he put the car into gear and started down the road. "By the way, name's Oslo."

"Simpson Jennings."

"What parts do you hail from Simpson, if I might ask? You don't sound like a traditional Northern Minnesotan."

"Tremont, Iowa -- it's in the northeastern part of the state."

"Ahh -- the middle of trout stream heaven."

Simpson smiled at Oslo's comment. Tremont was near one of his favorite trout streams. Fishing for trout could be as rewarding or frustrating as the days are different. Trout were the cats of the fish world. They did what they wanted when they wanted. Hit the hole on a good day and the stringer would be full in less than an hour. On a bad day, you could look down into the cool water and watch the trout race away from every type of bait and lure you threw at them.

"I like to think of myself as a cautious man, and a man that does a good turn where one is needed. You aren't dressed for winter hunting and most fall fisherman up here are long gone before the snow falls. I could try to believe you are an unfortunate first-timer that made a mistake, but I'd be wrong to do so. My guess is you have quite the story to tell. I'm also thinking you need to get somewhere and you kind of look like you're wearing a bad fit of desperation clothes."

Simpson didn't know what to say. Even more, he wasn't sure how to take Oslo's comment. Was he offering his help or needing an explanation. It was likely to be both. "You're a very intuitive man, Oslo. I'm not sure you would believe my story without thinking me crazy. I do need help to get home…" Simpson paused before going on and after a heavy sigh, he decided to share his story.

"My wife and I were celebrating our anniversary. On the drive home, we were in an accident that I couldn't -- I should've

-- oh hell -- it wasn't my fault. I've been blaming myself because I had one more drink than I should have, but the truth is that the accident was the fault of the other driver who ran the stop sign and collided with our vehicle. If I was drunk, it was love that made me so. I was paying more attention to my wife Vicky than I was to the road.

"I'm glad you feel like telling me the "what fors" and "what have yous", but Krofton is only a couple miles up ahead and I'm needing to know if I'm dropping you off or if I'm driving you somewhere. If I'm still driving, then you got time to finish your tale."

Simpson sat there with his mouth agape. Oslo was serious about driving him and Simpson believed it didn't matter how far. "I'm not sure that I can ask you to drive me all the way to Iowa. That would be beyond what I…"

"Deserve, want, need, hope -- fill in what you will. When I opened my door, I offered you my help. It still stands. Some will ignore others in need or only do the minimum necessary, leaving when there is still work to be done, I believe you have a responsibility to take care of those needing help. One day it might be me that needs it. I guess today it's you."

"Oslo, I don't know what to say or how I can thank you, but thank you."

"You bet Simpson. My father taught me well and I have always done my best to follow his example. I believe in helping others. And not just when it's easy or convenient to do so. What say we stop at the Gas & Go for some fuel and food? I'm thinking it would be better if you stay in the car. The way you look might just be enough for someone to cause us a little trouble. The last thing you need is a delay."

"Better safe than sorry," Simpson heard himself saying the old cliché. He looked out the window and could see the lights of Krofton looming up ahead. As the old Chevrolet Bel Air hit the city limits, Simpson studied the houses. Most of them appeared to be empty. The snow out front hadn't been shoveled and drapes were tightly drawn. Many of the residents had winter homes in warmer climates – that was fairly standard for those working in the tourist trade. Simpson was willing to bet that at least a third of the town had probably headed south by now. The Gas & Go was lit up in stark comparison to the relative darkness encompassing the rest of Krofton.

Oslo eased the car into the lot and stopped at the pump furthest away from the small convenience store. As he got out he asked, "Anything, in particular, you want to eat?"

"I wouldn't mind something with meat. Maybe a *Snicker's* bar and *Diet Coke,* too."

"I'll give it a look-see."

Simpson watched as Oslo closed the door and then removed the gas nozzle from the pump. In the overhead lights of the gas station, Simpson got a much better look at his Good Samaritan. Oslo stood nearly six feet tall and was thin. It might just be the baggy sweater giving him the appearance of being skinny -- it was hard to tell. His hands looked rough -- probably a skilled laborer of some sort. His fingernails were a vibrant white, much as his eyes were, and neatly manicured. His look and mannerisms were a bit of a contradiction to his overall appearance, thus making Oslo a man of mystery. His dark blue sweater had a spot where it looked like it had been repaired with mismatched thread. It made Simpson feel awful to think that he was beholden to the kindness of a man who may not have much to spare. He vowed that he would get his address and repay him for his expenses and time.

The moment that Oslo clicked off the gas pump, he headed into the store to pay and buy food. Simpson twisted around in his seat so that he could get a look into the back. There was a dark green insulated jacket and gloves -- nothing else. The inside of the car was spotless, not even a crumb on the floor or a wayward stain. When he opened the glove box, his first reaction was to close it quickly since being nosy wasn't something he enjoyed. But he also wanted to make sure that there wasn't a gun or something else in it that might be worrisome. It was as clean as the rest of the car. The only item inside was the car's manual, which looked like it had just been printed. Snooping around the inside of the car was doing nothing to alleviate Simpson's feelings of unrest. *There were no coincidences.*

Simpson consciously decided to trust Oslo. He really had no other choice. The man didn't give off a negative vibe. It was just the opposite. He wondered if Oslo restored old cars since that would explain the pristine look of the one he was sitting in. He settled into his seat, got comfortable, and before he knew it, Oslo was opening the door and calling his name. It took him an instant to remember where he was and who was talking to him. His rapid fall into a sound state of sleep had arrived unexpectedly and it caught him off guard. Now that he was awake again, he felt how tired he actually was. Oslo was handing him a sack and it took all his effort to lift his arm to retrieve it.

"Man, you were out cold. I had to call your name a half-dozen times before you even stirred. I hated to wake you, but you should probably eat the burrito before it gets cold. Experience has proven that when they're cold they make for better trash deposits than consumption."

Simpson had to fight his weariness to answer and the words came out sounding jumbled and fuzzy, "Tanks, it smalls good."

Simpson smiled sheepishly as Oslo began to laugh at him. There was no ridicule in Oslo's laughter. His was the full-body hearty chuckling of someone enjoying the best joke ever, the kind that made you laugh along without even knowing why it was so funny. Simpson's stomach began to rumble as his senses awakened to the smell of the burritos. He tore open the bag and pulled out one of the two wrapped burritos and it only took him five bites to demolish it. He was about to grab the other one when he thought that it might be Oslo's. He was buckling his seatbelt when Simpson asked him if the other burrito was his.

"Nope, both of them are for you. I had myself a good supper earlier. I try to make it my goal not to eat after eight o'clock. It makes for a better night's sleep -- at least for me. I figured you might need two to fill you up. Probably could have used three."

"Two should do it," Simpson replied as he took the other one out of the sack and began to unwrap it. "I can't thank you enough for your help. I want to make sure to get your address before you head back home so I can send you a check for the gas and your time."

"Wouldn't hear of it. A good turn's reward is in the doing -- not for compensation," Oslo stated as he twisted the key in the car's ignition. "One of these days you may be faced with your own opportunity to lend a hand. When you do, think of me. That will be my thanks. I know what you're thinking; Oslo must have been raised by a God-fearing mother who beat him with Bible verses."

This time it was Simpson's turn to laugh. "I had been thinking that you might be one of those wild wilderness pastors. The kind who drives along the deserted roads looking for converts."

"Not converts -- more like lost souls," Oslo said with a chuckle in his voice as he eased the Chevy out on the main road. Once he had the car headed out of town he added, "You're a good man -- could tell that right off the bat. The clothes you have on say you've been in a messy tangle -- but your eyes show compassion and conviction. We all make hasty decisions that lead us off our path. But sometimes those decisions were put in front of us, to test us -- find out if we're worthy to tackle the hard road ahead. I was only half-kidding about my mother. She brought me up to believe in the power of the Lord, and more importantly, to believe in the good inside of people. There's no doubt that the world has a boatload of problems -- people without responsibility, suicide, murderers, purveyors of destruction and malfeasance, but I still side with my fellow humans against the odds and hold to the belief that we are worth saving."

Simpson listened intently to Oslo as he spoke, mesmerized by the tone of his voice and the conviction within his words. He felt comforted by what Oslo said and by his company. Simpson had always tried to give his fellow man the benefit of the doubt, sometimes seeing the rewards as much as feeling the sting by those who continued to take any advantage they could gain. "I think you have a little preacher inside of you Oslo. So, what line of work are you in?"

Simpson watched Oslo as he thought about his question before answering. He pursed his lips together and tilted his head slightly to the left. "Kind of a tough question to answer. I'm a little bit of everything -- even a little bit of a preacher from time to time. Mostly, I do odd jobs. I have a knack for carpentry and fishing. During the summer, I occasionally guide the wayward fisherman looking for the hot spots and I take repair jobs wherever I can muster them up. This time of year, I hire on to keep a watchful eye on vacation homes and cabins. I grew up in Sibley, about thirty miles northwest of here. I was headed down to Minneapolis to pick up a part for my 1956 Ford Thunderbird." Oslo laughed as he added, "My work shed is twice the size of my house. It's the only way I can afford my hobby."

"My grandfather used to have a 1968 Chevy Bel Air, just like this one. With all that has been going on, when I saw the car, I thought you might be him."

"Sounds like an interesting story to me. Got plenty of time -- if you're up to telling, I'd like to hear it. Maybe you want to catch some sleep first?"

"Yeah, I could definitely use some sleep." Simpson even yawned to show he was telling the truth. He finished the second burrito and washed it down with half of the soda. With his stomach satisfied, he leaned his head back and with the comforting sound of the humming engine, he quickly nodded off.

CHAPTER 17:
The Road Home

———•·•◦⟨∞⟩◦•·•———

When Simpson woke, he found himself in a completely unfamiliar place. In his dreams, he'd been playing on the beach in Florida with ten-year-old Trent and his little six-year-old princess, Abby. Vicky was sitting under a large beach umbrella, reading a book while Trent scoured the beach between the breaking waves, looking for seashells and starfish. He and Abby were building a mighty castle where she could be protected from the trolls and giants that might want to attack. He would, of course, carry her away to safety before she could be forced to marry the "Dragon Prince," Artie Pelican.

Simpson knew why she had chosen Pelican as a name -- seeing them eating fish on the pier earlier had been an exciting discovery for her. But the name, Artie, was another matter. He prodded her, but couldn't get her to spill her secret, so he decided to play along and build a moat around her castle to protect the beautiful princess.

Isolation

Wherever he was, it was brightly lit, but he could tell by the temperature that it was far from beach weather. His neck ached and pain flooded through him as he raised his head. Remembering his recent flight from the wolves, Simpson looked out the car's window, seeing only gas pumps and bright fluorescent lights. It quickly came back to him though and he knew where he was.

Turning his head to look for Oslo, he spied him outside the car, holding the pump handle as he filled the car with gas. Simpson's body felt as if someone had beaten him with a baseball bat. He pushed himself up, wincing in pain as his left shoulder reminded him of what he'd been through. He rubbed the throbbing spot until it settled into a dull ache. Simpson heard Oslo returning the gas nozzle to the pump. Instead of walking toward the store or the driver's side, Oslo popped open the trunk of the Bel Air. Then, after a few seconds, he closed the trunk lid and made his way round to Simpson's side of the car.

Oslo opened the door and handed him an old Carhartt jacket. "Better put this on while we go inside to use the facilities. I'd keep my head down -- just follow me through the doors and into the restroom. I'm figuring it's time to clean yourself up some. Might want to use the arm of your sweater to wipe some of the dried blood and dirt off your face. It will make a world of difference."

Simpson took the extended jacket from Oslo without a word. Being cautious of his shoulder, he shucked off the outer sweater and then used it to wipe his face before he tossed it on the backseat of the car. He managed to wiggle into the jacket, which was on the small side. Stepping out of the car, he dug both hands into the coat's pockets to hold it semi-closed.

Oslo gave him a concerned look-over and then offered him a half-smile. "Better, but not so good." Oslo turned toward the store and Simpson fell in line behind him.

"Thanks again for all of your help," Simpson commented as he hurried to keep up with Oslo.

"You're welcome. Need anything from inside?"

"Some coffee -- and maybe a pack of gum. My mouth tastes awful," Simpson suggested as he ran his tongue around the inside of his mouth, feeling the thick coating of chalkiness on his teeth.

"Will do. I'll keep an eye out for you in the bathroom as you clean up, then I'll meet you back here at the car."

Simpson kept his head down and followed close behind Oslo. The gas station was one of the typical stops off most major interstates. The convenience store was separated from a restaurant by a long hallway that encompassed bathrooms and a bank of pay phones. An elderly couple moved to the side as they exited the doors leading into the bathroom area. Simpson noted out of the corner of his eye the stares that they gave Oslo. As for him, they never even glanced his way.

Once inside the doors, Simpson heard the civilized sounds of bustling activity coming from both the convenience store and the restaurant. It was strange but also welcoming to hear so much noise after the quietness of being at the lake. A large oval clock mounted on the wall to the right of the men's restroom showed six thirty-three.

The moment they stepped into the restroom, overhead lights popped on and he could see that it was a well-maintained and very clean facility. There was no lock on the door to the outside hallway since the restroom was too large to have one. Simpson moved to the nearest sink and reluctantly lifted his gaze to look at himself, feeling more than a bit afraid of what he would see reflected in the mirror. His eyes were red-rimmed with deep pockets of blue standing out against the white pallor of his complexion. The haunted face that looked back at him looked like someone to stay away from. The speckles of blood dotting his cheeks and the ragged line of raw-looking scratches snaking across his chin gave him an 'avoid at all costs' appearance.

He sighed and leaned in toward the mirror so he could get a better look at his eyes. Compared to Oslo's eyes, which shone brightly, his were dull and flat. He shrugged out of the jacket and let it fall to the floor behind him. Cupping his hands under the automatic water feed, he filled them several times as he splashed the warm water on his face, mixing it with scoops of the foaming soap that he had pumped from the dispenser.

Thankfully, the restroom had paper towels instead of air-dryers. It took Simpson several rounds of soaping and scrubbing and rinsing to get most of the bloody residue off his face and out of his scraggy-looking beard. The abrasiveness of the paper towels had made his ghostly white skin look wind-burned, but the overall result was better than what it had been when he walked in.

Picking up the coat, he slid it back on before stepping over to use the urinal. The door opened and a father and son entered the restroom while Oslo stood between him and the two new occupants. The boy and his father had seemed happy and animated as they talked to each other. But after seeing Oslo standing in the middle of the bathroom, they suddenly stopped talking and looked like they were trying to decide whether or not to continue into the room.

Oslo looked over at Simpson, giving him a curt nod, then made his way past the father and exited the restroom. The father and son had already walked past him and opened the door to one of the stalls. The boy couldn't be much older than six or seven, the father in his mid-thirties, and neither of them paid any attention to him. Simpson finished washing his hands, then, while walking out, he heard the boy ask his father if the man in the bathroom was really him. He didn't hear the father's response, but it made him smile as he remembered all the curious questions a once-curious Trent had asked when he was young.

Simpson didn't see or hear anyone else as he left the building and made his way back across the parking lot. It was still mostly dark -- the rising sun giving off the merest hint that it was ready to make its appearance. Suddenly feeling hungry as he heard his stomach growl, he wished that he had asked Oslo to bring him more than a pack of gum. He opened the car door and leaned in, rummaging in the sack for the candy bar. He tore off the wrapper to get to the gooey contents and downed it in three bites. But the sweet taste of chocolate had not satisfied his hunger and had left him feeling hungrier than before.

The air outside was damp but nowhere near as cold as it had been up north. He'd glanced at the map hanging on the wall just to the left of the exit doors, noting the red marker that pointed to 'you are here' and discovered that they were in White Bear Lake, a northern suburb of Minneapolis. It would take them at least another three hours to make it back to Decorah.

Although he'd been asleep for nearly four hours while Oslo drove, it had felt more like minutes. His thoughts returned to Vicky and his children. He was afraid of facing all of them, afraid of how they would react, and afraid they would see him for the coward he had been. It didn't matter because he knew he could willingly spend the rest of his life earning their forgiveness and enduring their judgment until he did.

"Simpson. Ready to hit the road?" Oslo called out as he walked around the back of the car and opened the driver's door.

"Any time you are," Simpson responded.

"I'm ready."

Oslo slid into the seat behind the wheel and handed over a cup of coffee and a pack of gum to Simpson. Simpson took them from his outstretched hand. The aroma of the coffee was heavenly. Snapping back the protective cover from the plastic lid, he inhaled deeply as the rich scents of hazelnut and vanilla wafted upward. "God, that smells good."

"Glad you like my choice. I pegged you for nut," Oslo jested, laughing heartily as he started the car.

Simpson grinned from ear to ear at Oslo's humorous tease. In a short time, Oslo had befriended him and comforted him in his time of need. Silently and privately, he promised himself that he would find the means to repay Oslo for his kindness and stay in touch with this savior who had rescued him. He already knew that there were people who popped into your life at strange times, who ended up being the friend or spouse that you needed at just that moment. Vicky had been both his friend and partner, but there was something unique about Oslo that made Simpson desire to keep him as a friend when all of this was over.

They made their way south on the interstate and Oslo looked peaceful as he drove. Simpson enjoyed the coffee and the apple that Oslo had tossed to him after they were a few miles down the road saying, "Thought you might like something besides coffee." Simpson could sense that Oslo was waiting -- but he wanted to hear his story. After taking the last swig of coffee, he felt he was ready to finish his tale.

"I'm going to tell you upfront that I'm not crazy and that I wasn't delirious with the flu or from drugs or from anything else. I've always been a calm, considerate, and rational man -- yet my ability to be irrational at the right time is what saved me from what has just transpired back in the woods. I told you we were in an accident -- well, that was just the catalyst that set me on my journey. You ever been married or deeply in love, Oslo?"

"Never married, but I did have someone that meant quite a lot to me. Our time was cut short."

"Sorry to hear that. You might understand then when I say that Vicky is my world. I love my children with all my heart -- but Vicky is the air that I breathe." Simpson paused and shifted himself around in the seat to face Oslo more.

"Some women can surely do that to you. They are rare and more precious than mere wealth. To have a woman like that is to have all a man's heart could desire."

Simpson smiled at the poetic way Oslo had rephrased his statement. Oslo may have been quoting from a book that Simpson was unfamiliar with, but Simpson felt as though he was speaking from his heart.

"After the accident, Vicky was in a coma, and then she had… complications. When she flat-lined, I lost it and walked away from everyone. I ended up here at my father's place -- actually, it's my cabin now. My dad passed away several years ago."

"I was absorbed in my grieving and the overwhelming feeling of guilt. On the evening of the accident, I'd had three glasses of wine over a five-hour period and plenty to eat. I wasn't drunk or even tipsy, but I still blamed myself because I was driving. I let that grief feed on my guilt and I ended up abandoning my kids when they needed me the most."

"Don't be too hard on yourself, or even doubt how the kids took it. They're probably more worried about you being safe than how you took their mother's passing."

"That's the strange part. I don't think she died." There was a silence and Simpson waited for Oslo to comment. When he said nothing, Simpson continued, "There are many things that I take on faith alone. Like you said earlier -- having the faith that people are generally good -- or that your kids will be fine without you and that God is watching and will be there when you need him."

Oslo turned to him, paused, and began to quietly answer. "Faith is a word that is often misused as we try to talk ourselves out of our doubts. I'm faithful, I believe, I can recite the bible passages until I've said them enough to believe I might have actually been there to hear them firsthand. But, you can't make yourself faithful -- you either are or you aren't. Sometimes things happen that allow your faith to become more cohesive – more tangible. It's okay to have doubts -- strong ones, weak ones. It's the seed of faith that you carry inside of you that matters most and not the idea of the word. When the time comes and you are faced with challenges, God will know the difference between believers and beggars and it won't matter a lick what level of doubt you were at."

Again, Oslo's words had brought immediate comfort to Simpson. The man had a knack for compassionate inspiration. Simpson was put at ease and found that telling the rest of his story without reservation was suddenly more bearable. Over the next hour, he told it as he best remembered it, detail by detail. He left nothing out. Oslo stopped him a couple of times to ask questions that could clarify the details, but nothing that he asked indicated either disbelief or agreement. When he'd finished talking, Simpson noticed that he felt both drained and purged.

"So you're thinking that the shadow wolves are some kind of inner-dimensional travelers that have telepathic powers which they use to confuse us and control animals. And this connection to them was made possible by your wife's comatose state and near death experience that somehow opened the door between realms. They had to kill you because you knew of their existence. Let's see -- Vicky is still alive because...?"

"When she was communicating with me, she kept imploring me to come back before it was too late. I don't know why I know it, but I do. So are you ready to drop me off at the loony bin?"

"If you'd tried to tell me that story when you were looking for a ride, I might have been tempted to leave you on the side of the road. But the truth is, I don't take you for a liar -- just the opposite. It's not for me to decide, but if it makes you feel better, I believe you."

"Thank you, Oslo. I have this strange feeling that you were just the person I needed to help me. Sounds strange me saying it, but I've come to believe that some coincidences are not random acts of probability at all."

Oslo let out one of his infectious belly laughs and Simpson joined in. Oslo asked a few more questions and then said, "No one really understands the universe. They've all got plenty of opinions and theories, but every day something new happens to blow a hole in them. I'm betting that if you ran an online search, you might be surprised by the number of individuals who've had similar experiences to yours. The truth is, no one knows for sure. It's kind of back to that little seed of faith. It doesn't mean that you should bury your head in the sand and avoid the evidence or pretend not to see things that raise questions. It does mean that you need to grow in your knowledge and trust in yourself to accept the tough things that you might never understand."

"You should have been a philosopher," Simpson said truthfully. "They have so many books and movies about what it would be like for someone from the Middle Ages to walk into the world as it is today. Imagine what we might feel being them and finding ourselves six-hundred years in the future. The world around us keeps expanding, changing, and becoming more complex."

"That's a good way to see it," Oslo commented. He added, "not only is the world expanding but so are we. Our ability to adapt to new ideas and amazing discoveries in science and technology will only lead us to places we've never imagined before."

"Always the optimist -- huh, Oslo?"

"Pretty much. I've been around long enough to have seen my share of *interesting* things. Seems to me that you can choose to embrace them, fight them, or ignore them. I don't go for ignoring a problem as a way to solve it. Never have seen one solve itself."

Simpson thought about Oslo's comment. If he'd ignored or embraced the shadow wolves, he'd be dead. Oslo was right -- sometimes you have to fight. "Now that you've listened to my story, I'd like your opinion on what might be coming down the road for me."

Oslo didn't say anything for a few moments and Simpson was just about to say, "You don't have to answer," when Oslo started speaking. "I'm not really sure. I kind of think that it might be up to you yet. I'm not sure that you are ever going to be out of the 'proverbial' woods. How can you encounter something like you have and then pretend it didn't happen? If you publicize it, then you just might end up in the psyche ward. You know that there is something out there and you're probably not alone in your knowing -- but knowing it and drawing a bulls-eye on your back are two different things. Me -- I'd try to find the meaning in what happened and adapt."

As Oslo spoke, Simpson found himself nodding his head in agreement. "Sounds right to me. I just hate the idea of looking over my shoulder or always wondering if the dog next door is keeping me under surveillance."

"Won't be the dog -- my guess, it will be the cat. Cats have that general look of consternation that helps them blend in and not be seen as out-of-place." Oslo chuckled, and then added, "Not that I have anything against our feline brethren, but cats didn't get nine lives by accident."

Simpson erupted with laughter, "Man…you can say that again."

They drove on in silence for the next hour, passing across the Iowa border and heading into the rising sun. The closer they got to Decorah Municipal Hospital, the more anxious Simpson began to feel. It was hard for him to sit still as one leg or the other bounced up and down in nervous spurts. He tried looking out the window and counting his blessings, but doubts knocked down the bricks as fast as he could stack them. He was worried, afraid, and hopeful all mixed up together.

They passed the highway sign announcing that Decorah was eight miles ahead and suddenly his fears turned into needs. He needed to see his wife, to hug his children, and to generally make things right. His head had begun to ache, which he took as a sign that all the stress he had felt and internalized was now overwhelming him. He closed his eyes and silently began to pray. When he finished and looked up, Oslo was smiling at him.

"I think you are going to be fine," Oslo said and turned his eyes back to the road. Ten minutes later, Oslo pulled the Bel Air up in front of the main entrance to the hospital. Simpson was stuck between two strong urges -- wanting to run to his wife and not wanting to say goodbye to the friend who had helped rescue him. He knew that the rescue had been more than just physical. All of Oslo's comments and interpretations had helped his damaged spirit as well.

Simpson opened the door and stuck one foot out. He looked over at Oslo. He'd donned a pair of dark sunglasses and now that they had stopped, he'd pushed them up onto his head. Oslo's eyes

Isolation

held nothing but compassion and it warmed Simpson to see that. He reached his hand across the divide between the seats to shake goodbye. Oslo smiled as he took his hand in his. In a final act of kindness, Oslo leaned across the seats and gave Simpson a long hug. Simpson felt Oslo's free hand patting him on the back and it made him feel unexpectedly better. Oslo broke the embrace and then said, "You better get going. They need you back inside."

Simpson said, "thank you" and "I'll be in touch" -- the usual types of goodbyes you say to someone you might never see again, but who had just helped you out of a jam. Oslo only nodded. Simpson twisted around in the seat to grab the backpack out of the backseat. He got out of the car and just as he was shutting the door, he heard Oslo call after him, "You're a good man Simple. I'm looking forward to seeing you again someday."

The door closed and Oslo put the car in gear, pulling away from the curb and leaving Simpson standing alone to face the end of his journey. A pleasant shiver rippled through his body when it suddenly occurred to him that Oslo had called him by his nickname.

CHAPTER 18:
Déjà Vu

Simpson stood outside the hospital entrance for a moment longer, knowing that he couldn't go inside with the knife and hatchet still secured to his belt. He moved away from the large glass entry doors and walked down the sidewalk to the nearest corner, ducking around the edge behind a cluster of shrubbery. He unfastened his belt and pulled it through the loops. Once he had freed the knife and hatchet, he restrung his belt, unzipped the backpack, and put them inside. His hand brushed the felt of Trent's old baseball cap. It sent a pang of regret coursing through him as he wondered how he could explain setting his father's cabin on fire. Would they be able to believe him or accept his story the way Oslo had done?

At that moment, Simpson really wished that he had a change of clothes and an opportunity to take a shower. In the state he was in, he would be lucky to make it past the reception desk. Simpson mulled over his limited options and mentally prepared a fictitious story to use if he was stopped as he tried to walk through the front

Isolation

entrance. As he stood there debating the chances of success, he caught something out of the corner of his eye and noticed a rising swirl of cigarette smoke wafting out from around the corner. Taking Trent's ball cap from the pack, he left the pack resting in the corner behind the shrub, stepped back out on the sidewalk, and started walking toward the cigarette smoke.

Simpson stopped abruptly and looked around. Something felt out of place -- *and it wasn't just him*. A deluge of questions surged through his brain. *Was he really sure that Vicky was still here? Why did it feel as if he'd just left and hadn't been gone for weeks?*

He understood why he had a déjà vu feeling. The trees lining the pathway to the side door still had their leaves and their color. The grass had recently been mowed and he could smell the familiar cut-grass scent. Time seemed to have stood still at the hospital while he'd been fighting off wolves in a snowstorm. The far north always succumbed to winter far earlier than where he was standing at that moment -- but everything felt distinctly strange nonetheless. His other concern was unexpectedly overcome by his budding seed of faith -- *he knew Vicky was still here.*

As he rounded the corner, two nurses were stepping on their cigarette butts, grinding them into the concrete pavement before they turned to use a key card to open the door. The heavy door had a handicap button and the nearest nurse pushed it. As soon as the door reopened, both nurses raced back in, chilled from being outside without having enough layers of clothing on.

Simpson raced to catch the door before it completely closed, knowing that a one second delay would have left him locked outside. He slipped inside, waited, and then slowly opened the door into an L-shaped hallway. A gurney was pushed against the left side of the hallway and straight on was a double set of doors that led back around to the front entry. Simpson wondered if Vicky was still on the third-floor wing -- or had she been moved to another floor or another room altogether.

As he untucked the flannel shirt from his pants, he noted that it was in better shape than his jeans were -- so letting it hang down covered some of the grime that he was coated in. He hugged the left side of the hallway as he cautiously moved forward, noticing that the end of the hospital he had just passed seemed to be mostly unused -- patient rooms with doors open and no lights on and an empty nurse's station sat three-quarters of the way down the hallway. From the nurse's station, another hallway with double doors at the end branched off to the right. Through the small windows in each of the doors, Simpson could see people moving around on the other side. Taking a deep breath, he moved hurriedly into a hallway that looked identical to the one that was behind him -- with one exception. At the far end, there was an exit sign – perhaps leading to the stairway up to the next floor.

With a racing heart, Simpson darted across the intersection of the two hallways and jogged toward the exit door. He could immediately determine that the door on his left lead outside and the stairs on his right did indeed go up to the next floor. He ran up the stairs, his footsteps echoing in the confined area.

When he got to the third floor, he opened the door a crack to see what was on the other side. Less than twenty feet away, he could see an orderly sweeping the hallway with a long dustbroom as two nurses talked outside a patient's room while studying a chart. It wasn't the intensive care ward after all -- that must have been down hallway opposite the nurse's station.

There was no way for him to avoid being seen since the floor in front of him had more people and more activity -- but Simpson took a deep breath, exhaled, and pushed the door open and walked through. One of the two nurses looked his way, frowned slightly, and then turned back around to continue her conversation with the other nurse. With an improvised air of confidence, Simpson strolled towards them, pretending that he knew where he was going, keeping his head turned away from them while focusing on the wall. Hopefully, they wouldn't stop him, but if they did, he had an excuse ready.

Neither of the nurses paused in their conversation as he strolled by -- and Simpson's luck continued when he arrived at the nurse's station and the one person on duty had her head down, deeply buried within her book.

Seeing the sign for the chapel, he headed in that direction since it was a part of the hospital that he knew well. He figured that he could regain his orientation with the hospital layout while he took a few deep breaths of relief.

A heavyset male orderly was pushing a cart down the middle of the aisle. Simpson had to flatten himself against the wall when the orderly moved past since the man showed no inclination to share the hallway. He wanted to yell something at him, but between his own disheveled appearance and his longing to see Vicky, he just picked up his pace as he strode toward the chapel and decided to let the man's rudeness go unchallenged.

Passing through the next set of double doors, Simpson felt relief that he knew where he was again as soon as he saw the chapel on the left. Almost unwillingly, he was drawn into the chapel while simultaneously fighting the urge to run straight to Vicky's room.

Standing within the chapel, Simpson saw that many candles had been lit, yet it was only occupied by one elderly couple. A strange sensation flooded through him as he stood there quietly and something familiar nudged the back of his mind. "*Time to go,*" a voice inside of him said. Hesitating for a moment longer, he looked at the altar and whispered, "Please Lord, don't let me be too late."

Simpson had already walked out of the Chapel and was approaching the waiting room where the picture of the cabin had first called to him. It suddenly hit him what had been familiar about the chapel -- the elderly woman inside. When he had visited the Chapel nearly a month earlier, she'd been sitting alone in the pew opposite him, wearing the same dark green dress and burgundy shawl. Now she was back with a man he presumed was her husband, wearing the same outfit, seemingly frozen in time. It didn't feel quite like a mere coincidence.

As he walked toward the waiting room, he felt as if he had just walked into a wall of reluctance and fear. Just like his hesitance at the door of the chapel, Simpson's body had the same response to the waiting room as it pulled at him to enter. Forcing himself to go through those doors, his head began to throb as soon as he had entered the empty room. The painting of the cabin kept a still and silent vigil over the room – but when he turned to leave, he discovered that it was impossible to do so. His unwilling legs moved him forward until he stood directly in front of the painting. Simpson's breath sucked in sharply and audibly when he saw them -- glowing red eyes peered out through the layers of darkened trees in the painting.

Startled by the sudden pain in his head, his eyes began to blur as his left arm ceased to move and hung numbly at his side and stabbing sensations coursed through his leg and hip. Simpson's mind raced in panic, thinking that Vicky must have taken a turn for the worse and was connecting with him as she suffered – as they both suffered the same pain. He wiped at his eyes with the only hand that still worked.

Taking a last look at the painting as he prepared to leave the room, he saw what had never been there before. Sitting in the window and backlit by the glow of a fire within was Sophie -- and racing along the side of the cabin toward the red eyes was Talini -- her tail pointing straight back and her mouth opened in a protective snarl. He blinked several times, but the two pets remained firmly in the same position in the painting.

He needed to get to Vicky – as quickly as possible.

Simpson broke free of the invisible bonds holding him in place and hustled down the hallway, hitting the button for the automatic door opener into the intensive care ward. As quickly as he could move with the pain coursing through his body, Simpson ran for IRR4, the room that Vicky had been in before. He didn't know why he knew, but he did -- *she was in there now.*

Stopping short, he sensed that something wasn't right and his head was spinning like a washing machine with too much laundry in it. It was the worst feeling of déjà vu he'd ever experienced. The large get-well bouquet of vibrant pink and white Stargazer lilies and orange roses was sitting on the counter, exactly as it had been on the day he left the hospital. The orderly with the broken finger was standing and talking with the nurse who had a purple streak in her blonde hair, just as he had been on that day. Simpson felt the knots tightening in his stomach. He turned to look down the hallway toward the exit doors, but they seemed to be receding, pulling back-back-back and moving silently away from him. Swallowing hard, he walked toward room four.

The door to Vicky's room was swinging shut just as Simpson reversed the motion and pushed it open. Stepping inside, he was unprepared for what he saw. The room was far from empty. Several people were standing inside and he knew them all. To one side of the bed, Trent and Abigail stood with Angela, the nurse whose nametag he had once read. Father Jacobson stood directly behind them, his hand resting on their shoulder.

He knew this scene -- he'd been here before. Dr. Parson was at the head of the bed and he and the other nurse were unhooking Vicky from life-support. After Simpson had left that last day, Vicky must have recovered enough to warrant being monitored, but now they must have been back at the point where a hard decision needed to be made. He had to let them all know that Vicky was still conscious inside and that she had reached out to him, asking him to save her.

Simpson moved toward the doctor, ready to do whatever he had to do to stop him from cutting off life-support when he heard Vicky speak. At first, he thought it was just in his head, like those times back at the cabin, but it sounded richer -- more real. He could even feel her warm breath in his right ear and smell her perfume as she whispered to him, "*The world needs everyone who can make such a positive difference -- it needs you. Time is running out and I'm scared. I don't know what to do. I don't want to be without you. You have to come back. Your life is in danger and I can't hold them off much longer. Please, Simple! Please come back to me...*"

Simpson stopped near the foot of the bed, unable to take his eyes off the broken body lying there. It made him want to cry as he looked at the damage -- a broken left arm and leg, the head wrapped in bandages, the body silent and unmoving -- almost dead, *but not quite -- this he knew.*

The doctor was removing the ventilator and Simpson tried to scream out for him to stop, but he was unable to utter any sounds or move at all. No one in the room paid any attention to him and his mind became panicked as his vision began to blur again. Simpson tried unsuccessfully to raise his arms to clutch at his chest as pain gripped him, but his arms had ceased to work. His throat burned and felt constricted, making him gasp for air. He was having a heart attack!

Simpson needed to save his wife and no one seemed to notice him as his heart suddenly stopped beating and he sank to the floor, his chin resting at the foot of the bed. Unable to breathe and fighting desperately to keep the darkness at bay as his vision began to fail, he knew he was about to die before saving the one person who meant everything to him. He wanted to shut his eyes and let the pain consume him -- *a death by the shadow wolves may have been more merciful.* The only person who acknowledged Simpson's presence in the room was Father Jacobson and even he made no effort to inform the doctor that he needed help. He looked right at him though, smiled as if Simpson was a long lost friend, and then mouthed, "Welcome back."

Simpson screamed at him, "Help me!" But no sound left his mouth. His throat relaxed allowing him to draw air, the darkness pushed back, and clarity returned. The scene before him was like a snapshot that captured a moment of great tribulation.

Trent and Abby were clinging to each other for support and tears glistened on Abby's face in the brightness of the fluorescent lights. Both of their knuckles were white from squeezing each other's hands in deathly comfort. The vacuum-like absence of sound and absence of pain made Simpson think that it must be what it felt like at the moment before death. He still couldn't move. *He was too late*, but it was ok because he was going to be with Vicky sooner than later.

A brief month earlier, Simpson had been blinded by anger and guilt that he directed straight into his own mind and heart. Then, in a moment of sudden clarity, he saw what he'd not seen before. There was a hand stretching across the bed and holding on to Vicky's hand. The hand holding Vicky's had deeply red painted fingernails and a glimmering diamond ring, so brightly new that the diamond captured all the light in the room and dazzled the eye with a kaleidoscope of colors. Simpson had finally allowed himself to see the full scene before him -- *to understand what he had not been willing to understand before.*

His gaze followed the hand up the slender wrist, up the arm to the shoulder that he loved to massage, toward the pretty neck that he kissed so lovingly and where she dabbed the perfume that never failed to call him into her loving arms. Simpson gazed at her through his own swollen eyes -- noticing the large scar that ran vertically from the corner of her eye. He thought to himself, "*Lucky she didn't lose the eye altogether.*"

The sound of the heart monitor altered as the metallic beeping first slowed and then screamed out one note of urgency. Simpson's eyelids grew heavy and his lungs could no longer draw in any air. Before his eyes closed completely, he promised Vicky that he wasn't going anywhere. She might never know how much her love *and her faith* had reached across time and the realm that he had been in, *not her*. He was the broken body in the bed. He was the one who had been given a glimpse of the *shadow plane*. He finally understood it for what it was -- a place of decision, or maybe, indecision.

Every episode since the accident had been a part of his own set of trials. His anger had masked the obvious -- he was the one who needed to decide whether to stay or leave. He wouldn't be allowed to take his guilt with him. The fight with the wolves had been a test of his resolve to fight for the rest of his life. The flight to the cabin had been his soul's journey toward finding faith, finding forgiveness, and finding purpose.

It had been a world of mixed cuttings, like a science fiction movie -- some of it computer generated, some of it shot in real time. However, the true crux of the matter was what real time had he existed in? It could have been 1998 for all he knew.

He'd been sensed by some of them -- Abby had seen him in this very room and fainted, the nurse in the infant wing had briefly seen him, as had the pastor. And then there was *Oslo*. Oslo had not only sensed Simpson, he had interacted with him -- the only one to do so. The way Oslo talked, the reaction of the young boy in the bathroom -- it all made sense if you had faith -- *and either you do or you don't*.

Simpson had never been one to walk away when things got tough and he hadn't done that this time either. He was right where he needed to be since his family needed him and Vicky needed him. In equal measure, he needed and wanted them – so what he would remember afterward didn't matter. If he was very lucky, he would remember enough to make him wonder at the unexpected for the rest of his life. In the far distance, he heard Talini bark and he would have bet that Sophie was somewhere close as well. Simpson felt at peace and let his eyes close.

B*eep, beep, beep, beeeeeeeeeeep*. Simpson was conscious of the sound of the monitor, yet it sounded dull, unreal. He couldn't open his eyes or move and wondered if he had actually passed out on the floor.

He willed himself fully to wake up, but his body wouldn't comply. Instead, Simpson only saw fragments of light and darkness through his closed eyelids as ghostly images danced within his mind. Memories or reality? He comprehended a truth, but couldn't quite place it. He tasted plastic air as his lungs fought to breathe and his senses felt dull, distant, and muffled. He must be near death -- no, not near death, but near life.

Simpson began to feel the bed below his broken body, the cast protecting the broken bones in his leg and arm. The pain wasn't too bad just then, but it would be soon -- attacking him with a vengeance. It was a reward of sorts and one that Simpson was willing to pay for.

She was there -- he felt her, sensed her. She was crying softly, her tears falling from her cheeks onto his neck. Simpson wanted to hold her and would someday. It sounded far away, but he clearly heard Sophie mewing and the guiding bark of Talini -- *he knew it was truly the two of them, but not why or how they were able to be there.* They had fulfilled a purpose to guide him to where he needed to be.

Simpson would never forget, but then again, that was a lie. *He was already forgetting.* Simpson prayed to the Heavenly Father and thanked him for everything, for Oslo, and for his life. It was time to sleep, to heal. The trailing sound of death's beep had gone silent -- it wasn't his time yet.

Trent spoke in the muddled darkness. Simpson heard him exclaim, "Abby, look there at the foot of the bed. I'll be damned -- it's my hat. How in the name of…"

Simpson didn't hear any more of the words that followed or Abby's reply, "How can that be the same hat, Trent? The cabin burned down in the autumn of 2008!"

Simpson's mind began to shut down – *but not forever.* With one last effort before he succumbed to sleep, he squeezed Vicky's hand and heard her gasp. In his mind, he smiled and asked her to dance.